OBIE
is Man Enough

Crown Books for Young Readers
New York

OBIE
is Man Enough

SCHUYLER BAILAR

Text copyright © 2021 by Schuyler Bailar
Jacket art copyright © 2021 by Dion MBD

All rights reserved. Published in the United States by Crown Books for Young Readers, an imprint of Random House Children's Books, a division of Penguin Random House LLC, New York.

Crown and the colophon are registered trademarks of Penguin Random House LLC.

Visit us on the Web! rhcbooks.com

Educators and librarians, for a variety of teaching tools, visit us at RHTeachersLibrarians.com

Library of Congress Cataloging-in-Publication Data is available upon request.
ISBN 978-0-593-37946-2 (hc)—ISBN 978-0-593-37947-9 (glb)—
ISBN 978-0-593-37948-6 (ebook)

The text of this book is set in 11.25-point Simoncini Garamond Std.
Interior design by Andrea Lau

Printed in the United States of America
10 9 8 7 6 5 4 3 2 1
First Edition

To every transgender kid who has wondered or
is still wondering if they belong here.
You do. And this book is for you.

OBIE
is Man Enough

Obie is a transgender boy who experiences transphobia throughout the story. If you are not transgender, please recognize that this transphobia does not represent all hatred and discrimination we experience. Still, it is an accurate representation that some experience. Certain moments in this book may be difficult to read for those who have experienced similar discrimination.

Please take care of yourself as you read, especially if you are also transgender.

Before

"You're never going to be a real man, Sarah," Coach Bolton says, using my old name. He's never really made the effort to use my new one, Obie. I cringe. It hurts every time. It says: *I do not see you; making you feel comfortable does not matter to me.*

His tone intensifies as he continues. "I don't know why you're kidding yourself. How are you going to compete against the boys? Are you insane?" He doesn't wait for me to reply. I don't think he cares what I have to say.

"Unless you can beat every boy on this team, I don't support this at all. I won't watch you throw away everything we've worked for."

"This isn't about being fast—" I try to interject, but I'm barely audible and Coach just plows on.

"If you're going to . . . to . . ." He falters, his face contorting. "Do *this* . . . pretend to be a boy or whatever, I won't coach you anymore." He rises from his chair as he talks. Or growls, rather. "Grab your snorkel and fins from the bin and leave before we start practice. I'll call your mother."

I sit there, glued to my seat. I hadn't even been able to respond. Coach just walked out of the office, seemingly taking my voice with him. I'd known telling him would be hard, but I hadn't thought it'd go *this* poorly.

The backs of my naked thighs stick to the sofa and I wonder why someone thought a leather couch in a swim coach's office was a good idea. Kids sit on it in their wet swimsuits all the time.

Today was supposed to be my last day in this suit—the one-piece that girls wear.

What will happen now that Coach just kicked me off the team?

———

When I see Mom's car pull up in front of the pool, I feel hot tears stinging my eyes. I pray she doesn't get out to hug me. I really don't want to bawl right here. I fight the hot anger bubbling in my chest. *Coach didn't even give me a freaking chance!*

Thankfully, Mom doesn't ask what happened. She must have gotten enough about it from Coach's phone call. She offers me the radio or an audiobook and I choose audiobook, hoping to be swept into a story and out of my life. But the tears come anyway. All of my friends are in that pool. If I don't go back to practice tomorrow, when will I see them?

Some of them go to school with me, I guess, but it's not the same. There's something unique about spending twenty hours a week training like we do. In a way, we're alone, each in our own underwater bubbles, but we're alone together.

I watch the BOLTON'S BARRACUDA AQUATICS sign fade into the distance and trace the BBA logo on my backpack with my finger.

We've done this drive thousands of times since I joined the team five years ago. But now it's different. I'm not just going home after practice. I'm leaving here forever. I sniffle and Coach's gruff voice invades my thoughts—"You're never going to be a real man, Sarah"—which somehow both stops and starts the tears at the same time. *Does crying make me less of a real man?* My throat burns with the sobs.

"Obie, do you want to talk about what happened?" Mom's nervously looking back and forth between my face and the road. The traffic is terrible, despite the fact that it's still early afternoon.

"Coach said I'll never be a real man," I choke out, "unless I can beat every other guy on the team."

"That's ridiculous," Mom says, her eyes narrowing. "That's absolutely *ridiculous.*"

"Where am I going to go? I don't have another swim team. . . . And Bolton coaches at school, too!"

"I don't know, sweetie, but we're gonna figure this out."

"But all my friends! All my friends are 'Cudas!" I am now— as my best friend, Lucy, would say—full-on ugly-crying.

When we get home, I kick my shoes off more violently than I mean to. They make two loud thuds as they smack into the wall, and the mud that had been stuck to the bottoms scatters across the floor.

"Honey," Mom starts but doesn't continue. I run through the kitchen and I'm halfway up the stairs when Dad calls after me.

"Obadiah—" my dad tries, louder this time, but Mom cuts him off.

"Let him be," I hear her say before I slam my door shut.

I drop my backpack on the floor and stare at the photo above my bed—Lucy, Clyde, Coach Bolton, Dad, me. My chest feels like it's about to collapse into itself. And I think I might vomit.

I've thought about taking the photo down for months— it's been almost a year since I told Clyde and he started acting like he does. Like I'm everything he can't stand. But I kept hoping maybe it would turn out different. Maybe he'd come around.

But I can't wait any longer. I rip the photo down. It tears at the corners where it had been taped, leaving four small triangles stuck to the wall. Clyde's foot gets trapped. I look at my face, my short hair, my XL tie-dyed sweatshirt from Spring Champs in 2017. As I'm ripping up the paper, it gets easier and easier to tear, and I realize that's because my tears are soaking it. I continue to rip little pieces off until just my own face remains. I stand, holding it.

There's a knock on my door. I don't turn around or say anything, but after a moment it opens slightly anyway.

"I don't want to talk," I almost scream, still facing the other way.

"O?" I hear Jae-sung say. *Oh.* I turn around, wiping my face.

"What do you want," I ask, but there's no question mark.

"I just, uh . . . Mom told me what happened—" he starts, but I cut him off.

"I don't want to talk about it," I say again. My voice climbs too high.

"I know, I know. I just . . . Um, I just wanted to say . . ." He hesitates. "I think that your coach is trash." He looks me directly in the eyes as he continues. "Even if he's a good coach, you know, with swim shit. A good coach becomes a bad coach when they're an asshole."

I stare at him, not knowing how I'm supposed to respond. Jae-sung's never been the serious type. He's the kind of guy who can make a joke out of anything.

"That's it. Just know I gotchu, O. I'm here." And then he's gone.

A good coach becomes a bad coach when they're an asshole, I repeat in my head.

But he is *the best coach. Does that make a difference?*

What if this means I'll never go to Nats—Nationals—like he said I would? I glance at the medals hanging over my dresser. The trophies from summer swim team. Some awards from end-of-the-year banquets. I take a few steps toward my bed and feel pieces of the torn-up photo stick to my bare feet. I kneel and collect them by the fistful and begin dumping them in my trash can.

A few pieces linger on the carpet—mostly parts of Lucy. In one fragment, you can still see her big smile. I think we were ten. We'd just finished our first Spring Champs. It was the first four-day championship meet either of us had ever competed in, and we'd each won at least two of our events. That was the meet I'd realized, *I am a Swimmer.* In the locker room after the last warm-down, Lucy and I'd been changing out of our suits when Lucy turned to me and said, "This was the best meet ever."

I'd grinned, nodding. "It was."

"I want it to be like this forever. Me and you, and Clyde, of course."

"Yeah, me too."

"Best friends, from the pool to school, we rule!" we'd shouted in unison.

One of the girls had turned to stare at us and there had been a moment of awkward silence. Lucy and I had looked at each other, then burst into laughter. The girl had given us a very condescending look before walking away.

"Are we getting too old to do that?" I had asked Lucy.

She'd waved her hand in the air. "Whatever. Who cares?"

I lie on the floor and stare at the ceiling.

A little while later, there's another knock on my door. This one waits for my answer.

"What?" I finally say quietly.

"Can I come in?" Mom's voice is gentle.

"I guess," I say, and sit on the floor with my back against my bed.

"How're you holding up?" Mom asks as she sits next to me. I look at her, my eyes burning from all the tears. They feel dried out, but that doesn't make any sense—tears are liquid!

"I know you probably are just processing right now," she says, "but I wanted to let you know that Dad's already started looking for other swim programs for you so that you'll miss as little practice as possible. I know you're worried about that." *Other programs?* It feels so strange that I won't be returning to Coach Bolton tomorrow morning. What if all the other coaches are like Coach Bolton? What if they hate me for being this way?

"I promise we're going to figure this out. If we have to hire a freakin' lawyer, we will," she continues.

"A lawyer?!"

"Of course. We will do whatever it takes."

"Why a lawyer?" Lawyers are for murder and other crimes, not mean coaches. . . .

"Discriminatory behavior. Coach Bolton kicked you off because of who you are. That's not allowed," she explains.

"Okay," I say. I'm still holding a fistful of ripped-up photo bits.

"What is that?" Mom says, staring at my hand. "What happened?" She looks really concerned. I just glance up at where the photo used to be.

"What if I lose all my friends, too?" I ignore her question. I'm looking at the piece that holds Lucy's smile. *Crap, I forgot to text her.*

"I doubt that will happen, honey. It just might be a bit harder to see everyone as often. It's going to be okay."

I nod. I don't believe her. But I'm too tired to argue.

"Do you want to come down for some dinner or shall I bring it up to you?" She must know today is a really bad day if she is not only allowing but *offering* me the choice to eat in my room.

"Up here, please?" I ask tentatively.

"Okay, I'll be back in an hour or so. Dad's still cooking."

"Thanks, Mom." She gives me a big hug before getting up and shutting the door softly behind her.

I call Lucy but get her voice mail almost immediately. When I hear myself giggle in the background—we set up our voice mail together, which mostly consisted of us rolling on the floor laughing because Clyde had tried doing several impressions of famous actors—I hang up. Gosh, that feels like forever ago.

Lucy's probably having dinner. Her mom is pretty strict

about tech at the table—at her house, we don't just put our phones away, we have to turn them all the way off and stack them on top of each other in the middle of the table. If your phone rings because you didn't actually turn it off, you don't get dessert. And Mrs. Weaver makes the *best* apple pie, so you do *not* want to miss that.

I hear Bolton's voice in my head again, *You're never going to be a* real *man, Sarah*—my old name is like a sucker punch to the gut.

I think a lot of people don't understand how painful it is to be called a name that doesn't fit. Some people even think it's okay to call me Sarah when they're talking about me in the past. But it's not okay. It's just as painful. I only ever want to be called Obie.

I drop the last bit of the photo into the trash can and slip under the covers. Normally I'd care that I'm wearing outside clothes in my nice clean bed, but today everything already feels dirty.

I lie on my stomach, my face turned sideways so I can breathe.

Suddenly, I'm nine all over again. My hair is long and matted against my forehead. I'm sweating and crying. I don't want to wake Mom and Dad, so I muffle my face in the pillow. And then the darkness is no longer just in my room, it's in my head, too. I wonder what it would be like if I just stayed like that—pressed into the pillow, unable to breathe.

What if I didn't turn my head for air. What if I didn't have to wake up every morning and be someone I'm not. What if—
My phone buzzes me back to the present.

> **LUCY, 5:45 P.M.:** Sorry was in din. You know mama W. I'm guessing it didn't go very well . . .

> **LUCY, 5:46 P.M.:** We all saw you leave. Are u ok?

Horrible? The worst day of my life? I kind of want to curl up and die?

But I don't type anything. Part of me wishes she were here and we could talk it through. But the rest of me just wants silence. So I stay burritoed in bed because even though Bolton wouldn't let me practice today, I'm still so tired. I switch my phone to Do Not Disturb and pull the covers over my face.

What did Coach Bolton tell everyone? Did he say he was kicking me off because he doesn't believe I'm really a guy? That he doesn't want me competing as who I really am? Or did he make up something else?

PEOPLE WHO BELIEVE I'M MAN ENOUGH:
1. Mom and Dad
2. Jae-sung
3. Lucy

PEOPLE WHO DON'T:
1. Coach Bolton

Chapter 1

"Take your mark"—a pause, and then the whistle blows. The guys dive into the water, splashing me and the others who are standing at the edge of the deck watching. Most of the team are at the other end of the lanes, cheering on the swimmers. Their bodies glow in the artificial light, the winter sun still sleeping.

"His butterfly looks like shit. How is he so fast?" Pooch laughs after the first lap. Pooch isn't his real name. It took me a little too long to get that. It's his last name, Puczovich, shortened. There was already a Samuel on the team when Puczovich joined, so everyone calls him Pooch.

"I know, man, I'm not sure," I reply. "It's pretty ugly, though." We both stare at the guy in lane 8—Jackson. He grew about a foot last summer, no joke, and now his arms are too long for his own good. They drag in the water as he heaves them forward with each stroke. You'd think that with all that friction he wouldn't go so fast, but he does. He's already about half a body length ahead of Sammy—the original Samuel.

"Think he'll die the last fifty like usual?" Pooch asks. I think about it for a second. Jackson does usually die, but he's also a good amount ahead so—

"Why are you over here gossiping about your teammates instead of down there cheering them on? Do you want to be the next for a two hundred fly, Mr. Puczovich?" Coach stands right behind us, just a tad too close. She's not very tall, but her voice makes us stand straight up.

"Sorry, Coach," we mumble in unison and then shuffle off toward the other end of the lanes.

———

It's been almost six months since I joined Coach Larkin's group at Manta Ray Aquatics and I still haven't decided what to make of her. She never yells at anyone for swimming bad races. She doesn't yell much at all, really. When I didn't go a best time at the first meet I swam for her, I'd hid in the warm-down pool for the better part of an hour, expecting her to yell at me like Coach Bolton would have. But she never did. She didn't even come find me. When I returned to the team area finally, almost sulking, she didn't even seem to notice.

Also, her practices have So. Many. Drills. And rest! We do rest *days* here! Coach Bolton would never have done that. I've been really worried that I'm not swimming enough yardage to be ready for upcoming meets. But Coach Larkin says everyone must at least start with trusting a coach's method, especially when switching to a new team. So, I'm trying.

But I miss Coach Bolton. And somehow, unbelievably, I miss the yelling. *How am I supposed to beat all of the guys without someone pushing me the way Coach Bolton did?*

Jackson and Sammy are nearing the wall, and Pooch and I lean down to yell in their faces as they do their flip-turns.

"Goooo!" we say together.

"Looks like he's hanging in there," I say to Pooch, nodding at Jackson. Coach is walking along the edge of the pool, shouting each time their heads break the surface. Every swim coach has a distinctive call, some more than others. Coach Bolton always used to make a big "BOO!" sound, deep and booming, emphasizing the *ooo,* that would carry his voice across the natatorium. You knew it was him. Everyone else on deck did, too, even the other teams. Coach Larkin's yell is a higher-pitched, quick "HUP!"

I know it shouldn't really matter, but I miss Coach Bolton's "BOO!"

The whole team cheers as Jackson touches the wall a body length ahead of Sammy. *Impressive.*

"Obie and Mikey, two hundred IM." Coach Larkin calls the next race.

"Aw, man, Coach L., why you gotta do me like that?" Mikey groans. "I don't have energy for one stroke and you want me to do all four?" IM means "individual medley." The 200 IM is a fifty of each stroke. I know he's being intentionally dramatic so I don't say anything aloud, but I definitely agree in my head. Plus, I already went; why do I have to go again? Also, against *Mikey*? Mikey is one of the fastest guys on this team.

"Miguel Garcia," Coach Larkin says sternly. I've only ever heard Larkin call him that. I suppose his mom probably does, too. When he's in trouble. "Get up on the blocks, boys," Coach Larkin insists, a grin on her face. *That's another thing about Coach L.,* I think. *Coaches aren't supposed to smile.*

"Take your mark—" My body tenses as I get into position. My mind goes blank. I take a deep breath, feeling the expected rush of adrenaline. This is one of the things I love about racing. It doesn't matter how much you feel like you've got or how tired you are. Nothing else matters except this moment.

Two hundred yards. Let's go. The whistle goes off.

The water crashes over my head as I pierce the surface. The world disappears for a moment beneath the rush of water. *Here I am,* I think. *Here. I. Am.*

I take six solid underwater dolphin kicks before I break for my first stroke. I don't breathe, Coach Bolton's voice in my head. *You never breathe on the first stroke of butterfly or freestyle. Keep your head down. Air later.*

Fly and backstroke laps go by in a blur. I grab armfuls of

15

water, Mikey right beside me the entire way. I try my best not to focus on him, but I can feel the excitement building with every turn. I've been afraid of him since joining because he's pretty well known in New England Swimming. The last time we raced each other, I hadn't even had a chance. I'd lost by more than four seconds. Honestly, that's nearly half a pool's length. But today, I'm right with him.

Don't get cocky, I remind myself. Breaststroke is my strongest. *Focus.*

Going into the last fifty, I am suddenly terrified I'll burn out. I've gained a hefty lead—I'm almost a full body length ahead of Mikey. But freestyle is my weakest leg. The previous two hours of work hit me like a brick and my legs begin to burn. My lungs beg for more air. I answer them with a sharp *no.* I push off the wall, my mind clearer than it's been in weeks. I collect myself as I hit one more underwater dolphin kick than usual. Seven. *Here we go.*

I pull farther ahead with each stroke. Mikey falls from my peripheral vision completely as I near the finish. I kick as hard as I can into the wall, diving for that last stroke, my fingers outstretched. I am grinning stupidly before I even raise my head from the water. I look up to see the team cheering. *I beat Mikey Garcia! I. Beat. MIKEY GARCIA!*

"Dude, where the heck did *that* come from—that was crazy!" Pooch is leaning over my lane, offering his fist. I bump it and realize just how sore my arms are. He steps over to Mikey's lane and bumps him, too.

"Thanks, Pooch," Mikey says, out of breath. "Wasn't my greatest. . . ." He trails off, looking at his hands holding on to the edge of the pool. He seems a little disappointed, but then he turns to me, flashing a grin. He sticks his hand over the lane divider to shake. I'm suddenly shy.

"Nice job, man," Mikey says. I hesitantly reach over, wondering why he doesn't seem upset with me. *Is the smile fake?* But he looks earnest. How strange. Most of the guys in the 'Cudas would have been livid and screaming by now. Especially Clyde. They were all sore losers. Didn't matter who they lost to. Although I think losing to me would kill Clyde. I shiver at the thought of his screaming.

"I'm pumped to race you at JOs this year," he says. "It's going to be dope." Crap—JOs! *Junior Olympics.* I haven't even dared to think about that meet.

"I mean, if I qualify," I say anxiously, but still smiling.

"Oh, come on, Obes, of course you will. Next meet, we'll throw down. Get you that cut." *Obes.* That's a new one. I like it. I make a mental note to add Mikey and Pooch to my journal list.

———

"So, munchkin, how was it?" Dad asks me as I hop in the car. He asks me this question every day after every single practice. You'd think he'd get bored. And yet, every time, he sounds genuinely interested.

"I told you, you can't call me that anymore," I say almost

reflexively. But I'm too excited about practice to be annoyed. "We did some two hundreds off the blocks and my first was meh, like it was fine, I swam breast. But then Coach made me do IM against Mikey, of all people—I don't know why—but then Mikey and me—"

"Mikey and I," Dad corrects me. I roll my eyes but I'm too eager to tell my story, so I just correct myself and keep going.

"Mikey and *I* had to do an extra two hundred IM and I was so tired, I thought I was going to pass out before I even got on the blocks, and Mikey was all pissed Coach made us do it." I pause, catching my breath. I've always been a fast talker. Sometimes so fast that I forget to breathe. The only time it ever slowed was during That Year. *Never mind. The race,* I remind myself. "But I won! I went a 2:09.6, and he didn't even break 2:10!" I grin from ear to ear.

"Wow, son, that's fantastic! That's so close to your best time, and just in practice."

"I know. Mikey thinks that I can make the JO cut at the Invitational next month . . . but I'm pretty nervous and . . ." I trail off, my excitement quickly waning.

"O, I'm sure you'll do great, but don't worry about it now. You can't control how the race goes when you're not even in it. All you can do is prepare the best you can, and if you do that, you'll put yourself in the best position to achieve your goals." Some of Coach Dad emerges as he talks.

But my performance is not the only reason I'm nervous.

Everyone from the Barracudas will be there. Including Clyde.

The winter sun still hasn't begun to peek over the horizon, but the sky has shifted to that early-morning dark blue as we drive home. It's like a whole day passes during morning practice—filled with people and challenges that are entirely separate from the rest of the day.

Despite how difficult 4:30 a.m. practices can be, I absolutely love the feeling afterward. I'm up with a total running start. A swimming start! Haha. But really—I've already completed the most difficult task of the day and most people's alarms aren't even close to buzzing. So right now, I feel great.

I try not to think about the Invitational. Or Clyde.

Practice first. Race later.

Chapter 2

At home, Jae-sung is still asleep and Mom is puttering quietly in the kitchen, making lunches for school.

"How was practice, honey?" She doesn't look up because she's slicing apples.

"Good," I say, grinning again. "I beat Mikey!"

"Really? That's exciting!" Mom doesn't know who Mikey is. She doesn't really follow my swimming the same way Dad does, but it doesn't bother me at all. I know she just wants me to be happy and enjoy it. I don't think she actually cares how well I do.

"What's for lunch?" I ask, surveying the kitchen and seeing the baguettes on the counter. "Sammiches?" I add with hope. These are my favorite.

"Turkey, lettuce, cheese, onion, and mayo!" She smiles.

"Go shower and get ready," Dad instructs. I scuttle over to Mom anyway and wait as she finishes the sandwich half she's working on. She seems to know why I'm standing there and lifts the sandwich to my mouth when she's done.

"Big bite," she directs. I take the largest chomp I can manage, enjoying the mayonnaise and onion. Mmmm! My favorite.

———

I shower, throw on some clothes, and run downstairs.

"Obadiah, it is forty-eight degrees outside. What are you doing wearing shorts?! Get your butt upstairs and put something warmer on, and while you're at it, wake up your brother!" Mom orders.

I groan. I like these shorts. And also, Jae-sung is the worst. He's so grumpy in the morning. Actually, he's so grumpy all the time these days. It used to just be in the morning, but lately it's like his life has become a never-ending morning. Mom says it's because he's going through *puberty*. But so am I, and *I'm* not like that!

"Obie—" Stern, non-disobey-able. I wordlessly move toward the stairs, but not before grabbing another bite of the second sandwich Mom's making.

"That's your brother's," she says exactly as I realize the same thing.

"Yuck!" I want to spit it out. Jae-sung likes honey mustard. I do not.

"That's what you get! No spitting!" Mom laughs. I chew with a disgusted face. "Go!" She nudges me.

"Okay, okay." And I run up the stairs.

His door is shut, unlike mine. I don't like the complete

darkness, but he apparently does. I don't knock. He won't hear it. I just walk right in with "Jae-sung, it's time to get up." I don't want to startle him, but I'm still too quiet.

"Jae-sung," I say louder. "Wake up!" Louder. He rolls over. *C'mon....*

"Jae-sung!" I nearly shout. "WAKE UP!" He groans. *Finally.*

He throws a pillow at me. I catch it and wish he were awake enough to have seen that. Maybe he'd have been proud. I've never been good at hand-eye coordination like he is. Hence swimming.

"I'm not going," he mumbles. I flick on the light switch. I used to jump on his bed, but last year he yelled at me, saying I'm too big. So now I turn on the lights.

"Aghhhhh. You're such an ass!" But he's reaching for his glasses and starting to sit up. See? Effective. Mission accomplished.

"Breakfast," Mom calls. I race downstairs. I'm starving! Post-practice hunger is a different beast. My stomach feels hollow, like it's maybe even starting to eat itself whenever I don't feed it right when I get home. I sit down at the counter and Mom places a plate in front of me with the rest of my already-bitten sammich.

"Thought you'd want it for breakfast, too," she says. "This is yours. Don't worry, no mustard."

Chapter 3

Even though I love being up early, I hate the beginning of the day at school. I mean, I *really* hate it. There are so many kids running around everywhere and they're all making so much noise and the snippets of conversations I overhear always manage to piss me off somehow.

"—no, dude, the Seahawks are totally going to win this year. Are you—"

"—so stupid, I don't even know why we have to—"

"—application is due, but I haven't even started—"

"I was up until *one* in the morning, finishing up—"

"Oh, what did you think? What did you get—"

I roll my eyes at the last one. I know that voice. Cynthia Broadman is always asking everyone else for their grades, even though she's always at the top of the class. She tries to mask it as "caring about others," but we all know she just wants to make sure she did better than everyone else.

"—a real boy, it's a girl—" I know that voice, too. My stomach turns and I stare at the floor. Which, honestly, isn't that different from how I usually walk. I think I've pretty much memorized the pattern on the linoleum tiles by now. I make a beeline for my first class even though it's only 7:45 and class doesn't start until 8:00. No chance I want to see the owner of that voice today.

The room is empty, as I expected. I spend a lot of time in this one because Mrs. Salmani is also my homeroom teacher. I always sit in the front. I like being able to see the board clearly. People make fun of me for being too eager, call me the teacher's pet. They're probably right, but I don't really care. Especially in Mrs. Salmani's class. She's my favorite teacher, even though I hate the subject. English. I'm terrible at writing, apparently. Before this year, I'd never gotten anything less than an A in a class. Okay, maybe I struggled with a few math lessons in fourth grade, especially those pesky times tables. But for the most part, I do very well in school.

But the first essay I turned in, in September, came back with a big red C in the top corner, right over my name. Above the letter, she'd written "Come see me after class" in her iconic flowing script. I'd never had to meet with a teacher because of a bad grade. I remember sweating through the rest of the class. When we finally met, Mrs. Salmani wasn't angry at all. Instead, she walked me slowly through each mistake I'd made and explained how I could do better next time. She wasn't too nice, like the French teacher everyone knows gives As just for handing in the assignment. But she also wasn't like the science teacher who shames you in front of everyone when you don't do well. October's paper was returned with a B, and I'd never thought I'd be so happy about getting less than an A.

I suppose the fact that I've spent a good amount of time with Mrs. Salmani outside of class makes me even more of a teacher's pet. But it's not all my fault. Mom and I met with Mrs. Salmani before the school year started because Mom wanted to make sure everything would be smooth for me. I'd only had one year—sixth grade—living as myself at school. So Mom was still concerned.

Mrs. Salmani was great, of course. She wanted to really get to know me, so we had a few meetings even before I got that C.

Since that first C, I've been meeting with her after school on Wednesdays for an hour to ask more questions. Wednesday is the only day I don't have afternoon practice, and I would usually prefer to use that time for something else, but our meetings have become one of my favorite parts of the week.

Everyone thinks Mrs. Salmani is weird or strict. But she's probably one of my best friends at school. I know that sounds sad because I'm almost done with middle school and I think I'm at that age when I'm supposed to hate adults. But she's one of the only people who makes me feel safe here. I'm determined to get an A on my next paper—not only for me but because I want to show her how much she's taught me.

"All right, class, take out *All American Boys* and turn to 'Quinn'—page thirty." We just started this book last week. In the first chapter, one of the main characters, Rashad, is beaten by a cop, presumably just because he's Black. I had never heard of anyone being attacked by a cop just because of the color of their skin. When I asked Mom about it, her eyes had gotten all faraway and she'd nodded and said, "Yes, honey, unfortunately police brutality is often rooted in systemic racism." I didn't know what systemic racism was, but we'd just gotten to swim practice and I'd had to go.

"Can anyone give me a three-sentence summary of the first chapter?" Mrs. Salmani likes three-sentence summaries. She says we need to be concise and know which parts are key to include when "distilling the narrative." I'm not good at this. My summaries are always very detailed. *The book begins with a small poem. I think it is designed to make you feel something.*

Mrs. Salmani also says we aren't supposed to provide opinions when summarizing. *The book begins with a short poem. The poem is not heavily descriptive or elaborative. Most of the sentences are fragments. The story opens in first person with a boy who does not get along with his father because his father wants him to do ROTC, but he does not—*

"Jason, let's hear it." Mrs. Salmani interrupts my thoughts.

"Okay, so the title of the book is, uh, *American Boy,* and—" Jason might be even worse than I am at this. First, he's telling us the title? Everyone knows the title. Second, he got the title wrong.

As Jason continues, I think about this month's essay. "Talk about a time when you felt a conflict due to your identity and explain what you did to resolve it—like Rashad, who learns to stand up for himself, and Quinn—" I stop reading because I'm worried it'll give away something about the ending. I don't know much about Quinn yet because we haven't gotten that far. I try not to read too much ahead.

"Okay, thank you." Mrs. Salmani tries to talk over Jason as he babbles on. "Thank you, Jason, thank you. That's enough now." She's firm but there is still kindness in her voice.

———

When the bell rings, I stay seated. Everyone else jumps up to go. In any other class, I would, too. But here, I wait until the room is empty and walk up to Mrs Salmani's desk. Mrs. Salmani's favorite color is clearly purple—her glasses, her shawl, and the little sand timer on her desk are all purple. I like purple, too.

"See you after school?" she asks, looking up at me. Her voice is gravelly, kind of like it's filled with rocks, maybe one for every year she's lived. She's pretty old. The kind of old that says weathered. Worn. Wise. Not the kind that says fragile, smelly, senile. . . .

"Yes, ma'am," I say, and give a small smile. My eyes

nervously flit to the door. She knows I'm not lingering only because I like talking to her.

"Tall and confident, Obie-jaan, he can never take you from yourself." Jaan means "life" in Farsi. Mrs. Salmani told me that when added to the end of a name, it's a term of endearment.

I nod in answer even though I'm not sure she's right. Sometimes I worry that Clyde could take everything from me. His dad almost did.

Pretty much everyone at school knows what happened with Coach Bolton. Mrs. Salmani is the only person at school who I personally told. She's the only person who really knows how I feel about it all. And I guess Lucy, too. But not a lot, since things have been weird between us lately.

In the hallway, the bustle is dying down as most of the students head into their classrooms. It's not an enormous school like some of the other public schools in the county, but it's large enough that it would be ridiculous to know everyone in my grade. I used to find that intimidating, but I kind of like it now. I don't have to know or be known. Sometimes, that's nice. Sometimes I think I hide too much.

Tall and confident. I repeat Mrs. Salmani's words in my head as I leave the room. *Tall and confident.* I lift my eyes from the linoleum tiles and stare ahead. I feel so awkward— where do people look when they walk down hallways like this? The popular kids always seem to be making eye contact with their friends, nodding, high-fiving, fist-bumping.

It's a short walk from Mrs. Salmani's class to my next one—math. It's just around the corner. But I have to pee. *Dammit,* I mutter to myself, and then immediately, *No cursing! Dad's gonna wash your mouth out.* I wonder if I can hold it. I start to turn into my classroom and someone bumps me as they exit, their backpack jamming into my bladder, and for too long a moment I'm terrified I'm going to pee myself. I set my backpack down in my chair—this time in the middle of the room. Mr. Devi is a nice guy, but I don't love his class. I quickly ask him if I can use the bathroom before class starts and he tells me to hurry.

I rush into the bathroom, which, luckily, is just across the hall. I'm about to press open one of the stall doors, but someone blocks my way. I stare at his shoes, praying someone else also has blue-and-orange Jordans.

No such luck.

"So, tranny, whatcha doing in the boys' bathroom, huh?" Clyde's snarl makes my stomach turn. *Damn.* One of the stall doors slams and Amar steps out.

"What's going on here?" Amar asks, giving a nod of acknowledgment to Clyde and then turning to stare at me.

"I just have to pee, guys. Let me be," I say, my eyes returning to Clyde's shoes.

"Yeah?" Clyde jeers. "Yeah, well, this is the *boys'* bathroom. Only *boys* pee in here." He spits the word *boys* and then takes a step toward me. I raise my eyes to his and straighten my back. *Tall and confident.*

"I know," I say, my voice sounding smaller than I want it to. "I *am* a boy." Amar scoffs, looking at Clyde.

"Yeah, right—" Clyde says. He moves as if he's going to take another step toward me. I flinch and take a step backward. He fakes shoving me and Amar laughs, clapping Clyde on the shoulder. I don't know what to do. I wonder if I could slip by Clyde, but he's standing so that he blocks both of the stalls.

"Stop looking at the stalls! If you're a real boy, you'll pee in the urinal," Clyde says.

"Plenty of men don't like peeing in the urinal. It doesn't make me less of a real boy," I say, repeating what Dad's told me a million times. *I don't need to pee in a urinal to be a man,* I tell myself in my head. I have to go so badly that the effort of holding it has me sweating now.

"Get out of here." Clyde's tone has shifted from taunting to angry. *What should I do?* I'm about to pee myself, and I can't use the girls' bathroom and I'm going to be late for class if I try to run down to the gym locker rooms—though I guess I'm already late as it is.

"I said get out!" I look up in time to see Clyde's angry face as he shoves my chest, hard. I stumble backward, knocking into the wall and paper towel dispenser behind me.

"You're such a gross tranny fag!" he shouts at me. I wonder if I'm imagining the tears in his eyes and suddenly an image flashes in my memory. We're in fourth grade, maybe third. We're walking to the car with Coach Bolton. When

Clyde reaches up to grab his dad's hand, Coach Bolton snatches his away with a gruff "Men do *not* hold hands." The memory of the sadness and surprise I saw in Clyde's face still makes my stomach tense.

"What? But—but, I—but we used to?" Clyde had stammered, his face falling. I remember my chest feeling tight.

"'Used to,' that's right. But now you're older. You're growing up and you have to man up, too. No more holding hands. Don't be such a girl." I remember feeling so confused. I think Mom and Dad would be thrilled if Jae-sung did that—they always complain he never lets them hug him. Also, doesn't every eight-year-old hold their parent's hand?

Clyde's eyes had filled with tears.

"Don't you dare cry, boy. Man up."

Clyde had slowed, falling into step with me instead of his dad. I walked with him, my shorter legs doing double time to keep up. He was tall then, too. I bumped him playfully, trying to get him to smile. He had looked at me, silently crying. I didn't know what to say or do so I gave him a hug, quick and silent, not wanting Coach Bolton to yell again.

In our seventh-grade bathroom, I see the same eyes. *He's sad? Or hurt?* I wonder what he's thinking—where the real Clyde just went—but he buries his fist in my stomach and everything blurs. I bend over, sinking to the floor. I wonder why I don't fight back—I know Jae-sung would have by now. My eyes closed, I hold my breath, waiting for the air to refill my lungs. There's that terrifying feeling you always get right when the wind is knocked out of you and you think, *Will I ever breathe again?* But all you can do is wait.

The bathroom is silent except for the sound of me gasping for air. Amar looks surprised. Clyde stands over me and I wonder if he'll hit me again. I keep thinking about his eyes. I don't think I hit my head, but I'm reeling and I don't see him winding up for another punch but he must because I hear Amar grab him and they struggle.

"What the hell, 'Mar," Clyde says through gritted teeth.

"C'mon, man. Let's just go." I catch Amar's eye for a moment. His expression is hardened, maybe even concerned.

"Little fag pissed itself," Clyde adds with a nasty chuckle as the door swings shut. *Itself.* I realize that the groin area of my jeans is soaked a darker blue. *Are you kidding me? What am I supposed to do now?* If I leave the bathroom, everyone will see that I've peed myself. If I stay here, I'll miss class. And I never miss class.

I tuck my arms around myself, holding my elbows, and feel something wet in my left palm. My hand comes away bloody. *When did that happen?*

I push myself up from the floor. There's a sharp pain in my side, kind of like the stitches I get when I eat too close to swim practice. But it doesn't get worse as I stand fully and slip into the stall, finally. Thank god no one else came into the bathroom. I let the rest of my bladder empty, cursing myself for not being able to hold it.

I must sit there for longer than I notice because then the end-of-period bell is ringing. *Crap.* Now what? Not only does this mean the hallways are going to be packed; I've also now missed an entire period. AND my backpack is still sitting in my chair in Mr. Devi's classroom.

———

I wait for the second bell, indicating the beginning of third period. Then I creep out of the bathroom, praying everyone is in their classrooms. I eventually find myself tracing my morning steps to Mrs. Salmani's room. The hallway is empty and I thank whatever god is up there that no one else is late to class today.

But god only has so much luck in store for me because when I get to Mrs. Salmani's room, it's empty. My heart sinks. Not knowing where else to go, I open the door and sit down at a desk. I rest my head on my arms. My elbow is still bleeding and I don't know what to do, so I just hold it. I hear my dad's voice from when I split my chin open in second grade: *Pressure. Apply pressure!* So I do. It hurts a lot now, but still I'm lost in my head.

I feel Clyde's hands on my chest, watch myself stumble backward, and feel the rage building. *I hate you!* I want to scream at him. *I hate you* and *your dad!* The anger gives way to my tears and I think about how close we used to be. I don't hate him. Actually, that might be the problem. I miss him—I miss how we used to be friends. *How can you be so different from then? What happened to me, you, and Lucy? Why are you such a jerk to me now? Where has Lucy gone? I—*

"Obie-jaan? My goodness, what happened?!" Mrs. Salmani rushes over to me with a short, round glass bottle in her hand. Martinelli's old-fashioned apple juice. It's her signature. She drags a chair over. When she touches my shoulder, I lose it.

"I, he—I tried—tall and confident—I tried—but—" I say through tears.

"Slow down, slow down. Deep breath. Good. I'm assuming we're talking about that rascal Clyde, right?" I nod. "Did he do this to you?" Her voice is taut, motioning to my elbow. I look. It's gushing now and there's a good amount of blood on the desk. And on my hand from applying pressure. It doesn't look so great.

"Shoved—and I had to go to the bathroom and—" The words all get stuck in my mouth and I feel a strange pain in my side.

"Take your time," she says encouragingly. I begin to cry again. When I don't stop and can't explain, she says, "I think the nurse needs to take a look at you." I know she's right, but the thought of leaving the safety of her classroom terrifies me.

"Listen, we'll go together. It'll be okay." *What if Clyde discovers I tattled and comes to find me later? I can't tell* anyone. But the words don't come. I just shake my head again.

"Obadiah," she says, her voice dipping like adult voices do when they think they're right and they feel bad for you in the good kind of way. "We have to explain what happened."

"No," I start. But I can't finish.

"It's going to be okay. I'll be there and I'll make sure Mr. Bolton is held responsible."

"Maybe I should have just held it—" My tears have started again. Mrs. Salmani raises her hand and tilts my chin up from looking at the floor.

"No. Zechariah-Obadiah," she says, suddenly stern and using my full name like my parents do when I'm in trouble. "You didn't do anything wrong. This is *not* your fault." Somewhere inside I think I know that. But still. If I'd just gone at a different time or to a different bathroom, this wouldn't have happened and I wouldn't be sitting here in my own pee, wondering if I'll ever belong anywhere ever again.

Mrs. Salmani hands me a tissue and I realize that in addition to my blood-soaked palm, the tears have dragged the snot from my nose, too, and I'm an absolute mess.

"Why don't you hang here for a few minutes while I give Principal Franklin a call?" *The principal?!* I look at her incredulously. I thought she said I wasn't in trouble.

But I don't think I have any choice so I just nod. "Okay," I say.

She pats my not-bloody arm and gets up. I hear her dial. The room is so quiet I can hear the muffled sound of Principal Franklin's voice, but I can't make out the words.

We get to the nurse before the principal does. I am indifferent about the nurse. She's nice, and the gender-neutral bathroom is in her room, so I've been there a few times, especially when I was first transitioning. But we've never talked much.

She cleans my elbow carefully. It stings and I wince, but I don't say anything.

"You're going to have to go to the hospital, Mr. Chang." I like that she calls me that. It makes me feel like an adult.

"This needs stitches. Did anything else happen?" She hasn't asked many questions so far. She'd just nodded when Mrs. Salmani whispered a few things to her when we first got there.

"N-n-no, well, y-yes," I stammer. "He punched me, too."

"Where?"

"My stomach," I answer, feeling the slug all over again.

"Hmmm, okay. Have you coughed or vomited anything up? Any blood?"

"No," I answer. *Coughing blood?*

"Okay, good—"

"Hello there, Mr. Chang," the principal says as she enters, and it doesn't feel nearly as affirming as when the nurse said it. "Mrs. Salmani." The principal nods with an expression I can't quite read.

"Hello, Deborah," Mrs. Salmani says, and I'm pretty sure her smile is fake. I get the sense that she doesn't like Principal Franklin all that much. I've only talked to Principal Franklin twice. And the first time didn't even really count because Mom did most of the talking. That was during That Year, after I'd told Mom and Dad and we'd had a meeting with Principal Franklin to tell the school, too. Principal Franklin was not like Mrs. Salmani—she was never going to give me a hug or call me honey. But she made it very clear that no discrimination would be tolerated in her school. I think she was also pretty afraid of Mom. That's fair. I would be, too. Mom can be scary when she's mad. Anyway, Principal Franklin is nice, I guess, but she's not the kind of person I'd ever want to spend time alone with. I think I'd turn into an icicle.

The second time I had to talk with her was when we were telling the school. Mom and I wrote The Big Email that Principal Franklin sent to all the teachers. It basically said that I'm transgender. We even added for the people who didn't know: "This means that even though the doctors assigned me female at birth, I am actually a boy." I hadn't known that sending it to all teachers meant all the coaches, too. That first practice after wasn't fun.

"Mrs. Salmani tells me there was a little incident in the bathroom today, Mr. Chang?" I nod. She's very matter-of-fact. Honestly, I think I'd like that, usually. I look at her. She's much younger than many of the teachers. Definitely younger than Mrs. Salmani. She's got freckles that sprinkle the bridge of her nose and I wonder if she's wearing contacts because her eyes are so blue that I'm not sure they're real.

"Can you tell me what happened?"

I look at Mrs. Salmani, who smiles encouragingly.

"No," I mumble, still sitting on the nurse's bench. *What am I doing?* I scream in my head. She doesn't *actually* care if I *want* to tell her or not. She just wants me to tell her. Principal Franklin's brows rise in surprise. I know she knows I'm a good student, which means I shouldn't be acting so refractory. *Refractory* is a new word that I learned in Mrs. Salmani's class. It means "resistant to control or authority." Mrs. Salmani says that it usually has a negative connotation, but sometimes you should be refractory. Like when Rashad's dad is telling him that he did something wrong in the second chapter of *All American Boys.* Rashad didn't do anything wrong, and he knows it, so he resists. I guess sometimes being refractory can be brave.

"Obie, I can't help you if you don't tell me what happened," Principal Franklin is saying, and I can hear the frustration creeping in. I look at Mrs. Salmani again.

"Honey," she says gently. "Tell her."

"I, uh, something happened," I start stupidly. Principal Franklin pulls up a rolling chair and sits at eye level with me.

"Obie, listen to me. I understand today was hard—I can clearly see that you had a run-in. I need you to tell me what happened so we can move forward quickly and appropriately." Principal Franklin carefully enunciates each syllable of the word *appropriately.*

"Clyde—Clyde Bolton. He's Coach Bolton's—" I begin again.

"I am very familiar with him," she interrupts.

"He, uh, he doesn't like me," I say. She looks at me, waiting for more. "I had to use the bathroom. But he was in there, too." I look at the door and through the small window. *What if he hears me and then tells his dad?*

Mrs. Salmani sits down next to me and wraps her arm around me and places her other hand on mine. I stare at her hand. Worn—like wise. Weathered—like practiced. I love old hands. As a kid, I always traced my halmoni's veins on the back of her hand because through the thin, old skin, they were raised and soft. Halmoni always let me. Mrs. Salmani squeezes my hand and I continue.

"And he wouldn't let me. He shoved me into the wall, called me names, and told me to get out because . . ." I trail off. *Tall and confident,* I remind myself. "Because I'm transgender—he kept calling me a girl and telling me to pee at the urinal. . . ." I falter, embarrassed. Mrs. Salmani rubs my shoulder and I take a deep breath.

"And then he shoved me and I fell into the metal towel dispenser thing, and that's how I got this—" I show her my bandaged elbow, which is bleeding through the gauze. "And then he punched me in my stomach and they—" I'm staring at the linoleum as I say this. I don't want to see their reactions—the pity or the fear or the disbelief.

" 'They'? 'They' who? I thought you said it was Clyde," Mrs. Salmani interrupts.

"Amar Arnold was with him," I explain. "But Amar

didn't touch me. He laughed at me and was, like, clapping Clyde on the back and stuff when Clyde was yelling at me. But in the end, I think he stopped Clyde from hitting me again and they left while I was still on the floor." I take a deep breath, looking at the veins in Mrs. Salmani's hands. "And I smell like the bathroom . . . because I, uh, I—" My cheeks feel hot and I'm sure they can see it all over my face. "I couldn't hold it."

"Oh, honey," Mrs. Salmani says, and pulls me into a hug.

"They called me the f-word a lot." I feel like a tattler, but everything's spilling out. "And some other mean things."

"Okay. I'm sorry this happened to you, Obie. I'm going to call your mom right away. She will need to take you to the hospital to get that elbow examined. I'll talk to her about further steps," Principal Franklin says, nodding. She's standing up when I finally find my voice again.

"No, no, please don't call my mom!" I say, my voice rising. "It'll just make her upset; I don't want her to know," I plead.

"Obie, I'm sorry, but it's school policy. I will need to discipline those boys and call their parents as well." Principal Franklin says all of this so evenly, like she does it every day. *Coach Bolton? What good is that going to do?* I should have just stayed locked in that bathroom.

"But—" I try.

"You have to go to the hospital, Obie," the nurse interrupts. I want to scream. *I feel fine. I don't need to go to the* hospital. *All the doctors care about are cuts and bruises and blood and all that. But a doctor can't make me unhear all the things Clyde said. Can't fix our broken friendship and bring him back. Can't make me stop feeling afraid every time I have to just pee. A doctor isn't going to take away this feeling I have. But my elbow will heal. What if my brain never does?*

"I'm sorry, I'm legally obligated to involve your parents," Principal Franklin is saying. "You can choose who I call first, if you like." I don't know if that makes it any better. I don't say anything.

"Okay, I'm calling your mom." She dials.

PEOPLE WHO BELIEVE I'M MAN ENOUGH:
1. Mom and Dad
2. Jae-sung
3. Mrs. Salmani

PEOPLE WHO DON'T:
1. Coach Bolton
2. Clyde Bolton

Chapter 4

When we get to the hospital, Dad walks me to the bathroom (which is single-stalled, thank goodness) so I can change into the clean pants and underwear he brought me.

When we see the doctor, she says I need stitches in my elbow—I guess the school nurse was right. On a silver tray, she lines up some needles that look a lot like the needles I use for my testosterone shots.

"This is lidocaine," she says. "It numbs your skin for when we sew the stitches. The first one will pinch—" I nod. "And the rest you won't feel." She smiles, her face stretched. I can tell she doesn't smile often. Someone must have told her about how I got the cut. I'm guessing she feels bad for me.

"Don't bend your elbow for a few days while it heals. No swimming or water—"

"What?!" I exclaim, knocking into the silver tray, sending it clattering to the floor. "Ah, crap," I say apologetically.

Dad shoots me a look and gets up to help but the doctor waves him off and bends down to pick up the tray.

"No swimming for how long?" I ask, trying to temper my voice. Invitational is next month. I can't take time off!

"At least two weeks," she says. "You need to let the skin close before you expose it to water. It could get infected."

"But I'm a competitive swimmer," I say indignantly. "Isn't there some waterproof bandage I can use?"

"Waterproof bandages rarely keep it one hundred percent dry, hon."

"What about if I kick on a kickboard and keep my arm out of the water?"

"Obie," Dad warns.

"Hmmmm. I guess that could work. I'll have the nurse come back and chat with you before you go." She leaves, shutting the door softly behind her. I wonder how many times a day she has to deal with argumentative patients like me.

"It's going to be okay if you have to miss practice for a few days. I'm sure Coach will understand."

"I don't care about Coach—plus Coach goes too easy on us anyway. This is about Invitational and JOs. I *can't* get out of shape!" *Screw you, Clyde. Maybe this was your plan all along—injure me so I can't even make the cut for JOs to race you.*

"You're not going to get out of shape in a week or even two. You're young. You're going to be just fine. And! You could cross-train. You know that's super good for you." The tears that have been clawing at the back of my throat burn a little less. Dad's right; maybe I could go running or something. Even though I hate running. I guess I could even go to practice. . . . Do drylands on the deck while everyone else swims. Ugh, that sounds horrible. But. It could work.

"That's true . . . ," I concede. Three knocks on the door.

"Come in," Dad says.

"So, I hear you want to swim sooner than the doctor told you you can?" the nurse says as she enters.

"Yes, I'm training for a big meet. I can't miss that much practice!"

"I'm sorry, bud, you're going to have to stay out of the water for at least ten days." Ever since I transitioned, people call me bud. I haven't decided if I like it or not yet. It's not like boss. That makes me feel important. Bud is what Jae-sung calls me when he's trying to make sure I remember he's older.

"I can't risk you getting an infection," the nurse continues. "That would keep you from swimming for a whole lot longer."

I grumble audibly, imagining Dad's eyes boring a hole in my head for being rude. But I don't care. *What am I going to do?*

"But—"

"If you take care of yourself for a few days *now,* you won't have to take off many days, or maybe *weeks,* later."

I nod begrudgingly.

"Maybe *next* Friday—in nine days—you can kick on a kickboard with a plastic bag tied over your arm. If you want to." I look up, excited.

"And then you come the following Wednesday—in two weeks exactly—and we'll see if it's safe for you to swim then. If so, you can go to practice the next day, depending on what time we see you."

"Okay." I nod vigorously. Two weeks is a long time off. But that's better than months, I guess.

"Thank you," Dad says, putting his hand on my shoulder. He squeezes and I know this means *Say thank you.*

"Yeah, thanks," I mumble. But I just wish I could sink underwater. *Not till next, next Wednesday. . . .*

We leave before the school day ends. I guess that's the benefit of getting beat up early in the morning.

———

Dad pulls the car into our driveway and puts it in park. He looks at me for a second. I don't like the concern. It scares me. It's like confirmation that something is really wrong.

"How are you really?" he asks. I stare at my lap. I don't have an answer. My elbow has begun to throb. The lidocaine must be wearing off. I stare at the clock: 1:45 p.m. An hour and a half left of school.

"Do I have to go back to school?" I ask, praying not.

"No, no, of course not. Why don't we get something to eat and you can watch TV for the rest of today?"

"Swim practice . . . ," I say, trailing off. That's really where I want to go.

"I know, O. I'm sorry, you're going to have to wait. I don't think you should do anything today. Today is for rest."

"What's going to happen next?" I ask. My eyes are suddenly heavy and the thought of having to go to practice or to school tomorrow morning is exhausting.

"Well, I've been texting Mom to keep her posted and she's going to meet us at home soon. She's been on the phone with Principal Franklin about what to do moving forward, but Clyde and Amar have been suspended until further notice."

"So they won't be at school tomorrow?" I feel a sliver of relief.

"Nope. You don't have to go to school tomorrow, either, Obie. I think we can play a little hooky, if you want. In fact, I think we're overdue." He winks at me and I allow a hesitant smile. Last time we played hooky, Dad took Jae-sung and me to Six Flags in Western Mass. I love roller coasters. Jae-sung loves funnel cake. It was the best day ever. I was only sad that Lucy and Clyde couldn't come. My smile dissolves.

"All right, why don't we go get a snack and then be home in time to meet Mom? How's that sound?" My stomach growls. *Crap, my backpack.*

"Ugh," I sigh.

"What?" Dad asks.

"I left my backpack in Mr. Devi's room before . . ." I trail off.

"That's okay. Your lunch box might be a bit smelly tomorrow or whenever we grab it. No big deal. Let's just go to Chotley's, okay?"

Dad backs out of the driveway and takes us to Chotley's Deli, which is only about five minutes away from our house. It's our place. Just me and Dad. Mom can't eat there because they don't have anything gluten-free, and Jae-sung doesn't like it because they don't have honey mustard. Yeah, I know, kind of strange for a sandwich shop not to have honey mustard. But I like that it's just a me-and-Dad thing. Dad's been coming here ever since he first moved to the US in the seventies. He says it was the first American food he remembers having. I wonder if it'll be my and my own kid's place someday, too.

We park in the small lot behind the store and walk in. The door rings the mini Santa bell that they've got hanging from it. Don't be fooled—they're not overeager about setting up their Christmas decorations this soon. That Santa bell is there all year round.

"Heyyyy, Richie Boy." Mr. Chotley's voice bellows from the register. Dad beams. I think Mr. Chotley is the only person in the whole world who calls Dad Richie. Dad's not really a nickname type of guy. He makes everyone call him Dr. Chang, or if they're friends, Richard. But I think

Mr. Chotley is special because he's known Dad since Dad was younger than I am.

"How's it going, boss?" Mr. Chotley asks me. Mr. Chotley is a big man. He's only an inch or two taller than Dad, but his shoulders are probably double as wide. He's thick, especially compared to Dad's wiry frame, and his belly could trick you into thinking he's Santa Claus if he were wearing the right colors. He's got the booming voice to go with it, too. And I'd definitely describe him as jolly. To everyone. Mr. Chotley is the kind of guy who doesn't care who or what you are; as long as you like his food, he's happy.

"I'm doing okay," I say. I can't help but smile as he offers me a piece of Armenian string cheese. He knows it's my favorite.

"What's going on with the elbow, boss?" Mr. Chotley bellows. "Not getting into any fights, are we?" I know he's joking, but today is obviously not the right day.

"No, sir. I, uh—"

"Oh, he just fell during gym class. You know how they are," Dad chimes in.

"I do, I do," Mr. Chotley laughs. "The usual?" he asks. We both nod.

I open the bag of jalapeño chips I grabbed from the counter. *What's going to happen if Clyde gets expelled?* He'll still be able to swim for the club team, even if he can't swim for our school. *Coach Bolton is going to kill me.*

"So, how is school aside from, uh, this?" Dad tries. I

remember suddenly that it's Wednesday and I'm supposed to have my weekly meeting with Mrs. Salmani.

"Dad, I'm gonna miss my meeting with Mrs. Salmani!" I exclaim.

"Shh, shh, don't worry—I'm sure Mom already talked to her. Mrs. Salmani will understand either way."

"Excuse me," says a cheery voice that is most definitely not Mr. Chotley's. We both look up. A girl with warm brown skin and striking green eyes who can't be much older than I am stands next to the table holding a tray with our sandwiches.

"Who are you?" I ask without thinking. I know every employee here. Dad and I come at least once every week. So who is this girl?

"Obie! Don't be rude," Dad interjects.

"Sorry," I mumble, but keep staring at her. She's still smiling at me, seemingly unbothered by my abruptness.

"It's okay. Hi! I'm Charlotte. Most people call me Charlie, though. Grandpa's my, um . . ." She pauses, thinking. "My great-uncle. I call him Grandpa, though. I just moved here last week with my mom and I'm helping out. Mom said Grandpa needed help." She leans in and whispers to us, but mostly to me, "Mom says he's getting creaaaaky!"

"But you look like you're my age," I say, ignoring the whisper. "Why aren't you at school?" It's still only about 2:15 p.m. and most of the schools in the area go until 3:15.

"Why aren't *you* at school?" Touché.

"I had, uh, an incident," I say, looking quickly at Dad.

"Oh, okay." Her gaze doesn't falter. She keeps her eyes fixed on mine. They're bright and excited and . . . beautiful.

"My school ends at two," she continues, "and I always head over here right after." She sets our sandwiches down on the table one at a time. I examine mine. Mayo, check. Jalapeños, check. Armenian string cheese, check. Red onions, check. Pickle on the side—nope.

"You forgot the pickle on the side," I say. It comes out a bit flatter than I meant it to.

"Please," Dad reminds me before I can add it. Then to Charlie: "I'm sorry, he's had a tough day today. You seem very sweet, Charlotte."

"It's okay," she says, seemingly unfazed. "I'm sorry—" She pauses and it takes me a moment to realize she's waiting for me to tell her my name.

"Obie," I say.

"Obie! Ooh, I like that."

She leaves and returns a few moments later with three pickle spears.

"A few extra, just in case," she says, grinning. The dimples in her cheeks deepen.

"You'll like her, Obie," comes Mr. Chotley's booming voice from the kitchen. "I know she's new, but I'm getting old so I can use the help. Give her a chance."

"You're not old," I respond loudly. He looks the same as

he always has. Plus, if this is going to be my own kid's place someday, Mr. Chotley can't get old.

I look at Charlotte, who is now standing behind the counter. She grins and gives me a tiny wave.

"You're blushing," Dad smirks. I shoot him my best death glare, hoping it looks like Mom's expression when Jae-sung forgets to take his shoes off and tracks mud all over the house. Dad just smiles.

Chapter 5

When we get home, Mom's waiting for us. She looks tired, but she wraps me in a tight hug.

"Ow!" I yelp as she pulls me in, putting pressure on my new stitches.

"Oh goodness, I'm sorry!" she says, releasing me quickly. She cups my face in her hands and kisses both of my cheeks and then my forehead.

"So," she says, looking at Dad, "I just got off the phone with Principal Franklin."

"Oh?" he says, setting his bag down.

"What did she say?" I ask.

"I think we should call the police," Mom says, ignoring me.

"THE POLICE?" I don't mean to, but I shriek.

"Okay, okay," Dad says, and pulls me to a seat at the kitchen table. "Listen—"

"EVERYONE IS TELLING ME TO 'LISTEN' TODAY," I yell. "BUT NO ONE IS ASKING ME WHAT

I WANT AND *I'M* THE ONE WHO GOT BEAT UP!"
I spit a little as I shout, but I don't care. I don't apologize,
either. Mom and Dad look surprised. Mom nods rapidly and
puts her hand on mine. I breathe heavily and the cut on my
elbow throbs.

"I'm sorry, honey—you're right. We're just, we're—"
She looks at Dad, who's looking at me. "You know what, it
doesn't matter. You're right. This is about you. What do *you*
want?"

I glance at both of them and then down at my lap. I don't
really know what to say. I didn't expect them to give in so
quickly.

"I don't know. I just don't want to make it a big deal. . . .
I just want all of it to go away, and you guys are making it
worse." I'm crying now. *Dammit.*

"Honey." Mom tries to pull me into a hug.

"AND STOP CALLING ME HONEY! I'M NOT A
BABY!" I yell.

"Okay, okay," she says, pulling back. I feel kind of bad
for yelling. I know she's just trying to help. But I just want
to forget it happened. I want Clyde to go back to being my
friend. I want to disappear into my classes and the pool. . . .

"Obie," she tries, "I'm so sorry those boys were so hate-
ful. I don't know where sweet little Clyde went." She looks
away for a moment and then back at me. "I'm so sorry," she
says again.

"It's okay, Mom," I pretend. Her face clouds.

"No. It's not," she says, and there's an edge to her voice. "It is *not* okay, honey. Don't ever say that. Don't let someone else tell you that. You're allowed to be okay or not okay or feel however you feel. But what those boys did—is never okay. Do you understand me?" I nod slowly, pretty surprised by her outburst. "I know you don't want this to be a big deal," she continues, "and you don't have to go blasting it on Snapcaps or Instagram or whatever—"

"Snap*chat*," I correct her through my sniffles.

"Snapchat," she says. "You don't have to post about it or tell your friends about it if you don't want to. But what those boys did was not okay, and they must be disciplined accordingly."

"Clyde should be, but Amar didn't touch me," I say. Amar wasn't exactly nice, but I'm pretty sure he's the reason I wasn't kicked to a pulp. "He actually stopped Clyde from hitting me again. Clyde was going for another, but Amar pulled him off and told him they should go." I pause, though, remembering Amar standing in front of the stalls, not letting me pass.

"He watched it happen," I add, "and laughed at me. But maybe he doesn't need to be suspended. . . ."

"I'm not sure I agree, Obie. As I understand it, Amar *saw* Clyde act violently before he stepped in. He shouldn't have just watched," Mom says skeptically.

"Regardless, suspension and expulsion are all the school

can do," Dad says. "Beyond that, we—Mom and I—can press legal charges. We could call the police, get a lawyer. . . ."

I stare at the backs of my hands. I rub the smooth skin of the small scar on my right middle finger. It's from the tip of a glue gun in third grade. One Saturday morning, Clyde and Lucy had come over after practice—they used to come over almost every day, we were kind of the three musketeers for a while—and we'd decided to make an enormous sign that read BOLTON'S BARRACUDAS in big wooden letters. While we were waiting for Dad to come help us, we had our favorite song—"Eye of the Tiger"—blasting on the speakers, belting out, "IT'S THE THRILL OF THE FIGHT!" together. We'd decided that Clyde would be in charge of the glue, I'd place the block letters, then Lucy would paint. I went to set the first "B" down but didn't realize that Clyde wasn't done outlining it. We reached over at the same time, Clyde's eyes closed, still singing, and he stabbed my middle finger with the glue gun. It stung pretty bad.

After he rushed back from getting me ice, Dad was so annoyed. I didn't get much sympathy at all.

"You were supposed to wait. You know that's the rule," he'd said with that adult shrug that is definitely *not* a shrug of indifference. It's a shrug of condescending I-told-you-so. We lost glue-gun privileges for a bit after that.

As I sit in our kitchen with Mom and Dad both looking at me, I feel the sting of that hot glue against my finger all over again and I remember how I'd screamed. And then how Clyde screamed and then sob-cried.

How could we be suing the kid who cried because he accidentally hurt me when we were eight? How can the kid who cried because he accidentally hurt me be the same kid who hurt me on purpose today?

"Well, we've got a meeting with everyone tomorrow morning, so let's hold off on making any more decisions until then," Dad says.

"Wait, so Coach Bolton is going to be there?" I ask nervously. "Do I have to go?"

"I think so, honey. But we'll be there together, okay?" Mom touches my forearm.

"Can Mrs. Salmani come, too?" I ask.

"We'll see. I'll give her a call." She picks up her phone and Dad stands. I get up from the table, too, cradling my elbow, which is really throbbing now.

"Do you need some ibuprofen?" Mom asks worriedly. Dad hands her the school phone book and I walk toward the stairs.

"Maybe in a little," I answer. "I'm going to go do some homework."

"Okay," Mom calls. "I love you." I don't answer.

———

In my room, I sit at my desk and unlock my phone. I click through Instagram stories. Jackson and some guys from the team goofing around after practice. Pooch and his dog. He really loves that dog. Mikey and his younger brother.

When Clyde's face appears, my stomach seizes. It's a selfie of him and the caption says "Faggots burn in hell" with a few emojis. I hadn't thought to delete him, even though it's been over a year since we've been friends. I guess longer than that. We haven't really spent time together since the end of fifth grade.

Before I can change my mind, I click on the Settings icon and hit REMOVE FRIEND. There should be a button for REMOVE EX-FRIEND.

I get a Snapchat a few moments later. It's from Lucy. I haven't heard from her since maybe Summer Champs? And even before then, we barely saw each other. Really since Bolton kicked me off the 'Cudas. . . . I hesitate before I open the snap. *Should I?*

I do and I find myself looking at a video of her cat, Sagwa, playing with a couple girls. I can't see who they are. There's a lot of giggling and my stomach twists. I miss her. Us. But I think about how we'd barely even said hello when we'd seen each other at the meet. I've told myself for months that the distance and weirdness is just because we're not training together anymore. But we could have easily hung out. But we didn't.

Just text her, ask her to hang out, I tell myself. *But I'm the one who got kicked out,* I argue back. *Lucy should text me.*

In her Snapchat video, you can hear one of the other girls

say, "Here, kitty, kitty," as she runs—or rather stomps—after the poor cat. I make an amused expression and then caption it, "haha, sagwa doesn't seem to like them, huh," and then, attempting to listen to Mom's advice, I type into the chat: "Hey, I was wondering if you had time to FaceTime today? We haven't talked in forever!"

I hesitate before hitting send. The blue chat icon almost immediately hollows, indicating she's opened my message—she must be on her phone. My phone notifies me that "Lucy Weaver is typing," and I wait. When no response comes, I close the app and reopen. Still nothing.

I crawl into bed, leaving my phone on my desk.

Chapter 6

"We're just waiting for the Boltons and then we'll get started," Principal Franklin is saying. I think I could vomit. Mom, Dad, and I are crushed into a couch that is the opposite of comfy. Maybe it's meant to be added punishment for the kids who get sent to the principal's office. Amar and his mom are in armchairs separated from us by a coffee table with nothing on it. Amar's dad, Dr. Arnold, is standing next to Amar. He looks very concerned—maybe even angry. Dr. Arnold's a nice guy, as far as I know. I mean, I don't know him well. He works at the university, like Dad. I'm not sure what he teaches, but I've seen him a few times on campus when I've visited or had to go to Dad's office for some reason. Dr. Arnold always says hello and smiles at me.

I hear footsteps approaching and the nausea gets a little worse. Maybe it's Mrs. Salmani?

No such luck.

"Hello," Coach Bolton grunts as he enters. He's sporting a beard, which only seems to add to the gruffness in his tone. Clyde follows. I swallow. They stand next to each other, Clyde almost as tall as Coach.

"What about Mrs. Salmani?" I whisper to Mom.

"I'm so sorry," Mom says. "I couldn't convince Principal Franklin to allow Mrs. Salmani to come." I sink into my seat.

"Thank you for joining us, Boltons," Principal Franklin tersely addresses father and son. Clyde grunts and opens his mouth to say something, but Coach Bolton puts his enormous hand on Clyde's shoulder and Clyde winces and stays silent.

"Where should we sit?" Coach Bolton asks.

"Grab a few chairs from the office next door and pull up around the coffee table," Principal Franklin says. Bolton wordlessly complies. I think again about Clyde reaching for Coach Bolton's hand years ago and I wonder again how we got here. *What happened to us?*

"All right, so I assume we all know why we are here, yes?" Principal Franklin starts. We all nod.

"As I understand it, the Changs have agreed not to press charges against the school or either of you two." She looks at Amar and Clyde. "But that does *not* mean you won't face other consequences."

"The school board has agreed that Clyde, because this is your first act of physical violence, you will not be asked to leave school. Instead, your suspension will last one week— effective as of the day of the incident. That means you may return next Wednesday."

Principal Franklin turns to Amar. "Amar, because you stood idle, watching an act of bullying, but did not yourself physically assault Obie, you may return Monday." Amar is already nodding.

"However," Principal Franklin continues, narrowing her eyes a bit, "before either of you is allowed to return, you must provide an official written apology to Obie. I will be reading this letter to decide if it will be sufficient. After you write this letter, both of you will cease all contact with Obie—at school, in class, in the bathrooms, and outside of school. If I or the school learns you've made contact without Obie's consent, you will be expelled immediately."

I try to focus on Principal Franklin as she speaks, but I find myself checking Clyde repeatedly. His face looks completely blank. I don't think I've ever seen him so still. He's always been such a loud kid. Often angry. Well, maybe not as much with me and Lucy. But in the world.

"Does this sound like something you can do, Clyde and Amar?"

"Yes, ma'am," Amar replies immediately. Dr. Arnold, whose eyes could probably bore holes in steel right now, does not seem happy with Amar. Amar looks at me, almost fearfully.

"I'm really sorry, Obie." I think he means it. I'm not sure—

"Well, I'm *not* sorry," Clyde interrupts loudly. "And I'm not writing a damn apology!" Clyde winces as Bolton's grip tightens on his shoulder again.

"What did I tell you about talking?" Bolton says in a low voice. I can see Clyde's jaw clench, but he doesn't say anything.

"Clyde will write an apology to *Sarah*," Coach Bolton declares, using my old name, of course. I open my mouth but before I can—

"Clyde. Will. Write. An. Apology. To. Obie." *Wow,* I think, shocked by Principal Franklin's immediate, cold correction. "Any apologies using the incorrect name or with the incorrect pronouns will not be regarded as an apology." I wonder what the principal would do if she knew why I no longer swim for Coach Bolton.

"Coach Bolton, if you and Clyde cannot respect Obie and his identity, this school is not the right place for you."

Mom glances at Dad. I guess there's my answer.

Coach Bolton's face clouds, but he doesn't argue. I can't read his expression.

"What happened to you, Sarah?" Clyde asks angrily. I see a moment of that third-grade sadness, still pleading. Mom and Dad open their mouths to correct him, but Principal Franklin's quicker.

"Young man, his name is Obie."

"What do you mean?" I ask him, ignoring his use of my old name.

"What happened to you?! Nothing was wrong with you and—and now you've just *destroyed* yourself. You're disgusting," he spits. His eyes are wet and he rubs at them frantically.

"Don't you dare—" Mom starts but I cut her off.

"I didn't destroy myself." I'm so calm I'm surprising myself. Everyone's attention is on me. Amar looks stunned.

"I was destroying myself *before*—living as the girl everyone else told me to be. Transitioning did not destroy me. Pretending to be someone I am not almost did." I waver as I get to the end. Mom rubs my back. Clyde glares at me. No one says anything. I wonder if I should have stayed quiet.

"You're sick," he says after a while. Coach Bolton clamps down on his shoulder again and this time, he yelps.

"Do you want to get kicked out of this school, you dimwit?" Coach Bolton says through gritted teeth.

"Clyde, you are not showing me you are capable of interacting appropriately with Obie," Principal Franklin interrupts. "If you cannot do so, I will expel you, effective immediately, and you will no longer be able to swim for this school. I know that's important to you." Clyde's face is darker than I've ever seen it.

"Clyde will do it," Coach Bolton declares, his voice low.

"I need to hear this promise from Clyde, Coach Bolton," Principal Franklin replies firmly.

"Well, Clyde?" Coach Bolton prompts impatiently.

"No!" Clyde erupts. "I want *Sarah* back! I hate you,

Obie, you ruined everything." He's shrieking now and I think I actually shrink as I feel my entire body contract.

The room goes silent. Even Coach Bolton is quiet. He looks surprised, maybe horrified or . . . afraid? I can only hear my own heartbeat in my ears and I remember Clyde, Lucy, and me listening to our heartbeats with one of Dad's old stethoscopes. Clyde had gotten so excited. *Dude, look,* he'd said. *I mean, listen! It's, like, proof we're alive—*

"Coach Bolton, this behavior is unacceptable. Clyde is no longer welcome at this school. I will communicate this to all of his teachers. Please escort yourselves out while the rest of us discuss further steps. Come meet with me first thing tomorrow morning," Principal Franklin finishes.

Chapter 7

We go straight home after the meeting. I try to relax, thinking about no school tomorrow.

Principal Franklin had said, "Go home, Obie, I'll talk to your teachers. Take whatever time you need."

I hadn't replied. I'd just followed Mom and Dad into the hall. I'd stupidly looked back toward the office and caught Coach Bolton's eye. He was furious. *This is only going to make him hate me more.*

At home, I'm curled up on the couch, watching TV. I probably should read more of *All American Boys* or work on my next essay, but I can't concentrate. Instead, I watch more *Friends* episodes. It's a silly show, I know. But Ross and Joey always make me laugh.

Mom checks on me every hour or so. At some point, she even brings us lunch to share on the couch. She's not a big *Friends* fan. I have to keep explaining who's who and what's going on, but eventually I'm laughing and being goofy and

I'm glad she's with me. I can almost forget why I'm at home in the middle of the day on a school day.

"Are you still up for going to your grandparents' for dinner tonight, honey?" she asks after lunch. *Shoot. I forgot it's Thursday.*

"Uhhh . . . yeah." Halmoni's Korean food actually sounds pretty great right now. "Did you tell her?"

"No, I wanted to ask you first. Do you want me to?"

"Not really," I answer. I don't want to talk about it.

"Okay. She'll probably notice your bandaged elbow, though."

"I'll just tell her I fell."

"Okay," Mom says, carrying away our empty dishes.

———

The door makes the same sound it always makes when I open it. A combination of air whooshing into the room and the rubber lining on the bottom squeaking across the wood floor. The smell of garlic and pungent Korean miso— daenjang—floods my nose. I think of worn hands with soft veins and making kimchi on the floor. (This is the traditional way.)

Halmoni rushes to greet us at the door like she always does.

"Hello-ooo!" she trills, adding an extra "o," in her thick Korean accent. "How are youuuuuu?" Her singsongy welcome. I smile.

"Good," I answer. "Have you been well?" I ask in Korean, giving her a hug.

"Yes, I've been just fine," she replies in Korean. Her eyes widen as she looks me over.

"Uh-mohhh? What happen to your arm?" Mom was right.

"I fell," I say in Korean.

"Hurt a lot?"

I'm glad I decided not to tell her exactly what happened. She's already concerned as it is. Although if I had said a fly hit me, she would probably be similarly worried that I might die, too.

"Ah-ni. I'm okay," I say.

She makes her classic upset face, scrunching her eyebrows together and frowning. She takes my hand and holds on tight, even as she moves to greet Jae-sung.

When she finally lets go, I head downstairs to find Harabuhji. He spends nearly all day in his study. Always has. I didn't know there was that much to learn. And even if there really is, I feel like he should have learned it by now.

"Hi, Harabuhji," I say from the doorway.

"Hello," he answers, barely shifting his gaze from his work to see me.

"Dinner is ready," I tell him in Korean.

"Okay, ready, I coming up, just minute," he replies in English.

"Okay, see you upstairs." I trot up to the kitchen. I help

set the table. Tonight, we're having one of my favorites, kong namul bap. Literally translated, this means "bean sprout rice," but Halmoni makes it so much more than that. Little pieces of salty pork mixed into soft, sticky white rice with sautéed bean sprouts, topped with a perfect vinegary soy sauce and pah—scallions. Mm. Delicious.

Mom, Dad, Jae-sung, Halmoni, Harabuhji, and I gather at the table. We don't technically have assigned seats, but we kinda do. We all sit in the same places every Thursday night. Halmoni leads with the Sign of the Cross. *In the name of the Father, the Son, and the Holy Ghost. . . .* She's really religious. Catholic, actually. I used to go to church with her a lot. I liked it. All the singing, everybody there for the same reason. It made me feel like people loved each other. Or at least loved *some*thing together. I used to pray a lot, too. Nowadays, I'm not sure I still believe in God. Actually, I'm not sure I ever did, really. I would never tell Halmoni that, though. I think it might break her heart.

The last time I really prayed was right after I announced I'm transgender, at the end of fifth grade. All my teachers knew by then. All my friends at school knew or were being told. Coaches—well . . . Coach. Coach Bolton, we were working on. But Halmoni and Harabuhji, not so much.

Halmoni used to give me dresses and pink skirts and lotions all the time. Every birthday, every Christmas, every celebration.

So I prayed. I prayed that Halmoni would still love me.

I prayed that she'd understand. I prayed that if she didn't understand, at least she'd still love me. I prayed that she wouldn't disown Dad. I prayed she'd still let me in her house. I prayed for forgiveness for every time I'd ever disrespected her. I prayed and prayed and prayed. And I think a tiny bit of my faith was restored when I finally got up the nerve to tell her that I'm transgender—that I'm actually a boy—and she said simply: "Okay. So, I have two grandsons from your dad. That's fine." (She's old; fine meant actually fine.)

That was the first time I'd seen Dad cry. I'd known he was nervous because, aside from marrying a white woman, he'd never done anything to disappoint Halmoni. He was your stereotypical Asian tiger mom's dream come true. He'd gotten straight As, gone to Princeton, graduated at the top of his class, gone to Harvard's MD/PhD program (because I guess just med school wasn't enough for him), and become a doctor. And not just any doctor. A pediatric gastroenterologist. Now he mostly just teaches at Harvard Medical School and does some emergency consultations every now and then.

Anyway. He was perfect. Until me. I think he was worried that my being different might somehow be his fault. That his mother would blame him. But instead, Halmoni had said it was fine. And really meant it.

"Obie had a great practice yesterday morning." Mom nudges me as she says this. "Didn't you, hon?" Everyone is staring at me.

"Wah," Halmoni says appreciatively.

"Yes, I did well," I say to Halmoni in Korean. She smiles excitedly. She knows almost nothing about competitive swimming.

"What about that asshole?" Jae-sung butts in.

"Uh-moh," Halmoni and Harabuhji say with sudden surprise at the exact same time.

"Jae-sung!" Mom reprimands.

"Um," I say to Jae-sung. "I only have to see Clyde at club meets from now on." I'm not sure what Mom and Dad told him about this morning's meeting. I know he's mad enough already about my elbow.

A grunt. And then: "Well, you should beat him up anyway. He's trash." I try not to smile. While Mom is not nearly as pleased with Jae-sung's comment, I love it. Jae-sung's compliments are like those fancy whiskeys Grandpa Jordan drinks: they look bad, they smell bad, but they're valuable and rare. At least, that's what Grandpa always says.

Chapter 8

Friday morning, my phone buzzes in my pocket and I resist the urge to check it.

Mr. Devi drones on about how to prove the congruence of two triangles with the Angle-Side-Angle method. He reminds us that Side-Side-Angle doesn't work. A few guys chuckle because if it's written Angle-Side-Side, its abbreviation is ASS. I'm sure Jae-sung laughed at that, too.

The bell finally rings and I gather my things. In the hallway, my stomach flips as I read:

> **LUCY, 9:31 A.M.:** Yo, someone said you pissed your pants at school, what happened?

Fantastic. The entire school knows. That explains all the stares and snickers in the hallways this morning. Even more fantastic to hear it from Lucy, of all people. Lucy, who's given me literal radio silence since the Snapchat of her cat.

Clyde must have told everyone before he got expelled.

But also conveniently avoided the part where he beat me up for no reason. Suddenly I'm furious. Lucy never replied to my Snapchat Wednesday night—even though I could see that she'd opened it. *Guess she was too busy saving Sagwa from those girls.* I roll my eyes. *Now she wants to text me for gossip?* The Lucy I knew would never leave me on read like that.

I probably should have stayed home another day, but I dreaded the makeup work I'd have to do. Now I'm second-guessing myself. My phone lights up again.

> **LUCY, 9:32 A.M.:** And did you hear that Clyde got expelled?!

I guess that's not surprising, either. News travels fast when kids talk. Plus, Clyde was pretty popular. Lucy and I haven't talked about Clyde since I came out to him in fifth grade. I'd told her first, afraid of what Clyde'd think, and then she went with me to tell him. When I finally got out the words *I'm transgender,* he'd just laughed. *You're freaking hilarious,* he'd said, rolling around on the carpet in my room. *I'm not kidding,* I'd said seriously, looking at Lucy for help.

It wasn't pretty after that. Lucy had gone after him when he'd run out of my house. I still don't know what happened exactly when she caught up with him because by the time she got back, I was curled up with Mom, crying. I thought I was losing one of my best friends. I guess I was right.

Lucy had texted me later that evening: I'M SO SORRY, OBIE. MAYBE HE'LL CHANGE? I'd thought, *Maybe. . . . Let's hope.* I'm not sure how much time someone needs when they "just need time," but, right now, it feels like forever.

Should I tell Lucy I know why Clyde got expelled? I wish I could just call Lucy like I used to. A couple years ago, she would have had the play-by-play updates. I would have texted her first thing. *But you did, Obie, and she left you on read.* True. Screw that.

> **ME, 10:15 A.M.:** Don't want to talk about it.
>
> Yeah, I heard.

> **LUCY, 10:16 A.M.:** Jeez, just asking . . .

> **ME, 10:16 A.M.:** Yeah, don't worry. I'm fine.

Of course, fine does not mean fine. Lucy will know that. I wonder if I'm being too harsh, but I'm too hurt to care. For some reason, I find myself thinking about the huge snowstorm we had at the end of third or fourth grade. It was just the three of us—Clyde, Lucy, and me—at practice. Coach had made us swim for only an hour and then he let us play. We ran outside in just our swimsuits and used those big blue recycling bins to build starting blocks of snow. We dove from them into the "pool" of snow. Of course, we totally froze. We raced inside to jump into the real pool and spent the afternoon laughing. Coach Bolton even cracked a smile. That was all before he and Clyde started to hate me.

———

The last bell rings. This might be my least favorite part of the school day. I know. It sounds funny. I hate the crowds of people and, unlike in the mornings, there is no way to avoid them.

I wait until at least the classroom empties, though. No use trying to be the first one to leave. I say goodbye and thank you to Mr. Roberson and step out the door. It's so loud. I wish I could cover my ears but I'm afraid of drawing attention to myself, so I do my usual stare-at-the-floor fast walk. As if ignoring visual stimuli can somehow dampen the sounds.

I turn the corner, nearing the last hallway before the exit, and I see Lucy standing at her locker with a couple girls. Ugh, Jenn and Chelsea. They must have been the two girls in Lucy's snap. Suddenly I'm so glad I didn't tell Lucy any more details when she texted earlier today. Jenn and Chelsea are the biggest gossips in the entire grade. Chelsea is the queen of the popular girls. She's also on swim team with us. Or, I mean, with Lucy. With Coach Bolton. Chelsea's not very fast. But that doesn't matter. She's the one whose chest grew before any other girls' did, making her immediately "cool."

I'm not really sure what the hype is, though. She's not particularly interesting and she's definitely not nice.

Okay, so Chelsea and Jenn have never been directly mean to me. But they were so mean to Lucy when we were younger. I don't understand why she's standing with them.

I catch Lucy's eye. I think she looks afraid. Jenn and Chelsea follow her gaze and see me. They giggle, covering their mouths. I don't catch Lucy's expression because she turns away with them and I'm pushed along in the throng of exiting students.

———

"How was your day?" Dad asks as I buckle my seat belt.

"I think everyone knows what happened," I say. "Even about how . . . you had to bring me new pants. . . ." I try to keep my voice level. "They think they're whispering, but I can hear them plenty." I wish I didn't care. In my mind, I see Chelsea and Jenn giggling and I think about how the only thing they know is that I'm thirteen and still peeing my pants. I wonder if Lucy laughed with them, too, after I left.

"I can call the principal—" Dad offers.

"No," I interrupt. "No, please don't. That'll just make things worse. It's fine. Whatever. People at swim team don't have to know." Dad nods, but I know he'll consult Mom later.

My phone buzzes.

LUCY, 3:01 P.M.: Sorry about that . . .

ME, 3:02 P.M.: Why were you with them?

LUCY, 3:05 P.M.: I guess we've gotten close recently?

ME, 3:06 P.M.: What?! After what they did to you??

LUCY, 3:10 P.M.: They're nice to me now, idk

Mom always says that anger is like holding hot coals with the intent to throw them at someone. You never throw them, so you're the only one who gets burned. I think it's a Buddhist saying. I guess it's true, but you could just put the coals down. You don't have to hand them to the person who made you want to throw them in the first place. . . . Lucy doesn't have to be angry at those girls, but she doesn't have to be friends with them, either.

I type WERE YOU LAUGHING AT ME, TOO? but then delete it, deciding not to reply. It's not like we're close anymore, so what does it matter who she hangs out with? I wonder if I can still consider her a friend even.

I sit quietly for the rest of the car ride. I'm thankful I

don't have to explain myself to Coach Larkin or the other swimmers. Mom already called Larkin about my elbow, and the others can just think I fell down or something. Since I'm not allowed to get into the pool for at least another week and then some, I'll be using the stationary bike in the gym attached to the pool.

My elbow starts to itch as soon as I step onto the pool deck, as if to remind me it's still healing.

"All right, boss, you're going to start with ten minutes' light warm-up, then do ten minutes at heart rate 130, ten minutes heart rate 140, ten minutes heart rate 150, and then five minutes easy. Then come get me and I'll give you the next set, okay?" Coach Larkin's all business, and it's exactly what I need right now.

"Yes, ma'am," I say, and walk toward the weight room.

I hop on one of the good bikes and set it to a reasonable resistance. The wall in front of the cardio machines is all glass and looks out on the pool deck. It's a very decent view. A nice pool is one of my favorite sights in the whole world. The blue water is like a giant translucent crystal.

Not without jealousy, I watch my teammates jump in. Coach must have given the go. Jackson and Pooch push off the wall in unison, kicking a few dolphins before surfacing, and I feel a pull in my stomach. *That's where I should be,* I think. *This is all Clyde's fault!* The anger stings and I pedal faster. *I! Want! To! Swim!* I think with each rotation.

I check the clock on the tiny bike screen: 3:00. *Three*

minutes? That's it? Land sports go so much more slowly than swimming. *All right, let's chill a bit. This is supposed to be warm-up.* I reduce the resistance a few levels and wait for the ten-minute mark.

Ten minutes feels like it takes longer than an entire swim practice, maybe two. But I finally finish the whole forty-five and get up to go ask Coach what's next. My knee buckles with my first step and I almost fall. *Holy cow, I guess this cross-training stuff is serious!* I grin, feeling hopeful. *Maybe I'll be able to keep up good training after all.*

I straighten myself and walk over to Coach.

"Finish up, Obie?" she says, not turning her head from the pool. She's got her stopwatch ready. Looks like the team's doing some timed stuff.

"Yes, ma'am," I say, nodding.

"Great. Next, you're going to do some sprints: thirty-second sprint, one minute easy, fifteen times." *Fifteen?* Seems brutal.

I wait while she shouts a few times.

"Sammy, 29.2, Jackson, 29.4, Mikey, 29.5, Pooch, 30.4." The guys are breathing hard. "Okay, easy one hundred. Do some backstroke." She turns to me. "Obie, injuries don't mean we work any less hard."

I nod.

"And we don't feel bad for ourselves, either. Injuries happen." She lowers her voice, softening a bit. "They shouldn't ever happen the way yours did, but they do happen. And now we are here. And so we move through it, okay?"

"Yes, ma'am, I understand." And I do. *Tall and confident,* I remind myself.

"Injuries mean you have to work harder than everyone else, got it? And harder doesn't always mean more. Sometimes harder means working smarter. It means different. Not being careless and making it worse. You're not getting back into the water even an hour earlier than the doc says. I don't want any infections. You'll cross-train. And you'll train harder and smarter, got it?"

"Yes, ma'am." I scurry over to the gym, feeling a tad lighter on my feet. *I got this.*

"You pedal that bike!" Pooch calls as I slip through the glass door.

———

Coach Larkin is talking to Mom through the car window when I walk outside after practice.

"See you tomorrow, Obes," Mikey says as he walks past me.

"Bye, Mikey," I say. "Bye, Pooch!" I shout to him inside the red car that's driving off.

"Bye, Obes." Pooch's voice comes from far away as they exit the pool parking lot. I cross over to our car.

"Hey, boss," Coach Larkin says. "I was just talking to

your mom about something that might be helpful to you. A former swimmer of mine, Tommy, is also transgender. He swims for Harvard now. I'm not sure if you've heard of him." I nod. I have. I actually follow him on Instagram. He seems cool, I guess.

"He's been pretty open about his experience," she continues. "Anyway, if you wanted, I could connect you and maybe he could help when you're struggling with things . . . especially like with what happened last week?"

I feel a strange knot in my throat and I don't really know what to say. I don't need them to baby me. I don't want to be treated differently. I just want to swim.

"I think I'm okay, Coach—" I say after a little too long.

"I think that would be wonderful, Jamie," Mom butts in. "Obie doesn't have many trans role models. Tommy sounds like a great resource."

"Mom, I'm right here. You don't have to talk for me! I don't need Tommy." Talking to Tommy will just make all this—Clyde, the bathroom, my elbow—so much more real. Make being transgender a problem. Make me even more different than I already am. . . .

"Honey, let's talk about this later," Mom says to me, her voice dropping into that stern tone that says I'm not allowed to argue. "Jamie, that would be lovely if you could get us an email or phone number for Tommy—if he's willing to chat." Coach looks at me. *What?*

"Obie, I'm not going to out you without your consent. Is

it okay if I ask Tommy for his number to give to you? I don't have to tell him who you are, other than another trans swimmer. How does that sound?"

I look at Mom. She's pleading with me.

"Okay," I grumble, agreeing more for Mom than for myself. Maybe I don't have to actually talk to him. Mom can just get his number and it can sit in her phone.

Chapter 9

"Mom, did you ever have a person who was a friend—but then stopped being a friend?" I stumble over the words.

"What, honey? Did something happen?"

"No, not really, I m-m-mean—" I stutter. I take a breath and start playing with a long rubber band I found on my seat. "Kind of," I concede.

"All right, what happened, and who are we talking about?" she asks, using her "I'm ready, hit me" voice.

"Lucy . . . well, Lucy." I'm not sure where to start. "Lucy and I don't really talk a lot now," I try. I turn to look at Mom. She's waiting for more. She knows this because Lucy hasn't been over in months.

I stare out the window as we pass the exit for our house, thinking about my first T appointment. Today will be my third. Lucy came with us to my first. I think it was only a week after Coach Bolton kicked me off the Barracudas last spring. Maybe that was the final time Lucy and I really hung out? I can't remember, but I mean I barely saw her during the summer because there was no school and I couldn't exactly see her at practice. . . . Is that why we don't talk?

"I don't know. I thought it was just because we aren't on the same team anymore, you know? But yesterday I saw her at school with Chelsea and Jenn—"

"Those mean girls from third grade?" Whoa, okay, Mom.

"Yeah, how did you—"

"Those two made Lucy's life absolutely miserable that year. Lucy's mom and I talked a great deal about Chelsea and Jenn. Of course I remember them." Wow, I had known they hurt Lucy's feelings a lot, but I didn't know that her mom knew. I'm not even sure Lucy knew her mom knew.

"So, Lucy's hanging with *those* girls now?"

"Uh-huh." I nod. Mom sharply sucks air through her teeth, making a little *tsk* sound. A car honks nearby and Mom adjusts her grip on the steering wheel. She hates driving in rush-hour traffic.

"And today," I continue, "when I was walking through the hallway, they saw me and were snickering."

"They were *what*?!" Mom's tone switches instantaneously from disapproval to protective anger, and I realize maybe I shouldn't have included that bit.

"It's okay, I was okay. Lots of people were laughing at me today because Clyde had already told the whole school I peed myself—"

"That bastar—" My face must look very surprised

because she stops mid-word, rapidly glancing between me and the road.

"I'm sorry," she says, straining to calm herself. "Clyde told the entire school, though?" So that also wasn't something I should have included. I guess Dad didn't tell her.

"Mom, please, I don't want it to be a big deal. I'll tell you if I feel unsafe, I promise. This is about Lucy."

"Right." She exhales. "Lucy is hanging with Tweedle Mean and Tweedle Meaner."

"Yes," I say, giggling at the nicknames. I'm not sure if moms are allowed to make fun of other kids, but it seems like if the kids are bullies to their kids then the answer is yes.

"And I'm not sure what's going on with Lucy." My smile fades. "I miss her."

"I'm sorry, honey. It sounds like Lucy might be going through some stuff. Why don't you text her and see if she wants to hang out? I'm sure she misses you, too. I know it's frustrating, but now that you aren't on the same team, you're going to have to make more of an active effort to see each other. That's both of your responsibility."

"Okay. Maybe you're right."

"Moms always are."

I roll my eyes.

"Text her after we're done here," she says as she parks the car. "C'mon." I hop out and follow her to the entrance to the doctor's office.

The glass doors slide open when we reach the top of the

steps and that distinct hospital smell greets us. You'd think it'd smell clean, but somehow it doesn't. Maybe *sterile* is the right word. *Too* clean.

"Helloooooo!" Jessica says as she leads us down the hallway to the exam room.

"Hi, Jessica," I say excitedly. Jessica is my favorite nurse. But she had a baby recently and hasn't been around as much, so I'm especially happy to see her. I give her a one-armed hug and she hugs me back.

"Your voice is so deep! And you're getting so tall," she says. I puff out my chest proudly and notice I'm almost as tall as she is. I mean, she's not that tall, but still.

"What did you name your baby?" I blurt. My voice cracks when I say *baby.* She laughs, but in a way that makes me laugh, too.

"Blair," she says, still smiling.

"Oooh, gender neutral. I love it."

"Yes! He's precious," she says, grinning. I sit and she starts taking my vitals.

"It's probably higher than normal," I say as she measures my heart rate. "I'm excited."

"That's okay. Don't worry about it." She pats me on the shoulder as she fits the blood pressure cuff around my bicep and it begins to inflate. I don't know if it's weird, but I kind of love the feeling. It's snug and the pressure feels comforting. Every time I get my blood pressure taken, I think that it would be nice to have a full-body pressure suit. I'd feel so safe.

As she's hanging the cuff on the wall, she's already talking again. "So, Obie." She sits down on one of the doctor chairs and rolls to face me. "Tell me how you're feeling—how are the shots? Still going okay?"

"Yes, they're good. Mom is still helping me with them— she gives them to me—but I don't really get scared anymore. I think I'm getting used to them."

"That's good," she says, nodding. "And are you getting your period?"

Mom took me to the doctor for the first time a couple weeks after I told her. That was when I was eleven. I'd just had my first period. That's really what tipped it all over That Year. The rest of puberty hadn't really hit me yet—I was flat-chested and straight as a bamboo stick, but blood gushed from between my legs as if to say: *IT IS I, WOMANHOOD! I HAVE ARRIVED.* I'd spent that whole day in bed, fighting a panic attack.

Much to my relief, the doctor Mom took me to gave me puberty blockers after a few visits and a note from my thera-pist, Libby, that I was good to go. The blockers stopped my period, prevented any breasts from growing, really stopped anything that puberty would have brought. . . . I was on the blocker until this spring, when I turned thirteen and the doc-tor said I was ready to start testosterone—or "T," as most people call it for short.

"No," I answer. "Thankfully." She nods, understand-ing. I think anyone who's menstruated can understand that

I don't want to have a period. Except maybe ten-year-old girls who seem to wait for it like it's the best present they could ever imagine. It took me a while to understand why. Mom explained that it's a coming-of-age thing. Girls who actually are girls—not like me—actually *want* their womanhood. And periods can be a sign of its arrival. But Mom had added, periods don't make you a woman. And not all women have periods. This is true. But I still didn't want mine.

"How about other effects? What have you noticed?"

"Well, Mom says I can be moody sometimes," I say, rolling my eyes. Mom rolls hers, too, smiling.

"Mhm." Jessica is smiling. "That is bound to happen. Taking testosterone is exactly like going through puberty— I mean, you *are* going through puberty. So you're going to be moody, and that's okay."

"Will I get like Jae-sung?" I ask, and Mom laughs.

"Hmmm, well, I don't know your brother that well," Jessica admits.

"True. Okay," I say, thinking about it. Maybe puberty has something to do with Clyde being such a jerk. He's pretty moody, but I'm not sure if that's the kind of moody that Jessica is talking about.

"What else?" she asks. "Anything you're excited about? How are you feeling about the changes?"

"Oh, it's good. Very good. My voice has changed—which is kind of funny sometimes when it cracks. And I'm getting more hair on my legs. I didn't expect that . . . well, because I'm Asian."

Jessica laughs. "It's genetic, though, so you got it from someone. Maybe your mom?"

"Your grandpa certainly is no naked mole-rat!" Mom chimes in.

"Ewwww," I say at the combination of my grandpa and *naked* in the same sentence.

"Almost no one calls me a girl anymore, and that's the coolest." I nod to myself. "I get to just be me. Obie. A boy." Mom's smiling.

"I also feel stronger, so that's pretty cool." I flex and chuckle at myself.

"And what happened here?" Jessica says, gently touching my elbow bandage.

"Oh." My face falls. "I, uh, I fell," I say, staring at the floor. They've got linoleum tiles here, too.

"Really? Did you fall because you fell or because someone made you fall?" I look at Mom, who looks sheepishly at me.

"Did you . . . ," I say to her.

"Yes, well, no," Mom starts. "Honey, our medical offices and hospitals are all connected, so your doctors can see your ER report. Dr. Lee called me to check in when she saw you'd been in the ER. I told her what happened, and she probably mentioned it to Jessica." Jessica tugs her seat closer to me with her feet. She takes my hand in hers.

"Obie, this isn't something to be ashamed of. You didn't

do anything wrong. Those boys should be expelled for any *one* of the things they did or said to you that day, okay?"

I nod.

"One actually did get expelled," Mom informs Jessica.

"Good," Jessica says emphatically. Then to me, "And it's okay if you don't want to talk about it yet." I nod again. "Are you still seeing your therapist?"

"Yeah, but just every other week now." A few months ago, Libby said I didn't have to come every week if I didn't feel like I needed to. "I'm doing okay. I also go to her support group once a month."

"Oh, good. Have you talked about this?"

"Not yet. My appointment is next week. Mom offered to change it to earlier, but I'm okay. I talked to my teacher about it at school."

"How are your thoughts?" she asks, tilting her head to the side. When medical people ask me this, what they're actually asking is "How suicidal do you feel? Have you thought about hurting yourself lately? Are you safe and can we leave you alone?"

"They're good," I say. And mostly I mean it. Surprisingly, even the Clyde incident hasn't made me feel like I did That Year.

"Promise me you'll talk to Libby about what happened at school?"

"Promise."

"Good." She takes a loud breath. "Okay, now we do the fun stuff." This is sarcasm. She means labs. But I don't hate them nearly as much as I used to.

"You're going to head down and they'll just take a couple vials like last time and then you'll be good to go. Any questions for me?"

"I think I'm good," I say.

"You wanna see a picture of Blair before you go?" she asks in a whisper. I think there's some doctor law that means you're not supposed to talk a lot about your personal life.

"Yes!" I say, lighting up.

Blair is adorable. He's in some baby kangaroo costume— Jessica tells me he was born over the summer, right after my three-month checkup, so he's still only a few months old.

———

Mom reminds me to text Lucy when I get in the car and so I do. Or rather, I try. I type and delete, type and delete. Nothing I write feels right. Finally, I give up and just send something simple. It feels empty, but it's all I've got.

> **ME, 6:30 P.M.:** Hey! I miss you. Hang soon?

Surprisingly, she responds within seconds.

> **LUCY, 6:31 P.M.:** Hey. Maybe . . . When?

> **ME, 6:31 P.M.:** Maybe this weekend?

LUCY, 6:35 P.M.: Cant, im grounded for the rest of november

ME, 6:36 P.M.: What?! Why?

Lucy is, like, a perfect student. But the nonboastful kind. She never breaks any rules. I've never heard of her parents disciplining her for anything, really. I wonder why she's grounded.

I don't get a reply until after dinner.

LUCY, 8:03 P.M.: I failed my bio test last week. Moms pissed.

ME, 8:04 P.M.: What?? How?

Like I said, Lucy's a perfect student. And, I mean, that bio test wasn't easy, but it definitely wasn't hard if you studied—

LUCY, 8:05 P.M.: I didnt study.

Well. I guess that would do it. But why wouldn't she study? Something's definitely wrong.

ME, 8:06 P.M.: Are you okay?

LUCY, 8:10 P.M.: Yeah. Im fine. I gtg.

Lucy is not Halmoni. She is not old. *Fine* does not mean fine. Months ago, I would have just called her. Asked her what's up and what was bugging her. That's what she would have expected. But now? I'm not sure where we stand. Six months ago, she would have called me after failing a test. I mean, Lucy Weaver, *failing* a test? Is the sky falling?

———

"Hey, honey. Remember that boy Jamie told us about today? Tommy? The one who's also transgender and swims?" Mom doesn't wait for my reply. "Well, Jamie sent me his number and I think it could be really good to at least text him."

"Mom," I grumble. Why can't she let it go? I don't need extra help.

"I know you don't want to make a big deal, so it doesn't have to be a big deal. Harvard is so close to us, maybe you can just have lunch with him one day and hang out?"

"He's, like, an adult, Mom," I say. "What am I supposed to say to him?"

"He's not that much older than you are, honey. He's still in college. He probably remembers what it's like to be in middle school."

"I have enough friends." I cross my hands over my chest and I know I'm being refractory. (Yay, vocab words!) To be honest, I'm not really sure why. I don't have any other friends who are trans *and* athletes, and maybe it could be cool to talk to him. But I don't want to be seen in public as The Trans Kids. *Will people stare at us?!*

"I know, but Tommy could be a special friend. Someone who will really understand what you're going through. Even though Dad and I try our best, we still aren't transgender. Look, your dad really loves connecting with other first-generation Korean immigrants because it helps him feel less alone. It doesn't mean there's anything wrong with being Korean. It just means that they have similar experiences that bond them in specific, familiar ways. They can rave about how they love the smell of daenjang and kimchi even though it makes non-Korean people wrinkle their noses." I laugh a little. Daenjang does smell. But it's also a cozy home smell.

Maybe meeting Tommy wouldn't be so bad. He's also kind of a celebrity, so I guess that's cool.

"Maybe," I offer.

"Okay, I'm going to text him," she says, tousling my hair. I grumble but don't protest.

Chapter 10

It's a dark and early Wednesday morning and I survived another cross-training workout. It doesn't give me quite the sense of accomplishment that a good swim workout does, but it'll do for now.

In the car going home, I finish the last few pages of the *All American Boys* reading assignment. In the book, we're reading from a new guy's perspective—Quinn, who was at the store where the main character, Rashad, was beaten up. Quinn watched it all happen. My stomach turns and I feel more than just hunger gnawing at me. I wonder if Amar felt like Quinn did.

I close the book before I can read further. We're almost home.

"How was practice?" Dad asks when he notices the closed book. He's been waiting to ask.

I smile. "Good. The cross-training isn't that bad. But I'm ready to get back in the water, so I'm glad the stitches will be checked—and hopefully fully dissolved—soon. One more week!" I pump my fist in the air.

"As long as the doctor says it's okay," Dad reminds me.

"I know, I know. But I did everything she said! It should be fine, right?"

"Yes, but I just want to make sure you don't set your expectations too high. Okay, son? Bodies heal at different rates, and if yours needs a few extra days, you have to give it that time."

I grumble and nod.

"Good." It's annoying having a doctor for a parent sometimes.

———

Mrs. Salmani is reading when I knock on the doorframe. She's wearing her half-lensed purple reading glasses. They magnify the bottom half of her eyes so that the top half almost peers over the lens. It's a funky old-lady-glasses look.

"Come on in." She smiles. I drag a chair over and sit next to her at her desk.

"So today we're going to review your last essay," she tells me. Her tone shifts into teacher mode. All teachers have this—a different voice they use when they teach. I think most kids only ever hear the teacher voice. No regular-person voice.

"Okay," I say. This last essay was the one I got a B on.

"Now, it was certainly better than your first essay." She gives me a stern look. That was the one I got a C on.

"That's good, right?" I say sheepishly.

"You still have a lot of work to do to improve your writing. Do you have the essay with you?" I nod and reach into my backpack.

We spend the hour dissecting my essay line by line. Mrs. Salmani says I do too much telling, not enough showing.

"You don't always need to *tell* the reader how you felt," she tells me. "You can just say what happened and they will feel the feelings, too. So I would delete the 'I was afraid' bit and let the reader draw the same conclusion from reading that your heart was beating quickly and your palms were sweating. Does that make sense?"

———

I say a quick goodbye to Mrs. Salmani before scuttling off. Then I run down the hallway—usually no other students are around at this time, so it's clear. I'm watching the linoleum tiles rush by me, one foot after another. Hey, maybe this cross-training stuff is paying off! Maybe I'll become a good runner. But I haven't looked up in time to avoid the feet I'm now toppling over. By the time I recognize Lucy, we're both sprawled across the floor. Standing above us are Jenn and Chelsea.

"Dude, like, what the hell?" Jenn says, already posing with one hand on her hip.

"Like, look where you're going?" Chelsea piles on.

"Are you okay?" I say to Lucy, who's gathering up her stuff. As I move closer to help, I notice . . . *makeup? Is Lucy . . .* wearing *makeup?*

"I'm fine," she says angrily. Again, Lucy is not old, so fine does not mean fine. She's wearing eye shadow and something black and goopy is collected at the edges of her eyes. It looks like an eight-year-old Lucy broke into her mom's makeup and tried everything on. Haphazard and lopsided. Although I'm sure Lucy's mom would be happy to see her like this. Lucy and her mom used to fight all the time about Lucy never wearing the right clothes or being "girly" enough. But Lucy never really cared what anyone else thought. I wonder if that's still the case.

Lucy quickly finishes collecting her things—her makeup bag exploded when we fell. I get up first and offer her a hand, but she ignores it.

"I'm sorry," I try again, but they're already walking off together.

I stare for a moment. Lucy is shorter than Jenn and Chelsea, and her hair is shorter. She's wearing the same jeans they are—which is easy to tell because the butt pockets have the same design on them. I've never seen her wear tight jeans before. She used to say they were so uncomfortable and athletic sweats were way better. *Has she changed? Or are they changing her?*

My phone starts buzzing. *Crap.* Mom must be waiting. I sprint to the car.

"Sorry, Mom," I say, opening the door, and she hangs up the phone. Mine stops buzzing in my pocket.

"What held you up? Are you okay?" Worry clouds her annoyance. My face must give something away.

"Yeah, no, I just ran into Lucy," I say. She seems to wait for more, but I don't offer.

"Did you text her last week?" she tries.

"Yeah."

"And?"

"And I didn't see her over the weekend because she said she was grounded." *Grounded.* Doesn't that mean she shouldn't be at school an hour after it's ended, hanging out with two friends and a giant makeup bag?

"But she's at school this late on a Wednesday?" Mom realizes, too. Wednesday means there are no sports after school. Usually the place is all but deserted by this time.

"Yeah." I look down at my lap. "I don't know, Mom, I don't think she wants to spend time with me. She was with Jenn and Chelsea again." I leave out the part about running in the hallway and knocking Lucy over.

"Hmm." We're silent for a bit.

"I could call her mom," she says with a mock evil look.

"Mom, please."

"Okay, okay. You let me know if I can do something, then. Okay, honey?"

"Yes," I grumble.

"Radio or audiobook?"

"Radio, please."

Chapter 11

Mom and Jae-sung are packing when Dad and I get home from practice Thursday morning. They're going to Chicago this weekend to move Grandpa and Grandma to an older-people's community closer to us. We're not supposed to call it a nursing home because Grandpa would *never* agree to that. Mom says Grandma's too old to keep mowing the lawn but "that old woman won't stop until she dies, and I don't want that to be the thing that kills her."

I'm not going this time because I can't miss practice. And Dad's staying with me so he can drive me.

"You're going to be well behaved while I'm away?" Mom asks me, combing my hair with her fingers. "And take good care of your dad?"

"Yes and yes, Mom."

———

That afternoon, Dad doesn't notice when I walk up to the car after practice. He's got his head in his hands and I can see his entire body heaving with the big breaths he's taking. My stomach catches and I'm frozen, standing at the passenger-side window. I don't know what to do.

He looks up before I have to decide. His eyes are wet and a bit red. They meet mine and he quickly looks away, brushing at his face. He unlocks the car and I get in.

"Um, Dad?" I ask quietly. "What happened?"

"Nothing," he says, clearing his throat. "Just, uh, got some tough news about a friend." He stares at the steering wheel.

"Did someone die?"

He hesitates before he says slowly, "It's just . . . a difficult situation."

"Oh." It must be someone he really cares about. I've never seen him cry, come to think of it.

"Hey, why don't we go to Chotley's and grab ourselves some sandwiches before going home. Perk us both up, huh?" He offers a weak smile.

"Okay." I'm never going to turn down Chotley's. Plus, I spent practice hoping he'd offer—since Mom's not home.

When we get on the highway, Dad clears his throat.

"So, Mom tells me you're having some girl trouble, huh?"

"What?"

"With Lucy."

"What? No! Lucy? Lucy's not a *girl*. I mean. Lucy *is* a girl. But she's not *girl* problems, not like that!" I can feel myself flushing.

"Okay, okay," he says, raising one hand defensively. "Okay, then *just-friend* problems." He nods to himself. "What's going on?"

"I don't really want to talk about it," I say, meaning it. I'm tired. What advice is he going to give me, anyway? Lucy is clearly avoiding me, probably because of Jenn and Chelsea, and I don't care anymore.

"Are you sure?" Okay, I mean, I do care. A little. But not a lot.

"Yes," I say firmly. "Tell me about the friend. Someone I know?"

"Let's talk about that later—" His phone saves him by ringing. It's connected to the car's speaker system, so Mom's contact picture shows on the screen. He reaches to hit the green answer button but hesitates and then presses DECLINE.

"Why did you do that?" Now I'm really worried. What if something happened between Mom and Dad?

"Don't worry, I'll text her later. I want to hear about how you're doing right now." I eye him skeptically.

"Are you and Mom fiiighting?" I say, teasing. Sorta. But not.

"No, honey, everything's fine between us," he insists. "I told you, just a tough call about a friend."

I think parents think they can lie to their kids and get away with it. They think because they're adults, if they smile enough and say something with enough fake confidence, kids will believe them. I'm not buying it.

"Let's just grab those sandwiches, okay?" Something *is* wrong.

I would argue, but we've arrived at Chotley's and I realize I'm starving. My stomach is for sure eating itself.

We wave hello to Mr. Chotley and I catch the eye of the new girl. I feel myself blushing. *Come on, keep it together, Obie.*

"Look!" Dad's whispers are not even remotely soft. "There's that girl—what was her name again? Cheryl? Sherry? Charlotte?"

"Charlotte. Who likes to be called Charlie." At least I can actually whisper. "And shhhh!" She's staring right at us, and I must look like a freaking tomato.

"Our usual," Dad says when we get up to the counter.

Mr. Chotley smiles and says, "You got it: the usual coming right up," in his booming, deep-bellied voice. "Charlie, would you help these gentlemen with their sandwiches?"

"Of course!" she replies, her voice just as cheery as before. "Extra pickles, right?"

I swallow and nod. My words feel stuck and my palms are sweaty.

"Cool!"

"Thank you, Charlie," Dad says, his hand on my shoulder.

"Thanks," I get out.

"Let's eat here," Dad says to me. I nod. "For here, Charlie, thanks." And we sit down.

"So, there's your *girl* problem," Dad says, winking at me. "You think she's a cutie, huh?"

"Ew, Dad, stop it!"

"All right. I'm just saying. You're blushing like I've never seen before. Maybe you two could go to a movie or something this weekend. Ask her!"

"I'm just here to eat my delicious sandwich," I say as Charlie walks up.

"That's right—two delicious sandwiches, riiiight here!" She sets them down in front of us and we thank her in unison.

I take huge bites of the sandwich, almost choking I'm eating so fast.

"Slow down, munchkin," Dad says, laughing.

"Don't call me that," I say, and the sourdough, along with a few pieces of precious Armenian string cheese, go flying from my mouth. "Sorry," I mumble. But Dad doesn't notice. His eyes are on his phone—he's texting someone pretty intently. I start to ask him what he's doing, but I feel someone standing over me.

"Is everything okay?" Charlie asks me. I think she means the food. My words disappear again. I take a big bite of my sandwich to stall.

"Mhmm," I say, rubbing my stomach. *What the heck, Obie? You're so cheesy. You look like such an idiot.*

"Can I get you anything else?" she asks. I shake my head no. She nods toward Dad. "What about him?"

I finish chewing and swallow. Finally.

"I think we're good, thank you." I smile, praying that there are no enormous chunks of food in my teeth.

"I'm going to take a quick call. Okay, munchkin?" I look over at Charlie, hoping she hasn't heard him call me that, but she's still standing right there. Embarrassed, I look at Dad, but something in his expression makes the annoyance wither and I nod wordlessly.

As soon as Dad steps out, Charlie's repeating, "Munchkin, huh?" *Darn it.*

"Yeah . . . they always call me that," I say dejectedly. "I hate it."

"I think it's cute. Munchkin." She smiles at me and my stomach does a flip. *You're* cute, I want to say. I mumble instead.

"What did you say?" She tilts her head as if she's trying to listen harder.

"Nothing. Never mind," I say, staring at my sandwich again.

"Okay. Well, if you need anything, I'll be at the counter."

I finish eating and stare at Dad's uneaten meal. He's been outside for longer than a minute. Parents never actually mean "just a minute" when they say that, though.

I get up and throw away my trash. I'm trying really hard

not to peek over at the counter, where Charlie is, but I want to know if she's watching me. I sneak a look and see that she's playing with a Rubik's Cube. Somehow that fits her personality, or what little I know of it. Mostly the colorful bit.

I sit down and begin browsing Snapchat stories.

Sammy's selfie that reads, "HUMP DAYYYYYYYYY" with a camel emoji. *I guess he forgot it's Thursday.*

Jackson and his brothers with frozen hair from after this afternoon's practice. *It was randomly cold today—I mean, Boston is cold in the winter. But November's kind of early for frozen hair.*

Jae-sung's airplane window shot flying to Chicago. *I hope he has a good time, especially with Grandpa—Jae-sung's always been his favorite, everybody knows. I kinda wish I had gone, too.*

Lucy with two girls at the movies. *Wait. Lucy at the movies? With Chelsea and Jenn? I thought she was grounded till the end of the month?!*

My stomach starts doing weird things again, but this time it isn't because a pretty girl is talking to me. What happened with me and Lucy? Why is she lying to me?

"Hey."

I look up and Charlie's standing above me again.

"You look upset," she says.

"Um," I say, taken aback by her directness.

"Sorry, it's probably not my business. My mom says I get into other people's business too much. But you seem so nice. And you look like something made you upset. And that

doesn't seem right. Do you want to try my Rubik's Cube?"
She talks fast. Faster than I do sometimes, which is saying
something. I don't know how I'm supposed to respond. I sit
there like an idiot. She extends the Cube to me.

"C'mon, try!"

"What, I—I—" I stammer. "I don't know how to do it,"
I finally get out.

"Oh! I thought you did; you've been staring at me holding it for a bit now." She grins. Caught.

"I—"

"It's okay. You're pretty cute when you're trying not to
stare," she says, nodding as she mixes up the colors. *You're
pretty cute,* I hear again in my head. Happy-stomach feelings
are back now.

"I am?" I ask weakly. It's all I've got.

"Mhm." She called *me* cute. I try to focus on the Cube
to stop the blushing. She pauses as she examines the colorful
squares. "Do you want me to mix it up some more?" I just
stare at her.

"Here," she says, her big green eyes looking at me. She
hands it over and I stare at it. It seems pretty mixed up to
me. Except there are a couple reds next to each other. A few
greens. I twist and turn, but doing so makes two blues and
two yellows line up together. I do this a few more times as
she watches. I feel myself begin to sweat. She's going to think
I'm stupid. I can't even mix it up right.

"See? You're cute," she says. I'm a tomato, is what I am.

"I figured you'd try to separate all the colors evenly. You can't do it all the way. There'll always be a few same colors next to each other."

"Oh." I still feel dumb. She takes it from me, her fingertips grazing my palm.

"Wanna see me solve it?" I nod. "Time me," she requests. I look at my watch. It's this enormous bright green one I got a few years ago that I love, but now that I'm looking at it in front of her, I feel like a huge goon.

"Cool watch—" I look up. She doesn't laugh or seem like she's joking. *Okay.* "I'm ready," she nudges.

"Okay. Go," I say. Suddenly her fingers are a total blur and she's whipping the sides around like crazy.

"Done!" She slams it down on the table just as the door bangs closed and I jump. "Sorry," she says sheepishly.

Dad's walking in as I say to her, "Wow, eleven point three seconds. How did you do that?"

"Practice! I can show you how to do it if you want."

"Kiddo, we gotta go," Dad interrupts, gathering up his sandwich.

"What? Already?" I say, disappointed.

"Come on," he says, his voice low. I look at him. It's like someone pulled down his entire face. Something is definitely wrong.

"I have to go," I say to Charlie.

"Next time," Charlie whispers. She jots something down

on her order pad. She tears off the sheet and hands it to me. "You can text me." And then she's gone.

Before I can melt because I just got a girl's number for the first time *ever,* Dad pulls me gently out the door and we head to the car.

The drive home is quiet and although I desperately want to text Charlie, I decide not to because Dad's upset and it doesn't feel right to pull out my phone. Instead, I hold the note's edge in my pocket. *I think you're cute, too,* I say to her in my head.

———

When we get home, the single light above the kitchen table is on, casting a warm yellow glow over the room. Usually this feels homey, but tonight, I feel cold.

Dad sits down at the table and motions for me to sit with him. I do.

"Honey," he starts, staring at his hands. "Grandma died

today." His eyes meet mine as everything stops. The words are ringing in my ears over and over. *Died today, Grandma died today, Grandma DIED today, GRANDMA DIED TODAY—*

"Grandpa called Mom right as they were driving to Barrington. Grandma didn't wake up from her nap this morning." He pauses and the ringing continues—*GRANDMA. DIED. TODAY—*

"She was gone by the time Jae-sung and Mom could see her." My hands feel bloodless. *Died. Died. . . .* I can't seem to stop. My hands tighten into fists in my lap.

"Why did she die?" I finally muster. "Did something happen?" Last I'd heard, Grandma was totally fine except that her hearing wasn't so great. But that was okay, you just shouted a little more around her. How could she be *dead*?

"She was just old, O." He runs his hand through his spiky hair and offers a weak smile. The kind adults give you when they feel bad for you but don't really know what else to do. "She went peacefully," he adds, as if it makes her less dead.

"What about Grandpa?" I ask, and I feel my voice waver.

"Well, I think he's very sad. But I think he's hanging in there."

"What happens now?" I ask.

"We will probably need to go this weekend for the funeral. Grandpa and your mom have already begun planning it." He looks at me again. "You'll have to miss a few practices, but maybe we can find a gym there for you and Coach Larkin can give you some land training to do."

"Okay," I say. I don't think there is another possible answer. "Will we see her . . . body?" The words stick in my mouth. *Body. Dead.* I have never seen a dead person before. *DEAD. DEAD!*

"Well, no. Grandma wrote in her will that she wanted to be cremated." Dad's phone begins ringing again. This time he answers it.

"Hi, honey. Yes, I did. He's here with me. Yes, sure, of course. Here—" He offers me the phone and I stand up to grab it.

"Hi, sweetie pie," comes Mom's voice. It's hoarse and heavy and that's when the tears come.

"Mommy, are you okay?" I sob as I realize this means my mother no longer has a mother. *What if* my *mom dies?!* Just thinking that brings so much pain, I crumple to the floor. My elbow throbs and I want all the feelings to stop, but the tears just keep coming. Dad takes the phone from me and says a few words before hanging up.

"It's going to be okay." He pulls me into a hug. But I realize I'm not crying just for Grandma. I'm crying for Mom and for Grandpa. The people Grandma left all alone. I think I'm crying a little for myself, too. For Lucy. Who should be here but doesn't even know Grandma's gone. Who I miss. . . .

Grandma would know what to do about Lucy. I wish I'd called her before it was too late.

I never really knew how to connect with Grandpa. He's more Jae-sung's vibe. But I could talk with Grandma for hours. I think about all the things I would tell her if I could until I fall asleep on the couch next to Dad.

Chapter 12

I bring my homework to do on the plane. A few geometry worksheets for Mr. Devi, some chemistry word problems (yuck), and *All American Boys.* I decide to start with the reading.

In the book, the students have all found out about Rashad's beating. Turns out that the cop who beat Rashad is an old friend of Quinn's, the guy who witnessed Rashad's attack. And Paul was practically a father figure to Quinn. . . . So Quinn doesn't know what to do.

The reading leaves me wondering what I would do if Jae-sung did something wrong like Paul did. I mean, I don't think Jae-sung would ever become a cop, much less a cop who makes terrible mistakes—but what *if*? I'm not sure who I'd believe or who I should believe. I wonder about the reverse as well and if he'd stand by me if I were accused. . . . I get myself stuck in a circle trying to figure these things out.

"Did you see her . . . like . . . body, her corpse—" I try to ask Jae-sung, breaking the cracker I'm holding in half. "Before they took her to the place?"

"Nah, Mom wouldn't let me. Says it's for grown-ups. Apparently, I'm not grown-up enough still. Can't do anything around here," he huffs. I'm not sure that's a grown-up privilege I'm excited about gaining.

But then I find myself whispering, "I kind of wanted to see it." I fidget with my suit tie.

"Why?" he asks. More gently than I expected.

"Because maybe then it'd feel real."

"Her dying?"

"Her being dead."

He nods. We're standing between a cluster of half-packed cardboard boxes and a narrow table filled with the food that one of Grandma's friends brought to the house after the funeral. I guess it's normal to have some kind of reception after a funeral so that everyone can pretend they're fine together while eating dumb cheese and crackers. Jae-sung eats another cracker, crunching loudly. I try to break one into fourths, but it just crumbles into my palm instead. I stare at the crumbs on the floor and in my palm, knowing I should clean them up. But instead, I'm crying again.

How can someone be there and then not *be there?* I want to scream into the universe. I don't know what to do with the contact on my phone that says GRANDMA FRIEDEL. *Surely if I just click that and call her number, she'll answer! How could she not?*

The tears this time are quiet, those enormous drops that roll down your cheeks so slowly they almost tickle. Jae-sung puts his arm around my shoulder. He squeezes and we stay like that in silence.

Jae-sung is still leaning on me when Grandpa wanders over a few moments later.

"How you two doing?" His voice is sorta like Mrs. Salmani's—gravelly but deeper. Less kind. Mom admits she and Grandpa didn't get along when she was a kid. Grandpa had trouble controlling his anger sometimes. That doesn't surprise me. Something's always broken when we come to visit. And Grandma never throws anything. *Threw.* Threw anything. *Dead. Gone. GONE. DEAD—*

"We're hanging in there, Gramps. Real question is how you're doing." I know Jae-sung's trying pretty hard to sound like an adult. Usually that would be annoying, but right now it's nice.

"I'm sad. But I'm okay. It's . . ." He trails off. "It's going to be different now."

I stare at him. He looks so broken—so different from the harsh man Mom describes. He's got these big bushy brows that remind me of Lucy's cat's whiskers. His eyes are deep set but somehow seem to bulge at the same time. He's got eyes you'll never forget. Well, Grandma's were even more impressive, somehow. But his are definitely striking—an electric-blue color that looks especially strange now, contrasted with the monochrome theme of everything else. Everyone in dark colors. All of Grandpa's things are gray. His watch, his hair, his cardigan, his socks, his shoes with the Velcro straps. Velcro because he's old, Mom says. "Because he doesn't really have the dexterity to tie them anymore." Even his skin looks a little gray. And all the shelves emptied, the walls bare, most of their belongings packed into boxes just adds to the depressing atmosphere.

I don't remember the gray when Grandma was here. Her eyes were a warm honey brown. Mom says that everyone romanticizes blue eyes—says they're better and more beautiful—but that brown eyes are just as beautiful. I agree. Grandma's eyes have—*had*—little flecks of green in them, too. I used to pretend they were miniature globes. Some 3D image of a faraway planet, undiscovered. During That Year, I thought if she looked at me long enough, maybe I could disappear into Grandma's other world somehow.

I wonder how her eyes looked right after it happened. Did they just stop seeing? Are eyes like a camera—even when the battery's dead, I can see through the lens of Dad's Nikon. Could Grandma's soul still see through her eyes?

Grandpa's giving both of us a hug. The slight discomfort reminds me he has never really known how to hug. It's like he jams his shoulder into my chest on purpose. But I know that's not his intent. He just doesn't hug people much.

"Boys, I think you're going to take off soon. Are you ready?" Mom appears to check on us next.

"One minute," I say. I run into Grandma and Grandpa's room and her perfume floods my nose. I'm crying before I shut the door. I fall to my knees, feeling the soft carpet beneath me, thankful that they chose that instead of hardwood floors in this room. I sit cross-legged and look up at the bed in front of me. It was always just tall enough that I needed a small hop to get me up and seated. I push myself up and hop on. I lie back and I can feel the mattress sag where each of them sleeps. Sleeps and *slept*. I sit up, my legs dangling off the edge, and I stare at the dresser. This is the only room that isn't filled with boxes. It looks like they left it to be packed last. It looks exactly as I remember it.

I'm on Grandma's side. Her dresser has five things on it. Her nightstand rosary beads—the traditional Catholic style, with silver metal and colorful plastic beads. Her eyeglasses—I don't think I've ever seen her wear those, though. A Bible so worn that I'm afraid that if I pick it up, all the pages will fall out. A red tassel peeks out from the top and I wonder what page is marked. A framed photo of her and Grandpa with a tiny baby Mom, who's crying. I wipe my eyes on the sleeve of my sport coat. I get nasty snot all over it, so I reach for the fifth item—a tissue box with Grandma's hand-crocheted cover.

Then, staring at the red tassel, curiosity gets the best of me and I pick up the Bible as carefully as possible. It's soft and

I have a sudden urge to smell it. Old-book and old-leather smells fill my nose along with something flowery. Lavender? Probably. Grandma loved lavender. I gingerly open the Bible to the tassel and find an index-card-sized Polaroid photo of three people. I look carefully—it's me and Grandma and Lucy. I think it's from Christmas when we were . . . eleven? Grandma's got an arm around each of us. Lucy used to come to a lot of our family functions. In the photo, I'm looking up at Grandma, who's got the biggest grin. Grandma's looking half at me, half at the camera. And Lucy's cheesing directly into the camera. She was always excited to be in any picture. But during that time, I'd refused to be in any family photos. It had made me nauseous. I didn't want to be remembered or seen as someone I wasn't. As a girl. But that day, Grandma had pulled me close and whispered: "You look really handsome tonight."

I remember beaming with my entire person, maybe the only smile that had made an appearance in That Year. I wonder if Grandma knew and that's why she kept this photo.

I wonder if Lucy and I will ever be in photos together again.

There's a knock on the door. I flinch.

"Obie, hon—oh! Sorry to scare you. Are you ready to go?" Mom's head peeks inside.

"Yeah," I say, staring at the photo in my hands and trying desperately to keep my voice level. I don't succeed.

"Oh, Obie—" I just close my eyes as she wraps me in a hug. "I know, honey, I know."

I shake as I cry. And then I'm confused—a part of me doesn't even know why I'm crying. This makes me cry harder. I mean, I do know why I'm sad. Grandma is dead. But crying won't bring her back. . . .

"Whatever you're feeling, baby, you're allowed to feel it. Let it out," she says, and I think she's talking to herself, too. She is hugging me, almost cradling me in her lap, and I feel her words shake in her stomach. I clutch the picture. We stay like that until there is another knock on the open door.

"Ready?" Dad asks.

"We'll be a minute," Mom replies.

She pushes me up and looks at me. Her face is wet with her own tears and her eyes shine. Kind of like Grandma's did. She gives me a kiss on each cheek.

"I love you," she says, smiling.

"I love you, too, Mom."

———

Jae-sung and I sit in the back of the rental car, waiting for Dad. I watch out the window as Dad gives Mom a long hug. She dips her head a little into his chest and I can see him squeeze her again. I wish she were coming to the hotel with us, but Dad says she needs to stay with Grandpa. If I were Grandpa, I'd want someone to stay with me, too.

A LIST OF REASONS I'M SAD ABOUT GRANDMA DYING:
 1. She's dead.
 2. Mom is sad.
 3. Mom doesn't have a mom anymore.
 4. If I didn't have a mom anymore, I think I
    would never stop crying.
 5. I never asked Grandma about herself. I wish
    I could know what things she worried about
    when she was a kid like me. Did she ever
    worry about boys like Clyde? What did she do
    about them?
 6. What about Lucy?
 7. Grandma would have known what to do about
    Lucy. And now I cannot ask her.
 8. I won't ever see her eyes again.
 9. What's going to happen to Grandpa?
 10. What if Halmoni and Harabuhji die soon, too?

Reminder: add Grandma to my list.

Chapter 13

I search for Mom's car for a few moments before realizing that I should be looking for Harabuhji's because Mom's still in Chicago and Dad has to teach tonight. I find Harabuhji and Halmoni's ancient tan station wagon in the corner of the parking lot.

Harabuhji is reading a newspaper when I knock lightly on the window. I think he's the only person I know who still gets a paper newspaper delivered every day.

"Oh," I see him mouth, and he looks down for the unlock button. I slide into the passenger seat and greet him in Korean.

"Hello, Jae-eun," he says, calling me by my Korean name. "How was swim?" he asks.

"Good, but I can't swim yet." I raise my arm in explanation.

"Still hurt?" he asks, and puts the key into the ignition. The engine turns over. (Why is it called that? Is the engine actually turning over?)

"No, it's almost all better. I'm supposed to get the stitches checked tomorrow," I answer.

"Mm." He nods. "Your brother already at home. Halmoni feeding now," he tells me.

"Oooh, what are we having?" I ask, my mouth already watering.

"I think Halmoni made kimchi-jjigae."

"Yesssss," I say, stomach now in full-on grumble. That's my absolute favorite.

"You know, when I was student in the 1960s, I had no kimchi. And no Halmoni to make food," he begins.

"Where was Halmoni?" I ask.

"In Korea. With your dad and Andy."

"Oh."

"And I did not know how to make kimchi. I lived next to MIT—I showed you building before, remember?" I nod. Every time we go to H Mart, Dad points out Harabuhji's old apartment. Or I guess where it used to be. It used to be diagonal, across the street. Now it's a Target.

"Why didn't you just buy it at H Mart?" I ask.

"There was no H Mart in those days," he says, laughing to himself. His voice is hoarse—it's always been like that, ever since I can remember. "So instead, I chop up raw cabbage—the hard, green, American kind—and eat with salt and Tabasco." He says *American* like Halmoni does. *Uh-mer-ee-can.* And Tabasco with each syllable isolated: *Tah-bah-suh-koh.* "Try to make kimchi that way."

"Tabasco kimchi?!" I say, incredulous. "Was it good?"

"No," he chuckles. "Eat with Uncle Ben rice, too. Bad American rice." I laugh. There's something special about Korean rice, for sure. I can't imagine not having Halmoni's cooking around all the time. That would be miserable.

"Were you lonely?"

"A little," he answers, slamming on the brakes. He's never been the best driver. "I was away from family for long time. But Halmoni move here after a couple years. She always supports me."

"And then you could eat *real* kimchi?" I giggle.

"Yes, that's right. *Real* kimchi." He smiles at me. "We have some tonight."

From the passenger seat I can see just how thick his glasses are and I think about how he always used to tell me his eyes were bad because he read so much as a kid. He used to joke with me that if I did too much homework, my eyes would end up like his. Halmoni always clucked her tongue at his warnings, telling me that that isn't true and that I should always do my homework.

Dad says Harabuhji is much more chill as a grandfather than he was as a father. Harabuhji never told Dad to do *less* homework, that's for sure. He was a lot harder on Dad, I guess. But he's just right for me. I like his dad jokes and silly stories. Although I sure am glad Halmoni knows how to make real kimchi so we don't have to eat the salt-and-Tabasco kind.

Chapter 14

"Hey, Obie." I turn toward the lockers. It's Lucy. I wait for her to continue. We haven't talked since she said she was grounded. "I saw your post about Grandma Friedel. I'm really sorry. That's so sad."

She walks toward me as if she's going to hug me. I slip my hands into my pockets and feel something crumple as I do. *What is that?*

"Thanks," I say. I don't even attempt to conceal the flatness in my tone. *She saw the post but waited* three *days to say something? She couldn't have even* texted *me?*

"Uh . . . ," Lucy says, looking confused and then a little angry. "What's with the attitude?" She says the word *attitude* like it's a sassy question. The Lucy I know would have mocked this tone. *At-ti-tood?* I don't say anything. I'm mad. And distracted, too, because I realize the paper in my pocket is Charlie's number. Crap, I totally forgot about it. I hope the number is still legible after going through the wash. . . .

"I'm just saying I'm sorry! I knew her, too, you know,"

she says, pushing. "Jeez." I stare at her, wondering if it's worth it. Wanting to just leave and text Charlie instead.

But suddenly I'm too angry to let it go. How dare she make this about *her,* telling me, "I knew her, too." She was *my* grandma.

"You knew her, too?" I spit, mocking her. "I made that post about Grandma THREE days ago, Lucy. You could have texted, you could have called, you could have even *commented.* But you didn't. *And* you said you were grounded last week! But I saw your snapstory! You lied to me!" I let it all out. She won't look at me.

"I, uh, my mom . . ." She falters. "I got un-grounded?" But it doesn't seem like she even believes herself.

"Yeah. Okay."

"Listen, I—Obie—" She sounds like she's going to cry. Half of me wants to hug her, I'm so sad, but the anger fueling the other half of me wins, so I turn and walk away.

"Obie, wait!" She rushes after me and tugs on my shoulder. "Obie, I—" Tears are starting to sting now and I don't want people at school to see me cry so I yank away from her, but she continues. "I was sick of being different and being made fun of, and I—" She stumbles over her words.

Sick of being different? Who does she think she's talking to? The King of Normal?

"And after you left the team—"

"After I was *kicked* off the team." I face her again, not hiding any anger now.

"After you were kicked off the team," she says, nodding,

wiping her eyes. "After that, I didn't have anyone else. I started hanging with them. With Jenn and Chelsea, and I guess . . . I guess we got closer. They're not as bad as they—"

"They're the ones spreading rumors about me, Lucy. I know you know that. I'm not stupid, and neither are you."

"I know, but they just thought it was funny—" *Funny?* I can't believe what I'm hearing. This is coming from the girl they made cry almost every day of elementary school. I'd known Clyde was gone, but have I lost Lucy, too?

"Do *you* think it was just funny? Do *you* even know what actually happened?"

Lucy's face twists. "You wouldn't even tell me! You said you didn't want to talk about it. You never tell me anything anymore."

"You never ask!" I'm almost shouting. "And it shouldn't matter what I tell you. You were supposed to be my best friend. Best friends stand up for each other no matter what—"

"I—" she tries. I can see the anger fading from her face as her lip quivers again. "I just. I don't want to be *different* anymore. I've stuck out my whole life, always getting bullied, and being around you means—"

Yup. That's it.

"Means you'll be stuck with the tranny." I cut her off, my right hand raised to stop her. "Yeah, I know. Gosh, you're so put upon, having a friend like me. Forget it, Lucy, you're hopeless. Have fun with Jenn and Chelsea." And I'm through the exit doors before she can close her mouth.

I keep Charlie's note safe in my pocket until I get home from the doctor. I'm disappointed I had to miss another Wednesday meeting with Mrs. Salmani, but I got my stitches checked and I'm cleared for swimming, so I'm pretty stoked.

Lucy has texted me, like, fifty times asking to talk, but I'm ignoring her. *The nerve she had telling me she's the one who felt bullied when that's literally been my whole life.*

Dad keeps asking why I'm so quiet, aren't I happy to be stitch-free finally? I tell him it's something else and I don't want to talk and he respects that. I wish Mom were home. She's texted me a few times asking about the doctor visit. I type a reply as I walk into the house.

> **ME, 6:11 P.M.:** It went well. I miss you. When r u coming home?

Mom must be waiting because she replies almost immediately.

> **MOM, 6:12 P.M.:** That's so great!

> **MOM, 6:12 P.M.:** I think by the end of this week. Probably Friday. Grandpa says he'll move into the assisted living place. It was a battle. He wanted to stay here.

"Dad, how far is the senior home from our house?" I set my backpack on a chair.

"It's a little north of Somerville. Why?"

"Just wondering," I answer, walking upstairs. *Does this mean we'll see Grandpa more often?* Somerville is only fifteen minutes away from Watertown without traffic.

When I'm finally alone in my room, I pull out Charlie's note. I can still read the numbers, thank goodness, which I copy into my phone. I'm staring at the photo on my desk. The Polaroid of me, Lucy, and Grandma. Mom let me bring it home from Chicago, but now I flip it over. I don't want to think about Lucy anymore.

> **ME, 6:30 P.M.:** Hey Charlie, this is Obie. From the sandwich shop?

I hit send and compose another message: I'M REALLY SORRY I DIDN'T TEXT YOU SOONE—

My phone immediately buzzes with an incoming message.

> **CHARLIE, 6:30 P.M.:** Hi!!! I thought maybe I was wrong about you. You took forever to text me!

I erase the message and begin to type a new one: I KNOW, I HAD SOME FAMILY STUFF COME— But she beats me to it.

CHARLIE, 6:30 P.M.: It's okay, I'm sure you're busy.

CHARLIE, 6:30 P.M.: I haven't seen you in a bit at the shop!!!

CHARLIE, 6:31 P.M.: How was your day????

Gee, she texts exactly like she is in real life. Fast talking and excited. I erase all the messages I've written and begin responding anew. Again.

"Obie, I cut up some apple if you want a snack," Dad calls from downstairs. I realize I'm pretty hungry.

"Coming," I respond. I grab my books and trot down the stairs, still holding my phone in one hand. I almost trip at the bottom, but drop everything to grab the railing.

"Obie . . . ," he scolds, "you know better. No texting and walking. You don't need another reason to go to the doctor."

I grumble, but he's right. I sit at the table and he sets a plate of sliced Honeycrisp apples in front of me.

"Thanks, Dad," I say.

"Of course. Do you want anything else?"

"No, I'm good, thanks. Just going to do some home-work," I say, not taking my eyes off my phone. I look up

to see his stern-Dad expression. "Sorry, just texting"—
I pause—"someone." He doesn't like it when I don't look up
from my phone while talking to him. Fair.

"Thank you," he says, replacing the sternness with a
smile. He leaves the kitchen and I return to Charlie's messages.

> **ME, 6:34 P.M.:** I'm sorry, long story.

Send.

I begin typing the response to her question about
my day: MY DAY WAS— *Terrible. My grandma died this
weekend and today I basically friend-broke-up with my
best friend since I was, like, born. I'm devastated but also
angry?*

> **ME, 6:36 P.M.:** My day was so-so. I had a fight
> with my friend.

Is that too much? Should I have just said it was okay?
How much information am I supposed to disclose? How
much is too much? How do I know?!

> **CHARLIE, 6:37 P.M.:** Aw, I'm sorry, Obie . . .

> **ME, 6:39 P.M.:** It's okay.

CHARLIE, 6:40 P.M.: Still blows.

ME, 6:40 P.M.: Yeah.

ME, 6:42 P.M.: So wbu, how was ur day?

CHARLIE, 6:43 P.M.: Pretty good. After I spent the weekend wondering if this cute boy was going to text me back

My stomach feels warm and happy and—

My phone rings and I snap back to the kitchen counter. All my books are laid out, still closed. The news rumbles softly on the miniature, ancient TV on the counter.

It's Mom. I answer it and place it on speakerphone so I can continue texting Charlie.

"How's it going?" she asks.

"Good . . . ," I say, distracted. Charlie's sent me a GIF of a girl tapping her fingers, waiting. I stifle a laugh.

"Yeah? What are you up to?"

"Oh, nothing. I'm just, uh, texting . . . my friend."

"Lucy?"

"No. No!" I frown even though she can't see. "Mom, I'm done with Lucy. She's being a total b—" I pause and decide I want to use a different word.

"A total butt."

"That was a good call," Mom says, and I know she means my language. "Do you want to talk about it yet?" She's pushing now. I give in.

"Lucy's hanging with those girls. I confronted her and she told me those girls thought it was funny, what happened. That I peed myself and all that. When I told her a real friend would have stood up for me, she protested and said she was tired of being different and sticking out all the time. I think she meant because of me. So I left. I don't want to talk to her."

"Sounds like a good decision," Mom says. "I'm so sorry they're being like that. I hope Lucy comes back around at some point."

"I don't care if she does. I can't be friends with her anymore."

"And that is totally your right." She pauses and I can hear her breathe deep. "If anyone ever makes you feel like you are less-than because of who you are, that is on them. That is about their character. And you don't need them. Don't ever let anyone trick you into believing there is something wrong with you, you understand?" Her voice is crackly through the phone. I wonder when technology will be good enough that phone voices don't sound like phone voices.

"I know," I say. "Thanks, Mom."

"And how's that homework coming, Obadiah?" Her tone is gentle, even though she's using my whole name.

"It's coming . . . ," I say, even though I haven't opened the books yet. But she can't see that. I should probably get started, seeing as I've read approximately zero pages of the reading for Mrs. Salmani's class. Which is tomorrow. "I should get to it."

"Okay, I'll see you soon. Also, I want to hear about this *friend* at some point." *What? How does she know?!*

"What *friend*? We're just friends. Okay, I love you, bye."

"Bye, honey." She laughs.

> **ME, 6:58 P.M.:** Ah, I know I'm sorry.

> **ME, 7:01 P.M.:** I meant to text you as soon as we left the sandwich shop . . .

> **MF, 7:01 P.M.:** You're cute, too.

> **CHARLIE, 7:09 P.M.:** thank you 😊

HANG OUT WITH HER, Dad screams in my head. *I don't want to be different anymore,* comes Lucy's tiny voice. I wonder if this Charlie thing is a bad idea. What if we hang out, she discovers I'm trans, and then she doesn't want to hang out with me anymore? If she's just going to leave, why not just save me the hopeful, optimistic feelings and just ghost her now?

But. On the flip side: Do I have to tell her at all? Also, I'll never be able to avoid her completely. That would mean never going to Chotley's, and I can't do that. Not to myself or Dad, and especially not to Mr. Chotley.

Screw it, I tell myself. *Just go for it.*

> **ME, 7:11 P.M.:** So do you think we could hang out sometime?

No going back now!

> **ME, 7:11 P.M.:** Like, not at Chotley's?

> **CHARLIE, 7:12 P.M.:** What?! Chotley's isn't your no1 date spot?!

> **ME, 7:12 P.M.:** Actually, I think it would be except we already hung out there

> **CHARLIE, 7:15 P.M.:** Hahaha ok. Fair.

> **ME, 7:18 P.M.:** What are you doing in three weekends??

I hope she doesn't think I'm avoiding her. I already took, like, five days to text her and I can't even see her soon. . . .

CHARLIE, 7:19 P.M.: Wait, what? Like after Thanksgiving?

I'm trying to type fast, but I can't match her texting speed.

ME, 7:20 P.M.: This weekend is Thanksgiving and I have to spend it w my grandparents and other grandpa. And then I have a swim meet in Maine. And then I'm free.

CHARLIE, 7:21 P.M.: Oh, gotcha. I didn't know u swim!

CHARLIE, 7:22 P.M.: But nothing! I just work at grandpa's until 5pm on sats and suns. Does saturday night work?

Phew, she doesn't seem upset.

ME, 7:24 P.M.: Yeah! Sorry to wait so long.

CHARLIE, 7:25 P.M.: No worries. I get it 😊

ME, 7:26 P.M.: So what do you want to do?

Should I ask her to see a movie? That's what I've heard other kids do. What does a seventh grader like me even do on a date, anyway? It's not like I can drive us anywhere. And Watertown isn't super walkable.

CHARLIE, 7:30 P.M.: Where do you live?
Maybe we can take a walk and get ice cream?

ME, 7:37 P.M.: I like ice cream!

ME, 7:38 P.M.: Walking is okay 😊

CHARLIE, 7:43 P.M.: Haha cool

ME, 7:44 P.M.: Heh

ME, 7:44 P.M.: So meet you at Moozy's at 7pm Saturday night?

CHARLIE, 7:50 P.M.: It's a date! In three weeks

ME, 7:51 P.M.: Great

ME, 7:51 P.M.: And happy turkey weekend!

She sends a GIF of a turkey gobbling.

"I think I know who that smile's for. . . ." Dad walks over and tousles my hair. He doesn't wait for me to answer. "It's that girl from the sandwich shop, isn't it?" He pokes me in my shoulders.

"Whaaat?" I want to be annoyed but I'm too excited. "Yeah. She gave me her phone number when we left Chotley's last weekend. Before you told me about—" My voice falters. "Before you told me."

"She was all over you the last two times we went," Dad says, almost with pride. Good thing Mom's not here. "So . . . are you *dating* now? I don't know how dating works these days."

"Um, no. Dad! Calm down."

"Okay, okay. . . ." He smiles, hands in the air.

———

I slide *All American Boys* over and open it to the bookmarked page. I always bookmark with a little sticky note. Mom usually dog-ears her pages. She says it gives her books character. I think it ruins the uniformity of the pages. I mean. It does.

I feel my palms getting sweatier as I read. I think about

my conversation with Lucy. How disgusted I'd been with her for not standing up for me and how, in *All American Boys,* Quinn is standing up for someone he doesn't even know. Standing up in the face of so much pushback that he's gotta run into the bathroom after having been slogged in the nose until bloody. I feel suddenly cold and nauseous. I imagine Clyde's fist buried in my stomach again, and even though my elbow is pretty much healed—the last of the scab fell off in the shower recently—I still feel the sting.

A LIST OF THINGS ABOUT LUCY:
1. I shouldn't have yelled at her.
2. My therapist says that sometimes anger is an act of self-compassion. It says: I do not deserve this.
3. My therapist also says that oftentimes, anger is a secondary emotion. Anger is actually jealousy or shame or insecurity or pain in disguise.
4. I don't know what kind of anger that was.
5. I think I'm mostly angry but a bit insecure, too.
6. I miss her.
7. I miss us.

QUESTIONS ABOUT CHARLIE:
1. What will she do when she finds out that I'm transgender?

2. (Do I have to tell her?)
3. ((If I don't, will someone else?))
4. Am I supposed to kiss her on Saturday?
5. HOW DO YOU KISS SOMEONE?!

THOUGHTS ABOUT CLYDE (LIBBY SAYS "WRITE THE
THINGS, EVEN IF THEY ARE SCARY."):
1. I'm not doing this. Never mind. Sorry, Libby.

Chapter 15

"So I hear you have a *friend*," Mom prods. Don't let anyone fool you into thinking it's just kids who gossip. Parents do, too.

"Yes. *Friend*," I emphasize defiantly.

"Okay, whatever you'd like to call her," she teases.

"We're going to get ice cream the weekend after Invitationals."

"Oh? We are?"

"No, *I* am. With her." *Ugh.*

"So we're letting Obie date now, are we?" she says to Dad.

"I mean, I guess so. . . . I suppose we'll have to set some ground rules, though." He pulls her into a side hug, his arm over her shoulder. She lets her head fall onto his shoulder. He kisses the top of her head and I say, "Ewwwwww," but I'm smiling.

"I guess he can go on one date. Then we'll have to have this girl over for dinner and see if we approve." *God no.*

"Dad!" I protest, but he just laughs and they turn together to go to the living room.

"Be ready in a half hour," Mom says as she sinks into the couch. "And be hungry!"

———

We all hop out of the car.

"I'll be back in about a half hour with Grandpa," Mom calls from her window. "Ask Halmoni to put that in the fridge so it doesn't fall." She nods at the Pyrex container I'm holding. It's filled with whipped cream we made today. Even though I licked the whisk this morning, I'm so excited to eat it atop the cobbler later.

"Yes, ma'am," I reply. Jae-sung punches in the garage code and we wander inside, with Dad leading.

Inside, I can smell the roasting turkey in addition to the familiar daenjang and kimchi smells. My mouth waters.

"Helloo-oooo," Halmoni trills, and I smile. "What do you have here?" she asks me, taking the container.

"Whipped cream!" I say.

"Oooh, for turkey?" She grins.

"No," I say, laughing. "For that." I point to the other Pyrex container that Jae-sung carries. "The cobbler."

"Oh, very yummy. Looks delicious." She nods to herself. "Where's your grandpa?" she asks Jae-sung.

"Mom went to get him. We can't all fit in the car," he answers.

"Can I help?" I ask her.

"Su-ure, of course," she says, drawing out the words. *Of course* sounds more like *ohb koh-sub,* because there is no "F" or "R" sound in Korean. "Come, we going to get kimchi and then you can chop." I nod and follow her downstairs to where the kimchi refrigerator is. Honestly, it's a pretty neat machine. I didn't know kimchi was such an industry that companies make things specifically for storing it.

Dad told me that in the olden days, kimchi was stored in large clay jars that Koreans buried in the ground. That blew my mind—*what about all the dirt?* Dad explained that the jars were well sealed and the earth—the dirt—actually kept the kimchi at the right temperature. Because dirt temperature doesn't change as much as air does through the seasons. He said it's basically a natural refrigerator. Pretty cool, huh? Anyway, because Halmoni's kimchi refrigerator keeps the right temperature all year round, she doesn't need to bury her kimchi. So no digging for us today.

"Yeah, let's take this one." She hands me an orange-brown plastic container. It's heavier than I expect it to be.

"It's full!" I exclaim.

"Yes, but last one. Have to make again soon. Maybe after Christmas." Making kimchi is a big production, usually. I've watched a few times but never actually helped.

"Can I help next time? I want to learn," I say, surprising myself.

"Of course," she says, grinning. "I tell you when I make

it next. I teach you. You have to come for whole weekend, though." I nod.

Kimchi is practically sacred in Korean households. Kimchi making is usually a two- or three-day process that requires a lot of prep and physical space. Halmoni makes kimchi one to three times a year, depending on how fast we eat it. There are three main parts to the process. First, buying the produce—the baechu (napa cabbage), mu (daikon radish), gochugaru (Korean crushed red pepper), garlic, and green onion. I've done this part the most because sometimes we do Halmoni's grocery shopping for her. Next is the pre-soaking. And last, the pickling.

———

Jae-sung pulls out Grandpa's chair for him and Grandpa sits slowly. I've never seen Jae-sung be so . . . respectful? He sits next to Grandpa. And I sit across from Jae-sung.

"Jordan, do you want to say prayer?" Halmoni asks Grandpa. It's always weird to hear his first name like that. He looks up. I don't know how to interpret his expression.

"Mm." He nods. "Dear Lord," he begins. I bow my head, staring at the empty plate in front of me. "Thank you for bringing us all together on this beautiful Thanksgiving. I pray that you are taking good care of my love up there. Please tell her I miss her dearly. I pray that we all cherish the relationships we have—every moment of them. I am so thankful for our family's health. For my grandsons and their youth, and for this wonderful meal that Celia has cooked for us. Let us remind ourselves there are many less fortunate and let us act with compassion always. Amen."

"Amen," we all say together.

I find myself thinking about something we learned last week before break. In social studies, Mr. Roberson said that many indigenous peoples call Thanksgiving "Thanks-taking" or even "Day of Mourning" because the white colonists killed nearly all the indigenous people when they came here. He says this doesn't mean Thanksgiving can't be celebrated—gratitude is wonderful. But we should understand that the holiday has a complicated history.

I'm not really sure I know what to do with this information, but I know that Halmoni and Harabuhji love any excuse to cook an enormous meal and celebrate our family. I make a mental note to ask Mr. Roberson more about it.

"So, Dad, how are you liking the new place?" Mom asks Grandpa.

"It's just fine, darling," he answers after swallowing. "Linda lives next door to me and she is one *cr-aazy* little lady."

"Oh no, is she bothering you?" Dad asks, concerned.

"Oh, not at all." Grandpa smiles mischievously. "Not at all. She's a joy. We've started a TV club!"

"A TV club?" Mom asks skeptically. "What is that?"

"It's the same as book club, but with TV. We all watch a show and then get together with some Scotch and peanuts and talk about it."

"Now *that* is something I can get behind," Jae-sung says, grinning. "Dad, can I do that instead of my homework?"

"Absolutely not," Dad replies. I can't tell if he's mad or just unamused. I don't think he and Grandpa have ever quite gotten along. Halmoni is frowning a bit, too. I can only imagine what she's thinking. *Tele-bee instead of homework? Blasphemy!* but in Korean.

Chapter 16

Pooch and I press through the pool doors at the entrance and walk a few steps down the short hallway. Other swimmers rush past us, shoving and pushing like at the end of school or between classes. But unlike school, I'm happy to disappear into the crowd today.

I've been to Bowdoin College's pool every year since I was nine. Everyone in our area goes to this invitational meet. The pool there is a pretty fast pool. "That's a fast pool" is really something I guess only a swimmer would say. It's always a good temperature, and the walls are really nice. But we're always tired from the three-hour bus ride up here, so the coaches make us do extra warm-up to loosen up our legs. We all grumbled about it upon arrival, but today I'm glad we did those extra thousand yards last night because my legs feel good right now.

We walk through the second set of doors and are met with the wash of the neon lights, which are even brighter than I remember. They make the pool look iridescent, the clear blue water inviting me in as I scan the deck.

"There they are." Pooch motions to the rest of our team, sitting underneath the scoreboard—somehow we snagged the best poolside seats. *Nice.*

"Dope," Mikey says.

I set my enormous backpack down on the bleachers with a thud. Pooch sits down with his backpack on.

"Ready to crush that two-breast together, Obes?" Mikey abbreviates "200 breaststroke" to "two-breast," as most of us do. He puts his hand up for a high five.

"I'm going to do my best," I say nervously. It's a good high five. The kind that leaves your hand on fire for a moment but the perfect slapping sound rings for a millisecond and you're like, *Damn. That was a good one.*

"Nah, man, you're going to crush it. Manifest yourself!" He grins. I'm not sure that's the right use of the word *manifest,* but I've only heard someone our age use it in fifth grade when we were learning about Manifest Destiny.

"Manifest myself?" I ask.

"Yeah, dude. Manifest yourself—you got this." He nods to himself, eyes closed, and puts his headphones on again.

Pooch looks at me and shrugs. Mikey's curly black hair bounces slightly as he rocks to whatever he's listening to.

"Beats me," Pooch says. I shrug, too, but make a mental note to google it later.

"How are you?" I ask Pooch, sitting down between them. I scan the pool deck nervously, looking for the Barracudas' team area. The panic is slowly rising in my chest.

"I'm good, not pumped for the two hundred fly, though, let me tell ya."

"Yeah, can't imagine you would be. Can't believe she's tryna make you into a butterflyer—everyone knows you're a backstroker!" I say. Coach Larkin has some strange plans sometimes.

"Yeah, but she's got a point. . . . My one hundred back has sucked for the past year. And my one-fly has been pretty sweet. So I'll try, I guess. Don't have a choice." Pooch chuckles. I don't envy him. I hate that race.

"I'll be cheering." I bump my shoulder against Pooch's.

"Thanks, man. How about you, how's it going?" he asks.

I'm terrified of my old teammates who are sitting right over there. The elbow cut wasn't because I fell. It was because Clyde beat me up and I'm afraid to go to the bathroom here alone. If I don't perform well enough, people won't see me as a boy. I'm terrified, I'm terrified, I'm—

"I'm fine," I lie, playing with the zipper on my lunch box.

"You sure? Dude, you're so jittery, you're making the entire bleacher shake."

"Oh." I hadn't noticed I was bouncing my knee up and down. "Sorry, Pooch. Yeah, just nervous."

"C'mon, man, you're going to do great, just like Mikey

said. Manifest yourself or whatever." Pooch grins. "You've been absolutely crushing it in practice."

"But then I had to take that break when I hurt my elbow," I remind him.

"Break? You were sweatier than we were."

"What?" I laugh. "You can't tell if you're sweating. You were underwater—I was doing my silly land workouts on the bike. It's different."

"Okay, but either way. You absolutely did not look like you were having the most relaxing time of your life over there. That was most definitely *not* a break." I force my knee to relax a bit and smile.

"Thanks, man. I . . . Honestly . . ." *Should I tell him?* It's not like my being trans is a whole secret. Everyone at school knows. Or, at least, knew. Sometimes people forget or it becomes irrelevant, I guess. (Which is kind of nice sometimes. I get to just be me.) But everyone on the team was told I'm trans right when I joined. To make sure that we wouldn't have another problem like Clyde.

Coach Larkin had said that if anyone had an issue with me, *they* could leave. That on *this* team, it doesn't matter where we come from or what our histories are; as long as we're all working hard in the pool, anyone is welcome and anyone is included. It sounded like some kind of fairy tale, I know. And, in some ways, it was. Although I think a few kids' parents did switch them to other groups before I joined officially. A few others have asked me strange questions about my private parts. Coach Larkin says she's here to help me work through any of these things if I need it, but Mom and I have talked a lot about this. Especially when I prepared for telling everyone at school.

People are going to have questions, Obie, she'd said. *And if you think you can answer them kindly, I think you should. People are so ignorant. Even us—even you and me. Remember when you didn't even know what being transgender was?* Of course. *So if you feel like you can, answer their questions. But also, always tell them if you don't feel like answering. You* never *have* to answer. *If the question is too much or too private, tell them nicely why you don't want to talk about it.* I had nodded again. This made sense.

When I meet people in Dad's office and they tell me about some of the classes they teach—complicated words and phrases like *neuropsychology* or *evolutionary biology*—I want to know more. I ask questions that probably feel stupid to them. But almost always, they answer patiently and explain what must feel so basic to them. Except for when I was eight and I asked Professor Pendleton how much money he made and if it was more than my dad. He'd gotten very angry with me, telling me that the question was inappropriate and I was a rude child. I'd cried and never talked to him again. Mom had explained to me that I wasn't supposed to ask people what their salaries are, but that Professor Pendleton should have been nicer in that moment. I'm not sure this is the same thing as people asking me whether or not I have a penis, but I guess it's a similar situation of uncomfortable, ignorant questions.

But in the end, Mom had concluded, *all of this is up to you. Do you want to answer people's questions? Or shall we come up with something you can always say to avoid answering? Both are valid responses.* I'd said I wanted to try to answer questions. Sometimes I think I was bolder then. Before all the bullying had really begun. As Pooch stares at me, I know he's waiting for more.

"I'm kind of scared to see my old teammates," I finally blurt.

"Oh," he says, staring at his bare feet on the pool deck. My heart sinks as his silence continues. Then he looks up.

"Why?" he asks. Even though people on the Manta Rays know I'm trans, no one knows *why* I left the last team. I think people suspect. Maybe. Maybe not. I don't know. I stare at him, surprised and encouraged by his earnestness.

"Well, the coach there, he—I . . ." My boldness disappears as fast as it had come.

"It's okay if you don't want to tell me," he says. "Either way, I gotchu. And I still think you're going to crush it."

"Bolton kicked me off the Barracudas because I'm trans." The courage has returned and I'm not really sure where it is coming from.

"What?!" His mouth hangs open for a moment. "That's awful. What the heck?"

"Yeah," I say, his empathy feeding my boldness. "Yeah, and my best friend since we were babies is now friends with Jenn and Chelsea, who are complete bullies, and one of the boys, he . . ." I falter. If I tell him about Clyde, does that make me a tattle? I wonder if it makes me weak. I'm so afraid Pooch'll think I'm not a *real* boy because I didn't fight back.

"What did he do?" Pooch asks, incredulous.

"I didn't actually fall when I hurt my elbow last month . . . ," I say slowly, almost whispering. I check to see if anyone else is listening. Pooch takes a sharp breath and I see Lucy walk through the entrance, sandwiched between Jenn and Chelsea.

"He beat you up?" he asks quietly. I nod. "Is that . . . Is that when you had that . . . accident?"

"What accident?" I switch between the tiles on the deck and his face and then back to the tiles.

"I didn't want to ask because I wasn't sure if I'd make you upset . . . but that girl you mentioned, Jenn, she knows Stacy—you know, from our group—and Jenn told her that you, uh, couldn't hold it one day at school." I think my heart stops. *They know, too? I know everyone at school knows— but my new team?* I grit my teeth.

"Hey . . . Heyyyyy." He waves his hands at me. "I knew it had to be more than what Stacy was saying. You're not a toddler, I know that." Noticing my defeat, he declares, "Jenn's a real asshole. And so is that kid. What's his name? You're going to have to beat him, you know. It's not even a question. You've gotta show him, Obie!" Pooch offers a smile.

"Ah, I don't know if I should tell you. I don't wanna be a gossip or, like, make you have a bad opinion about him—"

"Dude. What the heck, of course I'm going to hate this asshole, but a) he deserves it because he treated you like shit, and b) you're my friend regardless, so I don't give a crap about him. Your terrible experience absolutely makes me hate him and that's the way it's supposed to go." He grins. "So which one is he?" he asks, nodding over at the other side of the pool deck where Lucy is sitting.

They're in the lane 1 splash zone. I find Clyde almost instantly—he's taller than everyone else, with a mop of floppy brown hair that all the girls swoon over. I feel my palms sweating. I haven't seen him since that day in the principal's office.

"Clyde. He's the—"

"Clyde *Bolton*?!" he almost screams. I freeze.

"Dude!" I whisper-yell. I glance over at Clyde. He's putting his headphones on and it appears he didn't hear anything. Thank god for the echoey natatorium and the eight lanes that separate us. Swallows those shouts right up.

"Shit, sorry," Pooch says, clamping his hand over his mouth. "But seriously, Clyde Bolton, like Coach Bolton's son?"

"Yeah, that's him," I say.

"Well then. I really don't need to know anything else.

He's a flat-out jackass, Obes. The kid's a *lunatic.* And you know what, I bet it's not even because you're trans. I bet you he's just worried you'll whoop his ass." Pooch laughs to himself, but I can see he's serious.

"I don't know, Pooch. . . . We were super close when we were kids. Like, his dad drove us to practice together. After practice, he and Lucy came over *all* the time. It's weird because even though he's a jackass, I miss hanging with him, you know?"

"Totally." He's quiet for a moment before he continues. "My mom says sometimes, people are friends forever. That's when you're lucky. She says a lot of the time, though, people grow up and grow apart. And that's okay. But then *some*times"—he drags out the word *some*—"people grow up and into assholes. That's what happened to Clyde. And really, it doesn't matter why or how. He's a jackass. But you've got me and Mikey and the whole rest of *this* team, *our* team. You just need to chill with us more." He bumps Mikey, who slides off one of his earphones and says, "What?"

"Shouldn't Obes hang with us more?"

"Duh," Mikey says, grinning at me. "Why you never hang, man?" He then covers his ears again and resumes bouncing to his music.

Pooch shrugs at me knowingly. "See?"

"You're right," I say, smiling. "You're right."

A few moments later, a whistle blows and everyone starts

standing up, stretching, taking off their outer clothes. It's time to get in for warm-up.

———

The water feels infinitely safer than the pool deck. I strap my goggles on and I'm in my own world, held inside by the tight silicone cap. Sometimes I wonder why I've always felt safe in the pool, so exposed in my swimsuit, despite all the difficulty I've had with my body. But *this*—this feeling I have in the water—*this* is why. When I swim, the only parts of my body I can see are my hands—and that's usually only out of my peripheral vision and only if I'm watching for them. Ninety-nine percent of the time, when I'm swimming, I'm *just* swimming. I am the act of swimming itself, and that's it. I get to disappear into the movements, the water, the feelings. I don't have to be a body or a gender. I can just swim.

I sink into this, listening carefully to the rush of the water and the way my hands slice into the waves created by all the other swimmers around me. I've discovered over the years that focusing on how the water feels rushing against my skin, instead of focusing on the exact times I want to achieve or the people around me, actually makes me swim faster. Mom calls this a "mindfulness practice." I call it swimming.

We do some pacing and dive starts at the end of the warm-up and I'm on top of the world. I feel so smooth and powerful. I'm exploding off the blocks into the water like a little rocket. Coach Larkin tells me that everything looks great and I just need to repeat exactly what I'm doing now when I get up to race. I nod.

"Can I do one more start, Coach?" I ask. I want to make sure I'm gauging the depth of the pool correctly for my breakout. Breaking up too early or too late could cost me half a second.

"Sure, but after that you're drying off. I want you to rest a bit."

I hop out and hop back in line at lane 2. The announcer reminds us over the PA that lanes 2 and 7 are start lanes, lanes 1 and 8 are pace, and that we've got ten minutes of warm-up left. I bend around the line so I can see how many more people there are and notice Clyde is standing two ahead of me. He's tough to miss—not just because of his height, but also because of his signature bright yellow Speedo. *Maybe I don't need to do another start.*

No. Obie. You're not going to let him take this from you. If you want another start, you take it. *But what if he throws another punch? What if he comes after me? What if everyone here supports him and thinks I'm a freak again—*

STOP! I scream at myself in my head. I even feel my fists tighten, my jaw lock into silence.

"Yo, we're going to go and get ready now." A tap on my shoulder brings me back. I turn to see Mikey and Pooch grabbing their water bottles, about to walk to the team area.

"Dude, are you okay?" Pooch's face changes as soon as he sees mine. I try to loosen my jaw and my fists.

"Oh. Yeah. Sorry, just concentrating." I turn and look quickly at Clyde. He's up on the blocks now, towering over everyone else. Pooch is trying to follow my gaze. When I look at Pooch again, I know he understands.

"On second thought, I'm going to watch your start. See if I can channel some Coach Larkin in the background or something." He grins. "Mikey, you wanna wait with me or you wanna go ahead?"

"Sorry, guys, I gotta get ready—I'm in the first relay."

"Oh, totally, of course. Go, already! We need you there," Pooch says, and Mikey holds out his fist to both of us. Pooch bumps and then I do, too, before Mikey trots off.

"You didn't have to do this," I offer. But I'm so relieved. He might not be the biggest ninth grader, but he's surely better than just me.

"I know, Obes. But like I said, I gotchu. Plus, your start needs all the help you can get." Maybe it's a dig, but he's smiling. And he's right, it does.

It's my turn. I step up onto the block and position my feet the way I always do. Front foot with the big toe curled just a tad over the edge. Back foot a foot or so behind, staggered.

"Take your mark—" Coach Larkin shouts from the edge of the pool. "Hup!"

And I dive in. My breakout is absolutely perfect. I nail the distance and pop up exactly with that first stroke. I only take a few more strokes before stopping. I let myself sink for a moment and then slip under the lane line into lane 3.

I swim a couple easy laps before stopping at the wall. Pooch leans over and says, "That might have been the best start I've ever seen you do, my friend." We do that sideways hand slap that turns into a handshake and his hand clamps down on mine and he gives me a boost out of the pool.

"Thanks, Pooch," I say, and put my arm around his shoulder as we meander to the team area.

"So what do we have here. . . ."

Of course it's Clyde. Damn, I forgot their team area was right at lane 1. I resist the urge to run for my life. A few moments later, Clyde's enormous arms pull us each into a strange side hug on either side of him and I no longer have the option to run.

"Go away, Clyde," I say, trying to push him off. I'm working hard to keep my voice level.

"Aw, why can't we be pals like before?" he taunts as his grip tightens. I never knew what "sickly sweet" meant, but I do now.

"You. Need. To. Let. Go," Pooch says in a low voice I've never heard from him.

"Why did you have to turn into such an asshole?" I try again to step out of his grip. An official passes us but she is staring at her meet sheet and doesn't stop. *HELP*, I want to scream. But I'm afraid if I do, Clyde'll hit me.

"At least I'm not a tranny freak like you," he spits at me. "You don't have your cute little parents or principal to come protect you here, faggot."

"Oh, shut the hell up, man," Pooch says, his voice hard. Clyde looks surprised. Maybe a touch angry.

"So, are you a freakin' fag, too?" he says, dipping his head down toward Pooch, getting a touch too close.

"What's it to you? Are you interested in me?" Pooch counters, seemingly unfazed and now actually smiling. Clyde's face goes from smug, satisfied arrogance to what seems like sheer terror. He drops both of his arms and takes a step back, his eyes narrowing.

"Because if you are—interested in me, I mean—that's a terrible way to ask me out." Pooch spins around to face Clyde. He leans in so close that Clyde takes another stumbling step away.

"Also," Pooch continues. "I'm not gay, so that would just be a real bummer for you." He pauses. Clyde, for once, is speechless. My hands are clammy and cold. I suddenly feel especially naked in my swimsuit and I wish I had my towel to cover up.

"And, actually," Pooch keeps going, still grinning, "to be honest, even if I were gay, I'd never be into you. You're fast, dude, don't get me wrong, but you act like a total imbecile. All of New England Swimming knows it. Maybe you should think about why you're so angry all the time so you can stop acting like an asshat."

Unbelievably, Clyde says nothing.

"Obie, let's go." Pooch nods to me, turning around.

"I'm not angry," Clyde practically yells at Pooch's back.

A few of the swimmers sitting on the nearby benches look at him. His eyes flit nervously around.

"Both of you are such fags," he says under his breath. Pooch whips around, closing the gap between them.

He points his finger at Clyde and, with a kind of calm anger I've only ever seen Mom possess, says, "Don't you ever use that word to talk about my friend or anyone else again. I *will* tell an official and you *will* be disqualified."

"You can't do that," Clyde says, getting louder again.

"No?" Pooch stares at him hard. He leans in and says, "Try it again. And then watch me." His voice is soft but powerful. Even though he stands a good three or four inches shorter than Clyde, Clyde seems to shrink as they stare at each other. A few moments that feel like for-freakin'-ever pass, and then Clyde blinks and looks at the deck.

I'm out of breath and we haven't even gotten up on the blocks to race yet.

Pooch puts his arm over my shoulder. "C'mon, Obes, we've got some races to win," he says to me.

When we're far enough from Clyde, I ask, "Can you really get someone disqualified for saying things like that?"

"I have no idea," he says to me, shrugging, "but I knew it would scare him enough."

"It definitely did."

"And it definitely should be a rule. I'll bet it is. Remind me to ask my dad when we get back to the hotel." Pooch's dad is an official, so he would actually know.

"Okay, thanks. But don't tell him why you're asking?"

"No worries, Obes," he assures me. Then, after a moment, "Hey. I'm really sorry Clyde's like that. You're way cooler than he is."

"Thanks, Samuel," I say.

"Who's Samuel?" he says, and laughs.

Chapter 17

"Should we tell Coach Larkin what happened?" Pooch asks when we're back with the team.

"No, I—"

"It's okay, I get it. I promise I won't say anything if you don't want me to."

"Ugh, it's not that I don't want to. I'm just. I'm scared." I feel tiny. "But," I continue, "I also kind of, uh, want to see if I can beat him? And if he gets disqualified then I can't do that. . . ."

Pooch's eyes light up. "Hell, yeah! You so can beat him," he says. "Well. You just let me know. I gotchu, Obes."

"Thanks, man, I really appreciate it." I feel tears begging to be released but I hold them in.

"What took you guys so long?" Mikey asks. He's in his racing suit, ready to go.

"Sorry, man, we—" Pooch looks at me as if to ask if it's okay. I nod hesitantly. "We got caught up. Some asshat from Obie's old team tried to mess with him, called us 'faggots' and—"

"WHAT?!" Mikey yells. His face is turning red and he's

fumbling for words. "What the—?! Who is this guy?" he demands.

"Dude, dude," I say. "It's okay, I'm okay—"

"Hell, no, that's not okay," Mikey says angrily. I've never seen him like this. Mikey Garcia is, like, *known* for being happy-go-lucky. . . . I didn't think he had this in him.

"Are you okay, man? I agree that wasn't okay, but you're kinda flipping out?" Pooch puts an arm around Mikey and they sit down together.

"I'm sorry," Mikey says. He's breathing deeply. "My sister is gay. She used to get called all sorts of terrible names by the people at our church. I freakin' hate that word especially. It's, like, the worst. I mean, do you know where the word comes from?" *Mikey's sister is gay?*

"No, I just thought it was a bad word for gay people. . . . Uh . . . where?" Pooch answers.

"My sister says it's hard to know for certain but before the f-word was bad, it just meant a bundle of sticks used for kindling a fire. They used to burn gay people at the stake, though. Or say that they would burn forever in hell. So, calling someone an f-word is essentially condemning them to burn in hell or saying they are the kindling for the eternal fires of hell."

"Ohhhhhh," Pooch says. "Damn." *Damn is right.* Obviously, I'd known the word was bad, but I hadn't known it was *that* bad.

"Anyway. I'm sorry I freaked. And I'm more sorry someone is saying that to you. He's an idiot, Obie, whoever he is.

Let's beat his sorry butt." Mikey grins at me, his face returning to normal. He offers a fist and I bump it. Then he dashes over to the blocks for his first race.

"Obie." I hear my name and I turn around. Lucy. *Dammit*. I've been so caught up in worrying about Clyde that I totally forgot about her.

"Hey, Lucy."

"Hey, can we talk?" She cocks her head to the side. I don't move. Pooch stands next to me, his arms crossed, examining her Barracudas cap and clearly not approving.

"What do you want?" I say flatly.

"Alone?" Lucy adds.

"It's okay," I tell Pooch. "I'll be back before Mikey's relay." Pooch nods, giving me a high five, and I walk with Lucy toward the water fountains.

"What's up?" gets Lucy talking a million miles a minute.

"Clyde just came over to tell us that you were messing with him and he told his dad you were trying to make him throw the race, I mean I know you don't like the guy anymore but what the hell, Obie, that's so unlike you and—"

What the hell? I was trying to mess with him? Are you kidding me? I'm so over this.

"Are you serious right now?!" I interrupt her loudly. "Are you freaking kidding me?"

Lucy looks stunned. I never curse, at least never out loud.

"Wha-what?" she stammers.

"Are you serious, Lucy? You think that's what happened? You really think that I would ever actively try to mess with *Clyde*?"

"I mean, I—" But I'm not waiting for her answers.

"I thought you were my friend. I thought you'd stand up for me when someone was bullying me. Clyde has been making my life hell recently and you don't even know because we never hang anymore because you're too busy with the same girls that used to bully *you* and who are spreading rumors about me! Do you even know half of the things Clyde's said to me? DONE TO ME?!" I am trying so hard not to yell. We're in a corner of the pool deck and there aren't that many people around, but still.

"Aw, c'mon, Obie, don't take out all your pain on Clyde, he's not that bad—"

I really cannot believe she's saying this.

"How can you even say that?" I interrupt her. "What the heck do you know about him?"

"Don't pretend like you know him better than me. I'll bet you didn't even know he had a huge crush on you when we were kids!" *A crush on me? Clyde? What?!*

"You acted all high and mighty like you never knew anything about it, ignoring him while I practically drooled all over him, but he *never* noticed me. I spent our whole childhood hoping he would look at me just once, but he was always obsessed with *you!*" Lucy's breathing heavy, like she's running out of breath.

"What are you talking about, Lucy?" I ask, the confusion dulling my anger.

"Obie, how can you be so clueless?" she says, exasperated. "Did you *really* not know?"

I shake my head no. I have no idea what to say. *Clyde . . . liked . . . me?*

"He's like this because he was in love with you before. When you looked different. When we were kids. All the boys were. You were the coolest 'girl.' " She puts air quotes around the word *girl,* indicating that she knows I'm really a boy. I wonder if, somewhere, my best friend is still in there.

"All the guys had at least a small crush on you. You were pretty and you liked all the same things they did. . . ." She trails off for a second. "Of course, that's because you actually *are* the same as them. A boy. It just took you longer to be able to say that. And I know that. But seriously . . . it's no fair you got all their attention and no one ever looked at me. . . . And even after you came out. People still pay more attention to you."

"Lucy . . ." But I don't know where I'm going. Clyde having a crush on me when we were kids feels so foreign. Is she telling the truth? And if so, how did I not notice? Alternatively: How would I have noticed? It's not like I was paying attention to stuff like that. I was just trying to survive. And why didn't Lucy tell me she had a crush on *Clyde*? My memories begin to play in my head: we are jumping in the snow, riding to practice together, goofing around at swim meets, posing with all of our medals, hanging out on my eighth birthday at Halmoni's house. . . . I remember the first time Lucy told me about a crush—some boy in our fourth-grade class that all the girls thought was cute. I remember how I couldn't see it and how I wondered if something was wrong with me. I remember how we teased Clyde about a girl he liked at school. . . . And suddenly everything feels like a lie.

"Is there a problem here?" a deep voice says from behind us. *Dammit.*

"No, sir," Lucy and I say in unison as we turn around. The years of practice with Coach Bolton come rushing forth. I stand straight as a bamboo pole.

"YOU." He points at me. "Do NOT talk to my swimmers again," he warns harshly. "If I see you with any of my swimmers, I'll have to notify Jamie."

I'm not really sure what Coach Larkin would do, but I nod anyway.

"Ms. Weaver, let's go." They walk off together. Lucy does not turn around to look at me. I lean against the wall, sliding to the floor. I'm still wrapped in my towel, chilly because all I've got on is my Speedo underneath. Down by the lanes, the officials are gathering for the national anthem and I want desperately to just go home.

When the song starts, I push myself to my feet and stand with my hand over my heart. I watch as the meet begins, swimmers diving in after the buzzer. When I get back to the team area, I'm met by Coach Larkin's harsh stare. She walks over to me.

"Where have you been? You missed the first couple heats already—you're lucky we didn't have any swimmers in them."

"I'm sorry, Coach, I had a little bit of a run-in with . . ." I don't know what I'm supposed to say. And I also know there isn't much time to explain everything right now.

"With my old team," I finish.

"Ah . . ." She pauses long enough to let me know she got it in an instant. "Okay. I understand. Are you safe?"

"Yes, I think so. I need to just focus on my races. I'm hoping I'm not swimming in lanes one or two." I force a chuckle.

"Well," she says, perusing her meet sheet. "You're in luck. You're heat nine, lane six for IM and heat eight, lane eight for one hundred breast."

"Okay, thanks, Coach," I say.

"I want to hear what happened later, but I agree: let's focus on your races right now and then we can chat after. Otherwise they win, and I refuse to let that happen, okay? Sound good?"

"Yes, ma'am," I say. I didn't want to explain everything anyway.

"Great. Go get ready and we'll chat about this at the hotel tonight after dinner."

—

When I get up behind the blocks for my first race, I find myself looking for Lucy, despite everything. Ever since we were kids, this was our pre-race ritual. She'd stand at the end of my lane and do our dance. I'd stand behind the block and do it in response. Our dance was really dumb. We made it up when we were probably seven or eight. We'd raise our arms above our heads and wiggle our hands around in circles, bouncing our heads from side to side, and then after a few of those, we'd point to each other across the pool.

Today, there's definitely no Lucy on the other side of my lane. When she wasn't there at Summer Champs, I nearly lost it. I mean, I did lose, actually. I did terrible at that meet.

The official is blowing the whistle and we're stepping up on the blocks. My heart rate quickens and I give myself a mini pep talk.

You've trained for this for months. You got it. Nothing else matters right now.

I shut my eyes for a moment inside my goggles and imagine myself at the end of my own lane doing our dance.

This is it. Let's go.

———

I chat with Coach Larkin after a dinner of hotel pasta. Which is what we always eat at travel meets. How else are you supposed to feed thirty hungry swimmers?

Coach Larkin says that she'll talk to Coach Bolton about Clyde. I don't want her to make it a big deal, but she seems adamant that something has to be done.

"Pooch said that he was going to talk to his dad about it," I mention.

"He can still do that," she answers. "But I'm also going to

make sure Bolton is held accountable for his swimmers. His swimmers' behavior is unacceptable."

"Okay," I respond, tired and just wanting to get to bed.

Mikey, Pooch, and I take the elevator together to our rooms.

"You guys crushed it today," Pooch says as my phone buzzes in my pocket.

CHARLIE, 9:16 P.M.: How did it go??

"Thanks, man," Mikey answers, fist-bumping him as we exit the elevator. Pooch and I stop at our room and Mikey continues.

"See you boys en la mañana. Wish me luck, I might not survive Jackson's farts!" We all giggle and Pooch unlocks our door.

"So . . . how does it feel to be a Junior *Olympics* qualifier?!" Pooch asks me, jumping on his bed.

"Pretty good," I answer.

"*Pretty* good? Obes, man, give yourself a break! A few months ago, you were like 'no way' and now? You destroyed the cut." He's sitting up in bed, talking excitedly and waving his hands to make his point.

"I guess that's true . . . ," I admit, laughing.

"Of course it's true." He stands up and playfully punches me in the shoulder. "Lighten up, you're crushing it. Especially with all the other shit that happened today." He rolls his eyes and mutters, "That asshole."

"Thanks, Pooch, you're the best."

"Course I am." He grins. "And like I said, I'll talk to my dad tomorrow." My phone buzzes again and I pull it from my pocket—I forgot to reply.

CHARLIE, 9:23 P.M.: I hope I'm not waking you!

"Ooooh, who's that?" Pooch asks, watching me.

"Uh, just this girl—"

"A GIRL?!" Pooch almost yells.

"Ah yes, shhhh, we're gonna get a noise complaint," I say, but I'm smiling.

"A *girl*friend girl?" he teases.

"No—I—I don't know." He raises his eyebrows as he changes into pajamas. "I met her at this restaurant. She gave me her number and we're going to get ice cream next weekend. . . ."

"That's a *date,* man. Hell yeah." He pauses. Then, as if realizing something, "Text her back! Don't make her wait!"

I begin typing.

ME, 9:28 P.M.: Nah, not sleeping, just chatting with my roommate. I made JOs!

I don't explain what happened with Clyde. How would I? She still doesn't know. . . . Anyway, I don't really feel like talking about it anymore.

"Man's made his JO cut, he's got a cute girl he's talking

to. . . . He's set," Pooch is saying to himself as he pulls the covers over his head. He's so weird. He slept like that last night, too. "Good night," he mumbles as he turns off the light. "Happy flirting." He falls asleep in an instant. I know because he snores, too.

THINGS THAT HAPPENED THIS WEEKEND:
1. I made JOs! I MADE JOs!!!!!
2. I made Junior Olympics. As a boy. Heck, YES!
3. I told Pooch why I moved swim teams and he was really nice about it.
4. Pooch stood up for me when we were at the pool and Clyde was bullying me. Again.
5. Lucy told me that Clyde used to have a crush on me and that's why he's so mean now. I don't know what to do with that. I've never been so mean to anyone I've had a crush on.
6. Lucy told me that she had (has?) a crush on Clyde. I don't know what to do with that, either.

I just feel so confused. Can I hate someone but not hate them at the same time? How can I feel bad for someone who's been so mean to me?

Chapter 18

Practice on Monday is pretty easy. Coach Larkin likes to make sure we shake out the lactic acid that builds up in our muscles after a long meet, so we do a lot of longer, slower stuff. I like it. It gives my brain a break.

In the showers, Pooch says we should walk together so we can chat.

"I talked to my dad this morning," he reports. "I want to tell you about it."

"Okeydoke," I agree.

"You know how you said I shouldn't tell anyone about what happened at the pool with Clyde?" he says when we're alone, walking to the parking lot.

"Umm, yeah. . . ." *Uh-oh.*

"Well, don't worry. I didn't tell any coaches. But I did ask my dad what would happen if someone used words like Clyde did."

"Oh?" *Okay, so maybe not uh-oh.*

"And he immediately guessed it was Clyde." *Okay, maybe yes uh-oh.*

"And he also kind of guessed that the other person was you." *Okay, definitely uh-oh.*

"Did he guess or did you tell him?" I ask, trying not to let any anger show.

"I promise, man, I didn't tell him. I said, 'Dad, I'm not telling you any names. I just want to know what would happen if someone acted this way on deck.'" He nods, proud of himself. *Okay, maybe revoking definite uh-oh.*

"And he went with that?"

"Yeah, I think so." He motions for me to sit on the bench. We've finished practice early, which is perfect because we have some time until the parents arrive to grab us. "He didn't press. Anyway, that's not the exciting part. Clyde *can* actually get disqualified—at least for a little bit—for talking like he did. Dad said it's called 'unsportsmanlike conduct.' Here, look." Pooch reaches into his pocket and pulls out his phone. He clicks for a few seconds before turning his phone's screen to me, which shows a picture of a printed page.

"See?" He points to the top of the screen. I squint.

102.22.4 ANY SWIMMER WHO ACTS IN AN UNSPORTSMANLIKE OR UNSAFE MANNER WITHIN THE SWIMMING VENUE MAY BE CONSIDERED FOR APPROPRIATE ACTION OR PENALTY BY THE REFEREE.

"Huh, so what does 'appropriate action or penalty' mean? Also, what happens if we report it now and it's like a week after it actually happened?"

"He says 'appropriate action' could mean being banned from meets for up to a year. It could mean that he's not allowed to ever talk to you. Lots of things. And, hmm, I'm not sure about what else. Should I ask him?"

"Oh, I don't know. . . ."

"Obie, he's really an asshat to you. I think you should stand up to him."

"I know, I know. It's not right. But I guess I don't want him to use this as an excuse, you know? He'll totally make himself into a victim." I think about how Lucy had told me he wasn't that bad. I feel my fists tightening again.

"When I walked back after . . . after Clyde, Lucy—one of my friends from my old team—"

"Yeah, I was there when she came to find you. Lucy Weaver, right? She's super cute." He blushes. *Lucy? Cute?*

"Anyway, she and I used to be best friends, but stuff's been weird ever since I left. At the meet, she tried to tell me that Clyde's not that bad of a guy. She said I should stop messing with him because after we left him, he went and told the whole team that I was the one trying to throw his race so I could beat him." My voice cracks some when I get to the end. I look away.

"What? That's insane, man!" Pooch exclaims, no longer blushing. "Are you freakin' kidding me?"

"No, I'm not, and I don't want someone else to just not believe me. . . ."

"Obes, dude. I don't have to believe you—because I was a freakin' witness! Clyde doesn't have a witness. You do."

"That is true. . . ." He's right. I do. Maybe that means something. . . . "Coach also said she was going to talk to Coach Bolton about Clyde and his swimmers leaving me alone. Maybe that's enough?"

"Maybe," Pooch says. "Listen, why don't I talk to my dad and see what's possible. Maybe Clyde can just get some kind of warning—so he's not forbidden from racing, but he'll know *for sure* that if he says anything else, he will be. What do you think?"

"Okay, but when he gets that warning, he'll know I tattled and he'll come after me again."

"I thought you said he was expelled from your school?"

"He was . . . but I'm still afraid. I still have to see him at meets."

"I get that." He nods. "I won't push you. It's your call, Obie." He smiles. *Tall and confident,* I hear Mrs. Salmani say. Maybe "tattling" is a part of being tall and confident, actually. Maybe it's just asking for help, and maybe I should do that.

"Okay. You talk to your dad and tell him what happened," I say.

"You got it," Pooch says, turning to go. "Did you mention it to your parents?"

"Oh . . ." I trail off. I guess I didn't. "No. . . . I didn't want them to worry. You know, they get all freaked out about this stuff."

"I see. I think you should tell them, though."

"You're right."

Pooch's ride pulls into the lot and stops in front of us.

"OH!" he says as he opens the car door. "I'm excited for your date." He gives me a theatrical wink before he gets in.

———

Mom is clearly not happy I didn't tell her sooner, but she says she's relieved nothing worse happened.

"How are you feeling, honey?" Mom's asking as we pull onto the highway.

"Good," I say, and mean it.

"I'm sorry Clyde is still bothering you so much."

"It's okay, I think I'm getting better at dealing with him."

"You definitely are. And it sounds like Mr. Puczovich is going to help get you some justice."

"Yeah."

"Is that okay with you?"

"I think so."

"Good. Keep us posted."

Chapter 19

The week feels like it takes forever, but finally it's Saturday. My date with Charlie. I knock on Jae-sung's door. There's no answer. I knock again.

"Hello?" I call. "Jae-sung? I know you're in there." I hear some rummaging around.

"I need your help, please!" I try one last time.

"Ugh," I say to myself, and start toward my room. His door swings open. I turn around.

"What?" Jae-sung says, his hair standing straight up. He looks like he's just woken up even though it's noon.

"Does this look good?" I fidget with my button-down shirt and tie. He rubs his eyes.

"Dude, what the heck are you wearing?" he says dramatically. "Where are you going dressed like that?"

I shrink. "I have a date," I say quietly.

"What? With who?!"

"Whom!" I exclaim, letting a small grin emerge. *Haha, Dad.* A break from my embarrassment. Jae-sung rolls his eyes. I am nervous again. "A girl from Chotley's," I mumble, staring at my feet, which are mostly hidden by my pant legs, which are way too long.

"Ooooooh," he says in a teasing voice. "We're tryna look good for the ladies, huh?"

I nod.

"Well, is she cute? Let me see a picture."

"Uh," I say. "I, uh, I don't think I have any pictures, actually."

"Just show me her Insta or something, then." He holds out his hand for my phone.

"Um, I don't have it." Am I supposed to? I didn't realize that was part of asking a girl on a date. I thought getting her number was enough.

"Such a noob," Jae-sung says, shaking his head. "Okay, what's her last name? I'll search her up."

"Umm . . ."

"Dude, really? You don't even know her last name?"

"Chotley?" I say weakly. He bursts out laughing. "Hey, it's a fair guess. She's Mr. Chotley's grandniece or whatever."

"Okay, all right. You'll have to show me a picture later. Maybe you can find out her last name and some more stuff about her on your date tonight. But first, let's make sure she doesn't see you and leave. Take it all off. You're not going to a fancy ballroom dance, bud."

"Okay," I concede, and unbutton the shirt.

"Come into my humble abode," he says with an extravagant bow, laughing to himself. I smile and enter his room. It's a mess. But it always is. Clothes all over the floor—sweatshirts, mostly. He has more sweatshirts than socks, it seems, but what do I know about the right clothes? According to Jae-sung, nothing.

"All righty, li'l bro. Let's get you all dressed up." Jae-sung rummages through a pile of clothes in his closet.

"Don't worry. These are all clean. I just don't like folding things," he says. I nod, not believing his cleanliness proclamation. "Here. Throw these on." He tosses me a pair of washed-out jeans. They're light blue and frayed by the left pocket.

"Those used to be my favorite jeans. They don't fit me anymore—you know, because I'm so big and buff now." He flexes and I laugh. "But seriously, they're too small. But they're the sexiest. Girls love guys in jeans." He grins to himself.

I've never heard that before, but okay.

"Try 'em on," he encourages me. I feed my feet through the legs and shimmy them on. They fit perfectly, except they're a tad too long.

"Oh, don't worry," he says, kneeling in front of me. "They're supposed to be like that, because you're supposed to do this." He rolls up each pant leg a few times so the white inside shows.

"Perfect," he says, examining his handiwork. "Now, to

make you look truly like a K-pop star, we need those terribly ugly white shoes everyone's wearing."

"What? I don't—"

He puts his hand up in the air to stop me. "Say no more." He dives back into his pile of "clean" laundry.

"*This* is the winning sweatshirt." He hands me a dark gray sweater. It smells like garlic. I guess he wore it to Halmoni's last. Great. Garlic cologne. That's hardly a good idea on a first date. I'll definitely have to toss it in the wash before I go, though.

To his credit, it's the softest sweatshirt I think I've ever put on. It's got a tiny cartoon drawing on the front. I look down, trying to see who the characters are.

"It's Mario and Luigi, dumbass," he says. "It's perfect. Girls love that shit."

"They do?"

"I don't know, maybe." He laughs. "It's great. This is it. You don't look like you're trying so hard anymore. You're just like, hey, I'm a nice-ish-looking-but-not-better-looking-than-my-brother dude." There he goes with those rare backhanded compliments.

"Okay, are you ready for my five rules for a date?" He stands up tall and makes some strange motion with his arm, almost like he's conducting.

I laugh, not knowing this was an option.

"Numberrrrrrrr—" he says in a dramatic tone, but stops and looks at me. "Hey, help a guy out. Can I get a little drumroll, dude?" I make the sounds with my mouth and fake a drumroll motion.

"Numberrrrrr ONE," he announces, holding up his pointer finger. "Make sure you smell good. Everyone likes someone who smells clean and good." I make a face. "What, you don't think I know how to clean up?" He's indignant.

"Um, I think your room smells like dirty laundry and you do, too."

"Hey, man, I'm not the one going on a date tonight. I ain't got nobody to impress." He tosses a shirt that's on the bed onto the floor so he can sit down. He bounces and the bed makes a squeaking sound. "Okay. Moving along. Numberrrrrr two," he announces. "Always ask to share a romantic food. Like in *Lady and the Tramp*."

"What's a romantic food?"

"I don't know, man. Where are you and this girl going?"

"Ice cream."

"Perfect!" He leaps up. "That's perfect." I've never seen him so amped before, but I laugh and he laughs, too. I've missed the fun Jae-sung. I'm glad moody morning Jae-sung has taken a break this morning.

"Share an ice cream. It'll be romantic as heck."

"Okay."

"Number three." He holds up three fingers and does a backward belly flop onto his bed. His face is covered by his hair as he continues, "Always pay. Yeah, yeah, I know it's really heteronormative." He carefully enunciates *heteronormative.*

It's a mouthful. "And if you start dating dudes, we'll have to reexamine this rule. But for now. That's what I think. Let her know it's a date, and not just as friends. If she wants to pay, that's chill, too. As long as one person pays for both. Then it's a date." I don't know how to feel about this one, but I make a mental note anyway. And I add to the growing list of notes to ask Mom or Dad later.

"Number four," he says in a deep voice, like some kind of Disney villain. I giggle. "Everyone likes to talk about themselves. Ask her about herself. But don't be creepy."

"What counts as creepy?"

"Uhhh, don't ask about her medical history. Don't ask her about any sizes or clothing or body parts."

"Ew, what?!"

"I'm just saying. Don't. One of my buddies asked this girl how big her hands were, in inches, and she got pretty mad at him."

"Why would he even ask—never mind. I got it."

"Okay, last one. Numberrrrrrrr—drumroll, please."

I begin another drumroll.

"Numberrrrrrrrrrrrr"—he drags it out again—"FIVE!" He stares at me wide-eyed for a moment and I match him, gooning. "Be confident." He puffs his chest out and lowers his voice again. "BE. CON. FI. DENT," he repeats, emphasizing each syllable. "What's wrong with being, what's wrong with being," he sings Demi Lovato terribly off-key, parading around the room. I'm nearly in tears laughing at him.

"Everyone loves confident. Confidence is sexehhhh!" He stops parading, his back to me, and shakes his butt.

"Okay. I got it, I got it."

"Repeat 'em," he demands, now standing on his bed, wobbling a bit. He's never had great balance. He's got his hands over his head like the Y when you do the YMCA song.

"Smell nice, share food, pay, uh . . ." What was the fourth one again?

"Oh no, not number four!" He feigns terror, the back of his hand to his forehead, and falls onto his bed with a squeaky bounce. "You can't have a conversation without this one."

"Oh—oh! Ask her about herself," I say excitedly.

"Bingo. And last one?" He jumps off his bed and grabs me by the shoulders. Slightly startled, I swallow and look at him.

"Um, be confident?" I say.

"Be WHAAAAT?!" he almost shouts back.

"BE! CONFIDENT!" I shout.

"GOOD."

"Okay, you are ready, young lad. My job here is done. You are dismissed." He waves his hand, as if to make me disappear. I give him a hug. Surprisingly, he hugs me back.

"I hope you have fun," he adds gently, dropping the act for a moment.

"Thanks," I say. He lets me go.

"Oh, and also . . ."

I pause and turn around.

"I was wondering. Did you tell her yet?" He's leaning against his doorframe. I'm already halfway down the hallway.

"Umm . . . no. I haven't. I—" But I don't really have much of an explanation ready.

"You don't have to explain, bro. I'm not asking because I think you *should* have told her." He pauses and I wait. "I just, uh. I just. Well. When—I, I mean, if. *If* you do tell her . . ." He pauses, his eyes searching mine for a second.

"Yes," I affirm.

"If she has an issue with it," he continues, "then I have an issue with her." He's looking straight at me and his voice is firm. "Rule Number Six. If she makes you feel like poop, she's poop. Call me."

"Thanks, Jae-sung, I will," I promise, trying to keep my voice from wobbling.

"Duh," he says, returning to his usual flippant tone.

I take the sweatshirt and the rest of my dirty clothes to the laundry room and start the machine. When I'm in my room, I shut the door and sit at my desk. I've still got about seven hours to kill until I'm supposed to meet up with Charlie. Maybe I should text her to make sure she hasn't forgotten.

I text her, asking if we're still on for 7 p.m. Her response is immediate, as usual.

I'm grinning like crazy as I unzip my backpack and begin working on my geometry.

I take a break around 4 p.m. to switch the laundry and get a snack. I grab a few of the cookies Dad's making while they're still hot. I try to casually remind Mom and Dad that I'm going out tonight.

"Ummm, I'm finishing up some more homework before I go see Charlie."

"Ooooooooooh," comes Jae-sung's teasing as he descends the stairs. The cookie smells have brought him down, too. I roll my eyes but I'm smiling. I retreat to my room and lie down on the floor on my stomach and prop myself up on my elbows. Coach says we're never supposed to study this way because it's bad for our shoulders, but it's my favorite way to read.

This week we're supposed to finish *All American Boys*—so I do. I'm in a total rut when I'm done. Why can't the bad guys just be bad guys? Why do the bad guys have feelings and kids and parents and lives, too? Why do the bad guys have to have been innocent little kids once? It would be so much easier to hate them if they were just bad. But they're not. Paul was kind—almost a father—to Quinn, once.

And Clyde was one of my best friends—and apparently,

I was his first crush. But my history with Clyde doesn't—can't—override how he's treated me recently. I guess it just makes it all that much sadder. I'm not sure.

My phone buzzes on my desk and I force myself up to grab it. I see the time before I can read the message. 6:30 p.m. Crap. I'm gonna be late and I haven't even eaten dinner.

I race to the kitchen and inhale a granola bar before racing back upstairs to grab my phone and my clean clothes. I'm running down the stairs when Jae-sung sticks his head out of his room and shouts, "Don't forget to brush your teeth." He lilts on *tee-eeth*. I almost fall as I stop in my tracks.

"What?" I shout.

"Rule Number One, man, smell nice. This includes your breath! Or do you want dragon breath when you go in for the kiss?"

"Ew, what?" I say again.

"Stop playing. You'll thank me later. Brush your teeth or chew some gum," he advises. Then he slams his door. I stand on the staircase wondering if he's right. I look at my watch. 6:41 p.m. It takes ten minutes to walk to Moozy's. Okay, I still have time. I run back up the stairs to the bathroom. I squeeze an enormous gob of toothpaste onto my brush and begin scrubbing my teeth.

Jae-sung sneaks a look through his side of the Jack-and-Jill bathroom.

"Here," he says, handing me a pack of gum. I reach to grab it.

"Ah-ah!" He snatches it from me. "Just take one. Who do you think I am, 7-Eleven?" I groan but hold my hand out. He places a piece in my palm.

"Good boy. Now, you might want to get outta the bathroom because I have to fart." Before he gets to the word *fart,* he's already let one rip.

"Aw, c'mon, Jae-sung," I groan again. I try to say *whyyyy,* but my mouth is full of toothpaste foam so it ends up sounding like *wahhh.* He laughs.

"Seriously, get out. I have to poop," he says. I spit.

"Okay, okay, jeez. Bye," I say after rinsing my mouth and simultaneously trying not to breathe in his fart.

"Boy, BYE!" he says with mocking sass.

JAE-SUNG'S DATING INSTRUCTIONS:
1. Make sure you smell good.
2. Always ask to share a romantic food. Like the spaghetti dogs.
3. Always pay. Or make sure one person pays the whole tab. That's how you know it's a date.
4. Ask her about herself but don't be creepy.
5. Be confident. Confidence is sexy.
6. If she makes me feel like poop, she's poop.

Chapter 20

The walk to Moozy's is quicker than I expect, which is good because with all of Jae-sung's shenanigans, I definitely did not leave on time. But I'm still a tad early, and I don't know what to do with myself so I stand outside, leaning against the wall. I wonder if that looks cool. After a few moments I decide it does not and I sit on the bench and pull out my phone. There's a text from Pooch.

> **POOCH, 6:58 P.M.:** Bad news. My dad says we probably can't file the complaint about Clyde because we're not at the meet anymore, I'm sorry man

> **POOCH, 6:59 P.M.:** But if he says anything on deck in the future, we're definitely going to do something about it. Ok?

ME, 7:00 P.M.: That sounds good. Thanks, Pooch. I really appreciate it.

POOCH, 7:01 P.M.: Anytime, dude. Good luck on your date;))))

I feel like I should feel the opposite, but I'm actually more relieved that I don't have to file a report. It would have been like dealing with the school-bathroom-pissing-myself scenario all over again, trying to get adults to believe me instead of Clyde. And I don't need to give him more reasons to pick on me. Maybe this is good—I'll get to race him at JOs.

I cringe as I remember my last conversation with Lucy. I wonder how I hadn't noticed that Clyde had a crush on me . . . and maybe more important, how did I not know Lucy had a crush on *him*—

"Hey, Obie!" I look up to see Charlie's grinning face.

"He-hey," I stammer, and shove my phone into my pocket as I stand up.

"Heyyy," she says again. I take a step forward and am about to offer my hand for a handshake, but she gives me a hug. I freeze. I guess I should have asked Jae-sung how I was supposed to say hello on a first date. *How are you supposed to know if you're allowed to hug?*

Charlie pulls away and smiles at me.

"I'm excited for ice cream," she declares. "Are you?"

"Yes," I say.

"You're cute," she says, but before she can see me blush, she turns to enter the store. I follow.

"What's your favorite flavor, Obie?" she says, face almost pressed against the glass. This is why I never touch the glass. Too many kids put their hands all over it like she's doing right now.

"I really like rainbow sherbet," I say.

"Oooooh, me too." She grins.

"Do you want to share one?" I venture, following Rule Number Two.

"Yes." She nods.

"May we please have a large cup of rainbow sherbet with two spoons?" I ask the boy behind the counter. I'm pretty sure he's our age.

"My pleasure," he says with absolutely no pleasure. Charlie looks at me. I shrug. I can't imagine I'd love working in an ice cream shop on a Saturday night, either.

"That'll be five dollars and forty-nine cents," he says in the same monotone.

I hand him a ten-dollar bill. Jae-sung's Rule Number Three, even though it's heteronormative. (But Mom gave me the ten bucks. So maybe that cancels it out.)

"Where do you want to sit?" I ask, holding the ice cream. She takes the dish from me with one hand and points to a booth in the corner with the other.

"I love booths," she says. We sit down and she places the

ice cream in the middle of the table. She removes her spoon and takes a heaping scoop.

"Mmm-mm," she says, eyes closed. "This really *is* the best rainbow sherbet, isn't it?"

I take my own bite before nodding. It really is. "My mom used to bring my brother, Jae-sung, and me here all the time before I started swimming a lot."

"Swimming! Right. Congratulations again on making JOs. You're amazing!"

I can tell she's super excited for me, but I'm pretty sure she doesn't quite understand how important all this is to me. I realize we really don't know that much about each other. I mean, swimming is my whole life.

"You're really super good, then, right?"

"Um . . ." *I was when I competed as a girl, but now that I'm competing with boys, I have some catching up to do.* I hesitate instead of answering.

"I'll bet you are. I'll bet you win all the time."

"No." I chuckle. "Not exactly."

"Can I come to a swim meet sometime?" I don't think I've ever had a non-swim friend watch me at a meet.

"Maybe," I answer. "I have a bit of a break right now from meets because we're about to begin buckling down to train for Junior Olympics in March."

"Yes, yes. And I hope you know that I'm going to be coming to watch. I mean, Junior *Olympics*?" She's practically screaming. She grabs my hand from across the table. "That's so cool."

"Yeah," I say bashfully. *It's not as big a deal as it sounds,* I'm about to say. But there's no harm in her not knowing that. "So, what do you like to do?" Rule Number Four. Everyone likes to talk about themselves, so ask questions. (Also. Find out what her last name is so Jae-sung can look her up.)

"Hmmm, well . . . I'm not an athlete so nothing sporty. But I do have fourteen Rubik's Cubes." My eyes widen and she grins.

"Fourteen?!" I exclaim. "Why fourteen? Are they all different?"

"Well, of course they are. They're all different shapes with different numbers of pieces." I didn't know that Rubik's Cubes could be so diverse. But then again, I could never even do those enormous, sized-for-toddlers puzzles when I was younger, so Rubik's Cubes have never been my friends.

"I have one with me." She pulls a small, otherwise normal-looking Rubik's Cube from her jacket pocket.

"Oh?" I say, unsure of whether or not I am excited.

"Let's chat more first if that's okay?" She stows it in her pocket. "Unless you want to play with it while we talk?"

"I think I'm okay, but thank you," I say. "What do you like about Rubik's Cubes so much?" Charlie puts her spoon down and looks at me with those green eyes and I can't help but think how beautiful they are. How beautiful she is.

"Well, I like puzzles a lot." She's thinking hard. This is the first time I've ever seen her face look so calm.

"And I am a biiiit of a hyper person—" She grins again.

"I've noticed," I interject, smiling, with a little more confidence. Rule Number Five: Be confident. Everyone thinks confidence is sexy.

She blushes and her dimples emerge.

"Well, playing with the Cubes can settle me down a bit and allow me to focus. Also, sometimes I get nervous and it helps calm my nerves, too."

"*You* get nervous?" I say, incredulous. Charlie does *not* strike me as someone who gets nervous. I mean, she was the one who gave me her number without me asking.

"Of course I do. Especially around people." Well, that doesn't match up at all!

"But you're so friendly! And you came right up to me and started a whole conversation and then you even gave me your number!"

"This is true." She nods. "But I was nervous the whole time."

"No way," I say. "I could never do that."

"Sure, you can. I'm sure you do it all the time."

"I never talk to strangers."

"You talked to me." Hm. She's got me there. And she

knows it. She smiles and takes another bite of our ice cream. "Have some, it's melting!"

I take another spoonful.

"All right, all right. So then, aside from when strangers force you to talk to them by talking to you first or when I 'forgot' to bring you your pickle . . ." She puts air quotes around *forgot*.

"You forgot it on purpose? Why?"

"Because I wanted an excuse to talk to you," she says with satisfaction. "But you didn't let me finish. Besides that, I'm sure you do things even though you're nervous all the time. Haven't you ever gotten nervous for a swimming race?"

I nod.

"And then still swam it?"

"Yeah. . . ."

"See?" She nudges. "Then you can do things even if you're nervous."

"This is true."

"Tell me about the last time you got nervous," she demands. Uh-oh. Dangerous territory. My rule, the only one: Don't tell her I'm transgender until after a few dates.

"Um," I say. "Well, last weekend, I was pretty nervous for my two hundred IM."

"What's 'IM'?" she asks.

"It's where you do one lap of each stroke in the order

of butterfly, backstroke, breaststroke, and then freestyle," I answer.

"Okay, cool. So, you're at the two hundred IM."

"Yes, and I was nervous because I really wanted to go a specific time so I could qualify for the Junior Olympics." I can tell she's waiting for more, but that's all I have.

"Well, there you go!"

"Yes," I say with a sheepish smile.

"Yay!" she nearly shouts. "See?"

"Yeah, I guess you're right," I concede. "Okay, your turn."

———

We spend nearly three hours talking in that booth, completely forgetting we had planned on walking through the park. All for the best, though, because at about 9:30 p.m., right before Moozy's is closing, we get pretty hungry. Luckily Charlie also brought ten dollars so we buy ourselves some loaded fries to share.

We gobble them up and she tells me that she'd better get going soon—her mom will be waiting.

"Of course," I say. "Can I walk you home?"

"Sure," she says, grinning.

We exit the store, the cowbell ringing behind us as the door shuts. She walks close enough that her arm grazes mine with each step. At first, I'm inclined to step away—but then

I wonder if this is the moment when I'm supposed to grab her hand. Is she walking like that on purpose? Maybe she is just one of those people who can't walk in a straight line and is always bumping into the person next to her. I wonder if I am allowed to hold her hand on the first date. *Darn, I should have asked Jae-sung!*

Just do it, I tell myself.

Staring at the ground, I open my hand and find hers— warm and soft. I lace my fingers between hers. Her fingertips are rough, callused. I wonder why? But I tighten my hold. I continue staring at the ground, wondering if she'll snatch her hand away from me.

She doesn't. Instead, when I look up a few moments later, she's looking at me, a different kind of smile on her face— less exuberant, but with something sparkling in her eyes.

"You're different from other boys I've been with," she says quietly. I freeze. I can feel my palms immediately drawing sweat and I curse myself for holding her hand. It's not like I can pull away now.

"You're so shy but I feel like you have so many stories to tell me. I love how humble you are. You're not wrapped up in all the crap other boys our age are." I begin to relax.

"Thanks," I offer weakly. I don't know what else to say. She's nothing like anyone I've ever met before. But she doesn't seem to be waiting for a reply. We continue walking for a while in silence. I move my right thumb back and forth along her thumb, feeling the bumps of her knuckle over and over again.

"I like you," I say quietly.

"I like you, too," she says immediately. I feel a small smile creeping up the edges of my lips.

"When can we hang out again?" I ask her.

"Hmmm, we'll have to see," she says mysteriously, and winks at me. She stops walking and pulls us off the sidewalk.

"This is me." She leads me, my hand still in hers, over to the front steps. The porch lights are on, so I can see it's a brick house with a light blue door with big green polka dots.

"Grandpa let me paint the door myself once when I visited. When I was six," she explains. "He never changed it. Said it reminded him of me."

"That makes perfect sense."

We stand awkwardly for a moment before Charlie says, "I should probably go in. I told Mom I'd be home before ten-thirty, and she's a stickler for punctuality."

"Okay," I say. "I'll text you."

Charlie's still holding my hand. "Bye—" she starts, but instead of letting go, she tugs and I take a step toward her to avoid losing my balance. When I look up, our faces are suddenly very close and she's staring at me and because she's only a tiny bit taller than I am, our eyes are pretty much level. Her gaze shifts down a tad and it takes me a moment to realize she's looking at my lips. Back at my eyes. Lips. Eyes. And then she's leaning in.

Don't panic, don't panic, don't panic—

I shut my eyes and feel her lips on my lips and they are so soft and then we are kissing.

We are kissing!

I have no idea what I am doing.

And I'm not even sure if it lasts for a whole second.

When Charlie pulls away, I know I'm grinning stupidly. She squeezes my hand, then lets go.

"Good night, Obie," she says, and disappears into her house.

———

I text Pooch as soon as I walk away. I almost trip over a crack in the sidewalk even though it's fairly well lit.

> **ME, 10:31 P.M.:** So we kissed good night

> **POOCH, 10:31 P.M.:** Dude!!!! How was it

> **ME, 10:32 P.M.:** Good? Idk, never done it before

> **POOCH, 10:33 P.M.:** First times always weird. Did u have fun?

> **ME, 10:34 P.M.:** Yeah, she's really cool

POOCH, 10:35 P.M.: Heck yeah. Happy for u man. Lemme be the best man at the wedding.

I giggle aloud, startling myself. *Wedding. Ha.*

ME, 10:36 P.M.: Shut up

POOCH, 10:38 P.M.: ;)))))

I slip inside our front door and close it as quietly as I can. It still clicks. I feel like front doors are designed to make noise so kids can't sneak in or out. Although I guess I'm not really sneaking. I told Mom and Dad when I'd be back. But I don't want to ruin the perfect night by having to explain it all to them. Maybe later. But not tonight.

I creep up the stairs. It's about 10:45 p.m. Light pours out from beneath Jae-sung's door, so I know he's awake. Or he fell asleep with the lights on.

I skip the fourth and eighth steps. They creak.

I'm about to close the door to my room when I hear something.

"Psssst." Jae-sung's head peeks out.

"What?" I whisper.

"Uhhh, uh-duh, how was it?" he whisper-yells at me.

"Good," I say, thankful I haven't turned on my lights yet. I'm definitely blushing.

"Did you kiss her?" he demands.

"Yes."

"Woo-hoo!" he hollers without whispering.

"Jae-sung!" Now it's my turn to whisper-yell. But I'm smiling.

"I'm sure it was all because of my advice," he whispers.

I roll my eyes. "Absolutely," I admit. He grins.

"I'm glad you had fun, O. 'Night."

" 'Night."

I'm about to shut my own door when Dad's head pops out of theirs. *Were they* waiting *up for me?*

"Glad your first date was so much fun, munchkin." The hall lights are off, but I can see he's got on that goofy grin.

"Daaaad! Were you eavesdropping or what? Jeez." But I can only be a tiny bit annoyed, I'm so happy.

"Welcome back, Obie," Mom yells from their room. *They're both still awake?* "You can tell us all about your date in the morning, please. And, Richard! Let our son get to bed already. This is his one night to sleep in some amount."

"Goooooood night, honey," he says as he retreats into their room.

"Good night, baby," calls Mom.

The house is finally quiet as I close my door and drop my clothes. I grab the old shirt I wear to sleep in and crawl into bed. My phone buzzes on my desk.

> **CHARLIE, 10:53 P.M.:** I had fun tonight
> 😊

I smile to myself.

> **ME, 10:54 P.M.:** Me too!

> **ME, 10:55 P.M.:** When can I see you again?

> **CHARLIE, 10:57 P.M.:** I was going to ask you the same thing

> **CHARLIE, 10:58 P.M.:** That new Avengers movie is coming out soon??

I put my phone down. Movie theaters are popular date spots, I know. But it's also the place where you run into the most people you know. That makes me nervous. But so does Charlie and I guess that all worked pretty great. So, what the heck?

> **ME, 11:00 P.M.:** Let's do it.

Went on my first date with Charlie tonight. She's so cool. But I haven't told her I'm transgender. I'm really scared to. . . . I'm not ready yet.

Chapter 21

"COME SEE ME AFTER CLASS" is written in burning red letters at the top of the first page. I'm preparing for the worst as I flip the paper over to find my grade. I'm dreading the C or D or even F I'm about to see.

"A+, magnificent job & impressive improvement from your last essay, Obie." *What?* I want to leap out of my chair and do all that cliché jumping-for-joy crap. Of course I don't. *But holy cow, I really did it.* I feel the pride swell in my chest.

I spend the rest of the class in a bit of a daydream even though I know I should be paying attention. I wonder if Charlie is now my girlfriend and if we are "dating." I'm not sure when you're supposed to be sure or if you're just supposed to ask. I know other kids talk about "DTR"—*Define The Relationship*. I've heard all kinds of things about when it's appropriate to DTR. I think I even heard Lucy talk about it last year. I wish I could ask her about it. Well. Kind of. I wish we were friends like we used to be. Whatever. I'll ask Jae-sung again. I make a mental note.

When the bell rings, I stay in my seat as usual. I gather my things slowly as I wait for everyone else to file out and then walk over to Mrs. Salmani's desk.

"Obie-jaan, this one was quite the improvement. I'm so impressed with how you were able to shift the voice to show more than tell." She smiles. I imagine every smile she's ever smiled creasing her face with wrinkles over her lifetime. Wrinkles as evidence of smiles.

"I tried really hard," I say. "But why'd ya have to scare me like that, writing 'Come see me after class,' like I failed again!" We laugh. "So why did you need to see me?"

"Ah, yes. Well, I would have just waited for our weekly Wednesday meeting, but this is time-sensitive."

"Oh, okay?" I'm confused.

"There is an online essay contest that I think you should enter. It's created by the National Council of Teachers of English. NCTE. Every year they take several hundred submissions from seventh and eighth graders around the country. This year's theme is personal identity struggle. They're partnering with We Need Diverse Books—have you heard of them?"

I shake my head no.

"They're an organization that tries to get books about kids from diverse backgrounds and identities onto shelves so that *all* kids—like you, Obie-jaan—can see themselves in books."

"What kind of diverse backgrounds?"

"Black and brown and Native kids, Asian kids, queer kids, trans kids, bisexual kids. . . . All the kids that are often left out of mainstream stories."

"So . . . like *All American Boys*?" I ask.

"Yes, exactly. So, all of the submissions this year must deal with some kind of diversity, inclusion, and/or equity issues. And I think this essay would be perfect."

"To . . . submit?" A few months ago, I was barely writing papers worth a passing grade and now she wants me to send one to an essay contest?

"Yes, I think it's a great opportunity. If you win, you get a nice check *and* one week at a renowned writing camp for students."

"Wow." I pick up my essay and flip it over to look at my grade again.

"You don't have to decide *right* now, but pretty soon because I have to register you by first thing Monday."

"Like, in a week?" I've got, what, seven days to decide about a paper that took me two months to write?

"Yes, but then you'll have until mid-February to submit your revised essay. I don't think you have to change that much before you submit it," she assures me. "Of course, there's no pressure from me to do this. I just wanted to make sure you knew this is an option."

"Do you really think I have a shot at winning?"

"I cried when I finished reading your essay. I cannot

speak for the judges. But I think it is one of the most power-ful pieces of student writing I've read in my forty years being a teacher."

"Wow." I'm dumbfounded. "Thanks, Mrs. Salmani."

"Why don't you think about it and let me know some-time this week? Talk to your parents about it. I'll email them the contest information in a few minutes so they can take a look, too. Does that sound all right?"

"Sure, yeah. Okay."

"Great. Now go enjoy lunch. It's almost halfway over!"

———

"Still on for dinner after practice, dude?" Pooch says, out of breath between 25s. We're almost done with practice, fin-ishing up with several lengths underwater to work on our breath control and underwater dolphin kicks. These are my favorite.

"Yeah," I say when we surface at the next wall. "Where do you wanna go?"

"Have you been to Chotley's Deli?"

"Dude—" But it's my turn and I have to push off the wall. When I resurface at the other end, gasping for breath, I say, "That's like my favorite restaurant of all time."

"Perfect," he says before pushing off the wall. "Have you met the new girl who works there?" *Is he talking about Charlie?*

206

"Charlie?" I offer.

"I don't know her name, but sure?" he says. "She's super cute."

"Pooch, man, that's the girl I went on a date with on Saturday."

"No wayyyyy!" That was the last 25, so we're all stopped at the wall now. "My man's got game!" I can't help but grin.

"Chotley's it is, then. We gotta go say hello to your girl-friend," he says, and punches me lightly in the shoulder.

"Not my girlfriend—" I answer.

"Girlfriend?!" Mikey interjects from the lane next to ours.

"Yeah, dude, Obie's seeing this cute girl from the sand-wich shop. We're gonna go have dinner there tonight. You wanna come?"

"I'll ask my dad when we get out," Mikey says.

———

We all pile into Dad's car. He's offered to take us—probably because he wants a sandwich, too. As we drive, I wonder if it's weird that Dad's coming with us. I'm the youngest in the car, which never really matters. But both Mikey and Pooch are in ninth grade—Pooch is normal-age for a ninth grader, and Mikey is young because he and I are almost the same age. I'm old for seventh grade. So in theory, Mikey and I are both eighth-grade age. But I never really think about people in terms of school grades because on swim team, you're just with the people you train with—people who are your speed.

Dad pulls up in front of the entrance and doesn't turn off the engine. He digs his wallet out of his back pocket and hands me a credit card.

"Pay for the other boys and I'll be back in an hour," he says. *Oh?*

"You're not staying?" I ask.

"Nah, you have your time with your friends. I don't want to intrude. Call me if you need anything."

"Um, okay," I say, surprised. *Dad passing up Chotley's. I'm shocked.* "Do you want something to go?"

"No, don't worry about me. Your mom ordered takeout at home."

"Okay," I say, and follow Mikey and Pooch inside.

I see Charlie right away. She's over by the window table, handing someone a plate. Her hair is pulled into a tight bun and when she turns around to walk to the counter, she catches my eye. She looks surprised for a moment and then gives a little wave. *Is she feeling shy?*

Pooch nudges me in my ribs.

"Ooooooooh," he teases. I turn into a tomato. She's walking toward us.

"Hi, Obie," she says, grinning. "And who are you two?" she asks Pooch and Mikey.

"I'm Mikey," Mikey says, awkwardly sticking out his hand.

"I'm P—I'm Samuel," Pooch says. Mikey stifles a laugh and we exchange a look.

"These are some of my friends from swim team," I say, a strange feeling of pride swelling in my chest.

"Nice to meet you," Charlie says. "I think I've seen you here before," she says to Pooch.

"Yep, I come here a lot."

"Yeah, I don't know how we've never run into each other," I say to him.

"Well, I'll see if I can come catch up in a few minutes. I gotta go help Grandpa." Charlie skips off.

"So, how did you meet her?" Mikey asks me as we stand in line.

"Here," I answer. "I've been coming to Chotley's with my dad forever and she moved to Watertown a few months ago and I don't know, she just started talking to me. . . ."

"My man's got GAME," Pooch says. I shove him lightly.

"Stop it! She's gonna hear you," I say, but Pooch just laughs.

"You bold, man," Mikey says to me. "I could never up and ask a girl out. . . ."

"What? C'mon, of course you could!" I say. *Mikey Garcia thinks he can't ask a girl out?* He's basically like a Salvadorian Zac Efron. . . .

"Nah, too scared," he says, waving me off.

"Boys, what can I getcha?" Mr. Chotley says from behind the counter. "How's it going, Obie?" he says to me.

"Doing great, Mr. Chotley. How are you?"

"Oh, you know, just chugging along. The usual?"

"Yessir! And whatever they're having."

We are lucky to snag seats just as a couple is leaving. Pooch grabs a chair that isn't being used and sits down. A few moments later, Charlie brings us the sandwiches, handing me an extra small plate with three pickle spears.

"Extra pickles, of course," she says, smiling.

"Oh, you didn't have to," I say, but she's already walking away. "So, how's high school different from middle school?" I ask.

"More homework," Mikey says, his mouth full of roast beef.

"Yeah," Pooch agrees, and takes an enormous bite of his sandwich.

"Is it really that much harder than middle school? I feel like we get a lot of homework now, too," I say.

"Eh, it's not that bad," Pooch concedes. "Honestly, it's just math that's a lot for me."

"That's cuz he's Mr. Genius over here. Pooch's taking some calculus statistics shit with the eleventh graders." Mikey pretends to scoff.

"What?" I mean, I can't say I'm that surprised. Pooch has always seemed like a smart dude.

"I dunno, I guess math's my thing," he says.

"Fair," I say. "You do know, now, that I'm going to text you when I need help with my math homework."

"Hahaha, okay, I can handle it. Geometry was my favorite," says Pooch.

"Yick," Mikey says, making a face. I laugh.

"Gotta agree with Mikey on this one," I say, and take a bite of my sandwich. "Whooo! This is so meh-woh."

"What?" Pooch asks.

"Oh, sorry. *Meh-woh* means *spicy* in Korean. We just always say it that way at home," I explain.

"Oh, okay," Pooch says. "May-whoa," he tries, but the sounds come out all wrong and I giggle. Clyde used to say it that way, too.

"Not quite." I laugh. Pooch tries again and it's a little better.

"Are you fluent in Korean?" Mikey asks.

"Eh, not really. I can get by. Find the bathrooms, order food." I shrug.

"That's still pretty cool. I wish I spoke more Spanish," Mikey says. "My parents immigrated so young they barely speak it themselves."

"All that's left of my ancestors is my Polish last name." Pooch grins.

"Hey, boys." Charlie's suddenly right next to me. I look up at her. Gosh, she's pretty. She's got her hand on the back of Pooch's chair, gripping it lightly. I like how strong her hands look. Strong, like powerful. Powerful, like capable.

"Hey, Charlie," I say, feeling my face heat. *Every time.*

"Wanna pull up a chair?" Pooch asks, and looks around for a free one.

"I can't actually stay. I'm sorry, Obie. My mom just called and said she's here to pick me up a bit early today." She frowns. I don't think I've ever seen her frown before. Not that I've spent that much time with her.

"Oh, okay. No worries, I'll see you soon?"

"Of course. I'll text you later." She leans down and kisses me on the cheek. If my face was burning beforehand, it's straight on fire now.

"Bye," she says, smiling at Mikey and Pooch. "Nice to meet you!"

Chapter 22

"I guess I'm just nervous about people reading my essay," I say, thinking aloud as we're driving to Grandpa's.

"I mean, why wouldn't you do it if Mrs. S. says you don't even have to do more work?" Jae-sung's twisted around to face me from the front seat. He's got a point.

"It's your call," Mom says, glancing at me.

"Do it, do it, do it," Jae-sung chants.

"Okay. You're right," I say to him. "I think I'm going to submit it."

"Did you bring your laptop with you?" Dad chimes in.

"Yeah."

"Why don't you email Mrs. Salmani when we get to your grandpa's? And then you can stop worrying so much about it."

"I think I'll do that," I say.

———

Grandpa's assisted-living place is really more like a hotel. I'm not sure what I expected, but for some reason I didn't think it was going to be apartments. He's been here almost a month, I think, but I hadn't been able to visit since I saw him at Thanksgiving because of swimming, and now it's almost Christmas. Mom said that was probably best, anyway, because Grandpa's been needing some time on his own. She says he's still really sad about Grandma. Me too. I want to call Grandma and tell her to come back.

"Hello, Jae-sung," Grandpa says when he opens his door to my brother's eager face. Mom, Dad, and I are a little behind. "Hello, honey," he says, giving Mom a kiss on the cheek. "How's it going, superstar?" he asks me. "I heard you qualified for the Olympics."

I laugh. "*Junior* Olympics," I correct him as I follow Jae-sung and Mom and Dad inside.

"How are you, Dad?" Mom asks. "Are they treating you well here?"

"Oh yes, it's very nice. But I still say you're paying too much for this place," he scolds her, but he's smiling.

"Where's your nurse? Did she bring you your meds?" Mom looks around the room. It's a nice room—a small kitchen attached to a living room with a brown leather couch. It doesn't look particularly comfortable, but next to it is Grandpa's favorite chair. I wonder how they got it here all the way from Chicago.

"Boys, what's happening?" Grandpa settles into his chair

and motions for us to sit on the couch. It squeaks and reminds me of Coach Bolton's office couch. I shiver.

"Not much, Grandpa. We're just going to school. Obie's swimming, of course."

"Yeah? Are you liking school, Jay?" Grandpa almost always calls Jae-sung "Jay." He has trouble saying Jae-sung right. I think the *jae* sound is hard for non-Koreans and it always comes out *jay*. It used to make Dad furious because Grandpa was being kind of racist about Korean names, refusing to learn to pronounce them correctly. My uncle Andy says that some people don't change and if their intent is good, sometimes you gotta meet them where they're at. I think Dad tries to do that now.

"No," Jae-sung is saying. "I hate it. School sucks."

"Ah-ah-ah!" Mom interrupts.

"School is very unenjoyable," Jae-sung corrects himself with a fake smile and a robotic tone. "I would desire to halt attending the building of school." I giggle.

"I didn't like school all that much as a kid, either," Grandpa agrees.

"How did you get out of going?" Jae-sung asks, wide-eyed. I'm not sure I've ever heard an adult admit that they, too, disliked school.

"I didn't." Grandpa shakes his head. "It's just one of those things you gotta get yourself through, son. Play the game." Jae-sung groans. "Now," Grandpa continues, reclining in his chair. "What should we order for lunch?"

"You guys decide," I say, getting up. I pull out my laptop and sit down at the table with Mom and Dad. "Time to email Mrs. Salmani," I declare.

Dear Mrs. Salmani,

I decided I'm going to submit my essay. But I want to add to it. You said it's still a few hundred words under the limit and I was looking at the prompts. I want to combine the first two. I think I'm going to add a paragraph to end the essay about culture. My history. The people I come from. And how that shaped my identity. Do you think that would work?

Sincerely,
Obadiah

Chapter 23

ME, 10:35 P.M.: Merry Christmas! Happy Hanukkah! Merry Kwanzaa! Happy random Wednesday in December!

Charlie says she's technically Catholic but apart from being baptized, she's never done anything "particularly Catholic," so I send all the current holiday greetings. Well, Kwanzaa begins tomorrow, I think. But this year Hanukkah overlaps with Christmas.

CHARLIE, 10:44 P.M.: Merry holidays to you, too, Obie! How was your Christmas?

CHARLIE, 10:56 P.M.: I know u said ur harmony is super-duper Catholic (unlike me haha), what does that mean for Christmas? Did u go to church?

She misspells "Halmoni" and I smile at her attempt to anglicize the sounds. She's only ever *heard* me say "Halmoni." She's never seen it written.

> **ME, 10:56 P.M.:** Yeah, we all went with halmoni to midnight mass last night.

> **CHARLIE, 10:57 P.M.:** We had to do that, too. Do you like it?

> **ME, 10:58 P.M.:** Yeah, I like the singing but the incense gives me a headache. How was your day?

> **CHARLIE, 11:00 P.M.:** We mostly just spent time with family. My grandma made my favorite boiled yuca with garlic!

> **ME, 11:03 P.M.:** Ooooh that sounds amazing. I don't think I've ever had boiled yuca!

> **CHARLIE, 11:04 P.M.:** It's so good. My grandma makes it the best.

ME, 11:05 P.M.: Did you do presents and stuff too?

CHARLIE, 11:06 P.M.: Yup!! Today I got a new rubik's cube, surprise 🙃

She sends a photo of something that looks like a Rubik's Cube but is very clearly *not* a cube. It must have more than ten sides, jeez!

CHARLIE, 11:07 P.M.: A dodecahedron 😄

ME, 11:08 P.M.: Holy cow . . . How . . . What??

CHARLIE, 11:08 P.M.: It's 12-sided. It'll keep me occupied hopefully until school starts again. I'm already bored haha.

ME, 11:09 P.M.: That's fair. I always wonder what people do without swimming.

CHARLIE, 11:09 P.M.: Did you have to swim today?

ME, 11:10 P.M.: Well of course!

CHARLIE, 11:11 P.M.: Wow, even on Christmas!

ME, 11:12 P.M.: Always on Christmas 😜 but winter holidays means we do doubles—two practices a day every weekday. So today we got off easy because it was only one. And we got to sleep in. Practice wasn't unil 9am!

CHARLIE, 11:13 P.M.: Waaaaat that is not sleeping in.

ME, 11:13 P.M.: True. But compared to 4am it is.

CHARLIE, 11:15 P.M.: Oh right. But still. 9am's still early!

ME, 11:16 P.M.: Yeaaaaah. Oh but also today coach only made us do hard stuff for an hour and then we got to play water polo. And we used one of those enormous exercise balls instead of an actual water polo ball. It was super fun.

Turns out Pooch is a total whiz at this game, too. He scored all the goals. Which also kinda sucked because we weren't on the same team for that game.

CHARLIE, 11:17 P.M.: Oooh, that does sound fun.

CHARLIE, 11:18 P.M.: I'd be terrible at it, tho.
I can't catch a ball to save my life.

ME, 11:20 P.M.: Ah I bet you could if you practiced.

CHARLIE, 11:21 P.M.: hmmm not so sure ☺

Charlie and I text until Christmas is technically over and my enormous Christmas dinner finally settles me into a food coma.

Chapter 24

"We making kimchi this weekend," Halmoni had said over the phone. "You still want to learning? Or are you busy with homework?"

"Not busy," I assured her, thankful it was still winter break. "I want to come."

"Good. No missing homework. Tell your mom to drop you off my house in one hour. We go shopping first. There is special sale today, so we have to go today." Kimchi making is usually timed for when the baechu is both in season and on sale. Halmoni is especially thrifty with her grocery shopping.

At H Mart, Halmoni and I bought six baechu. The cabbage heads are larger than my own head and probably weigh the same, if not more. We also bought, like, ten pounds of daikon radish for the gakdugi—radish kimchi—along with several other ingredients.

As we were leaving, we ran into some of Halmoni's church friends, which made me nervous. They thought I was Jae-sung. She spoke to them in rapid Korean, maybe so I wouldn't understand, but I heard "transgender"—in Korean, the word is the same, just in Korean phonemes: teu-laen-seu-jen-deo—so I know she was explaining me to them. They made some classic Korean oh-moh-nah (oh my goodness!) faces but quickly softened when they saw me staring.

"Aiyu, aiyu, ahjoo moshida." How handsome. I know they were just saying this to cover any embarrassment—plus no one wants to anger my grandmother. I relaxed. It was fine. Halmoni fine. Not Lucy fine. Fine fine.

"Gamsahabnida," I said respectfully, and bowed my head a little.

———

As soon as we set foot in her house, Halmoni begins explaining. No time wasting here.

"We start with soaking," she says, leading me to the sink. "But first, must wash."

Halmoni hands a baechu head to me. "Shi-soh." Wash, she commands.

We scrub the cabbage in warm water and Halmoni shows me how to clean between the leaves, pointing out a few bugs wedged in between.

"Chingulohwoh!" I say. Disgusting!

"It's okay," she reassures me in Korean and then in English, "Extra protein." We giggle.

"Harabuhji told me he made it with Tabasco sauce in college," I say. She makes a face that's both a scowl and a grin.

"He sooo silly," she says, shaking her head.

"Can Uncle Andy make real kimchi?"

"No, I don't think so."

"You didn't teach him?"

"Ani," she says. No.

"And Dad doesn't know, either?"

She shakes her head again.

"Why not?"

"Well, you know, in Korea, men don't cook. Men not allowed in kitchen. That was tradition. Bad to have man in kitchen." I wonder if she only allows me in the kitchen because I'm transgender. *Does she not think I'm a* real *man?* I think about my list. Maybe I will have to cross Halmoni off?

"But you know, Uncle Andy cook very good now. And so does your appa. Just not Korean food." She nods to herself as she stretches the sink hose over to a large plastic vat on the floor. She begins filling it with warm water. "Times change. Different now. Men can cook, too. So, I teach you." My smile hurts my cheeks. She'll stay on the list.

"Okay, give me salt." I hand her the salt carton, which she opens and begins pouring into the water with no form of measurement.

"How do you know how much, Halmoni?"

She waves me off. "Mix."

I do as instructed.

"Just tasting." She sets the carton down and dips her finger into the water. "Good. You try."

I lean down to taste. It tastes like salt water. (It *is* salt water.)

"See?" she asks.

"Mmm," I say.

"Okay, get baechu now." I gather the two heads I've cleaned into a large stainless bowl and bring them to her.

"So, I have not see Lucy recently," Halmoni says to me, but it's a question.

"Oh. Yeah," I say, not knowing where or if to start. "She, um . . ."

Halmoni squats and places the cabbage heads in the salt water. She shakes them.

"So water and salt get everywhere," she says, looking up at me.

"Got it. Lucy has new friends now."

"Oh? New friends cannot be friend with you at same time?" she asks, frowning. "Bad friend," she concludes, nodding to herself. We each grab another cabbage head and submerge it.

"Bring *your* new friend." She looks at my hands and commands, "Shake." I shake.

"What new friend?"

"Charlotte?" She pronounces the *ch* like the *ch* in

chocolate. Dad must have mentioned Charlie to her. I feel my face begin to redden. *Is there something wrong with my face? It does this so often these days.* I have to ask Jae-sung if it's normal and also if it's normal to talk about girls with your grandmother.

"Oh, Charlotte," I say awkwardly. "Um, you want to meet her?"

"Yes, of course," she says, standing up.

"Um, okay. Soon," I offer, knowing she won't take no for an answer. "Soon" can be whenever.

"We can package some of your kimchi for her, yes? You take to her."

"But, Halmoni, kimchi smells—" I don't want to offend her, but a lot of non-Korean people don't like the smell of kimchi. The fermentation and garlic kind of make it smell like a fart to unaccustomed noses. I've been made fun of plenty at school for how it smells. Jae-sung has refused to bring it in his lunch since, like, fifth grade.

"If she really like you, she can eat," Halmoni says. "We pack her some when it's all done."

"Neh." I nod, giving in. Maybe she'll like it, who knows. She seems like a pretty adventurous person, right? I'll ask Jae-sung what he thinks.

"Okay, now we leave everything here. Today, that is all." She stands up slowly. "Time for nap," she announces. "When your mom come to get you?"

"Whenever I call her. I'll call her now and you can nap. What time tomorrow should I come?"

"Same time. Lots to do tomorrow, though. You sleep good tonight."

I laugh. "You, too, Halmoni."

Chapter 25

Halmoni is already cooking something that smells amazing when we walk in the door on Sunday. We're almost fifteen minutes late, but I think she expects that now. Mom isn't big on being on time.

"Are you hungryyyyy?" she trills.

"Of course." I didn't eat breakfast because I knew she would feed me. Halmoni thinks that I will starve without her food. She's convinced there's never enough to eat at our house. Mom used to get super offended, but Dad says it's just a cultural thing, so now Mom just rolls her eyes to herself. (And to me, sometimes.)

She serves us both some fried rice, which really is just old rice mixed with bits of leftover Peruvian chicken, but somehow she makes it taste amazing and I ask for seconds. Halmoni loves that. And before we're even done eating, Halmoni is piling a plate with fruit. It's not a real meal without some fruit, according to her. She says it's shyunhae. Refreshing.

I watch her peel the Korean pear. Her knife moves deftly

around the fruit, shedding it of its skin. I marvel that she does not slice her own skin. Her hands are kind of like Mrs. Salmani's. They're old, like weathered, like wise, like experienced. I love watching them move. She finishes removing the skin and then chops the pear in half, then quarters, eighths. She hands me a slice.

"Eat," she commands in Korean. And I do. Korean pear is my favorite fruit. It's such a perfect combination—it's got the crunchiness of the best Honeycrisp apple, combined with the juiciness of the best pear. With none of that mushiness.

"I need to do some grocery shopping, then I'm taking Jae-sung to his tutoring. I'll come back before dinner with him and Dad, okay?" Mom says.

"Okay, see you later," I answer.

"Bye, Katherine." Halmoni uses Mom's full name and pronounces each syllable independently: *Kath-uh-reen.* And so proudly, too. I know their relationship began a bit tough at first because Mom isn't Korean. But that's sure changed over the years. Dad always jokes—and he had better be kidding—that if he and Mom ever got divorced, Halmoni and Harabuhji would probably choose to keep Mom over him.

"You take pear with you, so you don't go to grocery while you hungry. You grocery hungry, then you buy too much junk stuff and that bad for kids." Halmoni wags her finger at Mom and she's kind of joking, kind of not. Mom walks out the door with a napkin full of wet fruit.

Halmoni and I finish off the rest of the pear in comfortable silence. I keep thinking about what I'm going to submit for that contest. The first option said: *Write about a memorable experience in which your identity was questioned, challenged, or rejected. What did you learn about yourself through this experience? How has this experience influenced your view on the world and how you walk through it?* Mrs. Salmani is right—the essay I wrote for her would answer this perfectly, but I remember liking the second prompt as well: *Write about how your identity does or does not conflict with your ancestry and culture. How does your identity connect you to or disconnect you from your ancestry and your history?*

My ancestry and my history. Hmmm. I guess I come from Mom and Dad, who come from Grandma and Grandpa, and Halmoni and Harabuhji. Where did Grandma come from? I remember I did a project about her last year and learned that she grew up in Nazi Germany, but that's really it. . . . I wish I could ask her more questions. But at least I still have my halmoni and harabuhji.

"Halmoni?" I ask as she peels another Korean pear.

"Uh," she answers. Yes.

"How old were you when the war started in North Korea?"

"There was no North Korea at that time. Only one Korea," she answers.

"Dad said that other countries invaded, though, to make

North and South and that's why you had to leave?" I barely paid attention last time he explained this to me, and it's not like they teach us about it at school.

"Yes, the Russians, the Chinese, the Americans, all wanted Korea. Dividing. The Korean people could not agree how to make own country. The war is what make North Korea and South Korea. But even before that, the Japanese controlled Korea for almost my whole life. I was your age, about . . . thirteen, when we were forced to leave our home," she says. "Korea has had some of most terrible history."

"And what happened to you? To your family?"

"The Russians and Chinese came. We live in Pyongyang then. Soldiers stay in my house a little while. But then everybody leaving. Leaving, leaving. So fast. They just left. Leaving everything. So, we leave, too."

"Where did you go?"

"To Seoul. We had to get away from Russians and Chinese. We had to get away from bad leader who want us to be Communists. We had to get to American side of country. So much fighting everywhere. And then they make a line and divide the country. They call it DMZ." The Z she pronounces like *jjee*.

"How did you get to Seoul if there were soldiers everywhere?"

"Walking!"

"What? You walked all the way? How many miles is that?" I try to imagine my makeup-loving, Chanel-bagged, very fancy Catholic grandmother walking hundreds of miles during a war.

"No choice!" she exclaims.

"Were you scared?" I wish I spoke more Korean.

"Sometime. But. That doesn't matter. It just was. You just go. My mother, your halmoni-halmoni, she was a very, very strong woman. We go with her and we just praying, praying." She pauses to take a sip of her boricha, barley tea.

"We stay in houses. On the way. Everyone just left," she says, partly in Korean. "The bap all there. So we eating their food and stay in their homes just a night here and there." I nod, thinking of the picture book I read when I was a kid about the Korean girl whose dad doesn't make it over the border and gets stuck. The last page is a drawing of the girl crying in her new home, waiting for him. Sometimes I feel almost nauseous thinking about it. I can't imagine having to wait for my parents like that. And then never ever seeing them again.

"Did you leave anyone there, Halmoni? In North Korea?"

"Yes, Min-jun. Nae dong-saeng. My younger brother. Somehow when we walked, he got separated from us. I have not seen him since." She gets a faraway look on her face. I've never heard this part of the story before.

"Do you—"

She waves me off. "No more war talk today. It's time to make the stuffing." Not wanting to upset her, I nod respectfully and stand as she does.

We spend the next couple hours stuffing the slivered daikon radish mix in between the cabbage leaves and then squeezing the heads into kimchi containers. My hands reek of garlic, but I kind of like it. We seal all of the containers and I carry them downstairs one at a time and place them gently into the kimchi fridge.

"Wah," Halmoni says when I come for the last one. "You did great." I grin.

Chapter 26

My phone buzzes and I flip it over to see Charlie's goofy grin filling my screen.

"Hiiiii," Charlie says when I answer.

"Hi," I say, suddenly nervous. *She's never FaceTimed me before.*

"Whatcha doing?" she asks. "Ooooh, is that your room?"

"Yeah, wanna see?"

She nods. I flip the camera around and show her my desk.

"It's pretty messy," I explain. "They're loading us up with post–winter break homework."

"Me too," she groans. "Show me the rest!" I point the camera at my bookshelf and my closet and then my bed.

"Whoaaaa," she says, eyes wide. "Did you win *all* of those? Move closer!"

I lean toward the medals.

"Wait, I can't read what they say," she complains, but I panic and suddenly swing the phone away to a family photo on the wall.

"And here's my family," I awkwardly cut her off. The medals read, *Bowdoin Invite, Girls 200 IM Champion. Bowdoin Invite, Girls 100 Breast Champion.* And so on.

"Wait, what were the medals for? You didn't let me see."

"I-it's just boring swim meet stuff. I—I'll show them to you later," I stammer.

"Umm, okay." She frowns.

"This is my brother, Jae-sung," I say, pointing to him in the family picture. She brightens.

"How old—"

"Did I hear my name?" Jae-sung interrupts from my doorway.

"Have you been spying on me?" I ask, annoyed.

"No, your door was open and I live literally next door." Fair. "So. Are you gonna introduce us?" he says, gesturing to himself and my phone. I look at Charlie. She's nodding eagerly.

"Charlie," I say begrudgingly, "speak of the devil himself. This is my brother, Jae-sung."

"Hi, Jae-sung," Charlie says.

"Hellooooooo," he replies with a salute.

Wait, why? What a goon. "Jae-sung, this is Charlie." I lean over to him so he can see her. She waves.

"Okay, kids, as much as I'd love to stay and make this awkward for O here, I'm going to go now. Just wanted to say hi. Nice to e-meet you, Charlie, you should come over for dinner sometime. I'm sure our parents would love it."

Jae-sung salutes again before leaving. I shut the door behind him.

"Sorry about that," I start.

"He's silly." She smiles.

"Yeah, he's always loud like that. I'm the cool, calm one."
I'm going for Jae-sung's Rule Number Five: Be confident.
I try to add a wink. But both my eyes shut and then I stupidly
try again and I think I look like I'm farting.

"Are you okay?" she asks.

"Yeah, I, uh . . ." *What do I even say?* I sigh. "I was trying
to wink but I . . . can't."

She bursts into laughter. "Awww," she says. "It's okay.
Winking is hard," and of course she winks.

"Whoa, okay then, we've got a badass over here," I say in
a deep voice, mimicking the meme.

When we catch our breath, she says, "So, I actually was
calling to ask you if you wanted to come over for dinner this
weekend. My mom really wants to meet you—Grandpa talks
about you all the time and now that you're my boyfriend—"

"I am?" I ask, trying to contain my excitement.

"Oh yeah. Oh, I just assumed. I'm sorry!" Now it's her
turn to blush.

"Oh, no, no. It's okay, I just wasn't sure how to ask you
and how this all works. I've never done this—"

"Me, neither," she says.

"I *want* to be your boyfriend," I say, looking at my feet.

"Yeah?" she asks.

"Yeah." We're quiet for a moment. "Sorry I made that awkward," I add.

"Oh, stop it. I'm awkward, too. I think you're cute. So. Do you want to come over for dinner this Saturday? Or do you have practice Sunday morning?"

"We do have practice, but I can still come to dinner. I just have to be home before ten, I think. Let me ask my parents and I'll text you?"

"Sure, that sounds great."

"Okay, I'll talk to you in a bit."

"Okay, I'm going to hang up."

"Okay. Bye!"

I run over to Jae-sung's room as soon as the call ends.

"Dude, Charlie just invited me over to dinner with her family. What does that mean?!"

"Oooo-ooooh!" Jae-sung all but sings. Then his face rapidly shifts to a very serious one. "It means you're getting married. You're trapped forever. RIP, OBIEEEEEEEEEEEEE," he says dramatically. I roll my eyes.

"Okay, okay." He puts his hands up. "It just means she likes you, O. It's a good thing! Wait, is Mr. Chotley gonna be there? Have you . . . told her yet?" My stomach drops. *Mr. Chotley. He knows. . . . Of course he knows. He's known me since practically before I was born. Has he already told Charlie?*

"Oh . . ." is all I can muster.

"No, no, no, no. Don't get like that, no, no! It's gonna

be fine, dude. If he told her and she knows and nothing's changed, then it clearly doesn't matter. And if he hasn't, then we're back where we were five minutes ago, before you hadn't thought about any of this."

"I guess," I say, skeptical. "What if her mom doesn't like me, or what if I don't eat right, or what if Mr. Chotley says something or—"

"Breathe," Jae-sung interrupts, one hand raised to stop me. "Take a breath."

I obey.

"You're going to be fine. If someone doesn't like you, they're a dumbass. The only person who doesn't like you is me and that's my job." He grins. "The real thing you gotta worry about is what are you going to *wear*!"

Chapter 27

I walk up the steps holding the container I filled with the kimchi I made with Halmoni. She said a few weeks of fermenting would be perfect to bring to Charlie—not as strong as when we ferment it for months. I knock on the polka-dotted door. My heart is pounding and my hands are sweaty.

"Hello, Obie," bellows Mr. Chotley when he opens the door.

"Oh, hello, Mr. Chotley." I wonder again if he's told Charlie about me.

"Charlie, Obie's here," he announces into the house. Then to me, "Come on in, boss." I close the door behind me as Charlie comes bounding down the stairs.

"You're here! You found it okay?" Charlie asks.

"Of course, your door is hard to forget," I say.

"I'm assuming she told you about painting that when she was six?" Mr. Chotley asks me.

"Yessir," I answer.

"She begged and begged that whole week visit." He chuckles to himself. "And I finally caved. Turns out it's pretty useful as I've aged and gotten forgetful. Pretty hard to miss my house now."

"Whatcha got there?" Charlie asks me.

"This is homemade kimchi. It's a Korean—"

"I *love* kimchi!" Charlie exclaims. *Phew.*

"Hello, Obie—" comes another voice. Charlie's mother emerges from the neighboring room wearing an apron.

"Mom," Charlie cuts her off, "Obie brought homemade kimchi!"

"Wow, thank you, Obie. How sweet of you. Did you make it yourself?"

I nod. "With my grandmother," I clarify. "But some people think it's smelly. Just a warning. Sometimes folks don't like the—"

"Oh, we don't mind at all, Obie. We *really* like kimchi, so don't you worry," Charlie's mom reassures me. "It's so nice to finally meet you. I would hug you but I'm too messy right now from finishing up the burgers."

"Nice to meet you, too, Mrs.—" *Oh no. . . .* I freeze, staring at Charlie.

"Mrs. González," Charlie helps. "Don't worry, seriously. I've never told you my last name." Mrs. González waves her hand in the air in dismissal.

"Call me Maggie," she insists. Her smile is identical to Charlie's. Complete with the dimples.

"Okay," I say hesitantly. "Nice to meet you, Maggie." It feels strange to call an adult by their first name.

"You kids sit at the table and I'll bring you some appetizers." She disappears into the kitchen. Charlie grabs my hand and pulls me to the table.

"Appetizers?" I whisper incredulously to Charlie. "We never have those at my house!"

"Yeah, my mom's big on multiple-course meals. I promise you will not leave hungry."

"I promise you will leave absolutely stuffed," Mr. Chotley chimes in, patting his belly. "Mm-mm."

"I take it cooking runs in the family?" I ask as we sit.

"No, actually, it's just Maggie and me," Mr. Chotley says. "But I wouldn't consider my sandwiches 'cooking.' That's fancy, skilled assembly." He winks at me. Maybe winking runs in the family, too.

"I mean, you know your sandwiches are, like, my favorite thing in the world, no matter what you call 'em," I say.

"So, first up, Charlie told me you like a side of pickles, huh?" Mrs. González—I mean, Maggie—has returned with a platter of something. They look kind of like mozzarella sticks. "So, I thought I'd make you a specialty of mine. *Fried* pickles."

"Whoa!" I exclaim. "No way, these are *pickles*?"

"Yes! Spears—which, if anyone asks, are much better than coins," Charlie declares.

"What?" I ask, confused.

"Don't worry about it. Just try one," she urges.

"And here's my special sauce—you're not allergic to anything, are you, Obie?" Maggie asks.

"Nope, I eat everything," I say, and take a bite. It's hot, but it's amazingly good.

"Wow," I say almost involuntarily. "I have to say . . . I wasn't sure if I'd like it because hot veggies are not my thing, but this is delicious. . . ."

"Right?!" Charlie bites into her own and closes her eyes to savor it.

"I'm so glad you like them," Maggie says as she disappears into the kitchen again.

"Eat quickly or I'll eat them all," Mr. Chotley warns, reaching over and grabbing two spears.

"Leave a few for me," Maggie calls.

———

I'm so full I think I might explode. Mr. Chotley was right.

"So, Uncle David was saying that he's known you since you were a kid?" Maggie asks me as she scoops ice cream into bowls for our dessert. I look at it almost in a daze. Even my extra ice cream stomach might be full. . . .

"Uncle David?" I ask, puzzled. *Who's David?*

"That's me," Mr. Chotley says, his chuckle rumbling deep. Charlie bursts out laughing.

"Oh," I say, nervous now. *Did Mr. Chotley tell Maggie about me?* Everyone's looking at me.

"Whoops. . . ." I try to smile. *Does everyone know?*

"Boss and his dad have been coming to get sandwiches at the deli forever!" Mr. Chotley says, squeezing my shoulder. "Ever since he was a little boy!" He grins at me and I relax.

"Yeah, my dad always jokes it was my first meal after finally being done with baby food," I add.

"Wow, really?" Maggie asks.

"Well, I'm not actually sure. Legend has it. But probably not. I probably ate rice and kimchi first."

"Charlie's first meal was probably ropa vieja." Maggie laughs. "Her dad always tried to feed it to her, even when she was a baby! It was his favorite. . . ." *Was?* I want to ask more, but when I look up from my bowl and see Charlie's face, I decide not to. She looks like a mixture of afraid and embarrassed. There must be a good reason she hasn't mentioned her father yet.

———

CHARLIE, 10:01 P.M.: Hey, thanks for coming over. My mom loved you.

ME, 10:05 P.M.: I had such a great time! Thank you for having me.

CHARLIE, 10:06 P.M.: Also . . .

CHARLIE, 10:06 P.M.: I'm sorry about the dad comment. I know that was kind of awkward. I should have explained . . .

My phone still says she's typing but I respond anyway.

ME, 10:07 P.M.: It's totally ok. You don't have to tell me anything you don't want to.

CHARLIE, 10:10 P.M.: Thanks, Obie. You're really sweet. Maybe we can talk about it next time.

CHARLIE, 10:11 P.M.: . . . Speaking of which.

CHARLIE, 10:11 P.M.: When is next time??

We make plans to actually go see a movie in a few weeks like we originally talked about. I know I should go to bed but we're Snapchatting and she's sending me the most ridiculous snaps of her and her Rubik's Cube. I wish I could stay up all night talking to her.

Around 11:30, I finally force myself to say goodnight and put my phone on my desk to charge. Morning practice awaits.

A LIST OF THINGS I FEEL WITH CHARLIE:
1. Happy.
2. Free. Not so heavy and weighed down by all the trans stuff.
3. Scared. What if I tell her and she doesn't want to be my girlfriend anymore?
4. Nervous. But not in a bad way? I guess that's what people call butterflies?

Chapter 28

"Wooooooo!" Everyone is cheering. Jackson punches Mikey in the shoulder.

"You ready for some hard-core drills, bro?" Jackson says. We're all pretty stoked we don't have a difficult race set this afternoon. Just some drills to work on our form. We're about three weeks from JOs, so practice has just barely begun to ease up.

"You bet your racing suit I am," Mikey answers, laughing.

We get started on our 20x50s drill on the way down, normal swim on the way back. Coach suggests doing IM order, which means we'll do five 50s of fly, five of back, five breast, five free.

After a few, I notice Coach Larkin talking to someone who looks so familiar, but I can't quite place his face. He's probably my height with jet-black hair. It's wavy and falls in his eyes a bit. He looks young, but I notice some stubble on his chin and he's got a faint mustache. He's wearing a gray athletic T-shirt that says **HARVARD SWIMMING AND DIVING**, jeans, and brown leather shoes. He laughs at something Coach Larkin says. Then they both look over at me. I look behind me. I'm the last one in the lane. And I've missed my send-off. I push off the wall late, glad I'm at the end of the lane. No one behind me to ride my tail.

When we get to number eleven, I switch to breaststroke. I focus on lengthening my arms into a perfect streamline with each drive. In breaststroke, you do one kick per stroke, but in this drill, you do two kicks. I love this drill. The water is so quiet. I snap my legs together in that frog-kick motion and zoom forward. *Whoosh.* I wait until my body slows, the water almost pulling me back. I take the second kick.

When I get to the wall, Coach Larkin is standing behind my lane. She catches my eye and motions for me to hop out.

"I want you to meet someone." Mikey and Pooch look at me quizzically. I shrug and jump up onto the pool deck. I'm a little annoyed. I've still got four more 50s breaststroke. I don't like missing my favorite stroke.

"This is Tommy," Coach Larkin says, putting a hand on the boy's shoulder. *Tommy? That's why he looked so familiar.* Mom didn't tell me we had a meeting today?

"Hi" is about all I can muster.

"Obie, hey! How's practice going?" He offers me his hand to shake and I stare at it for a moment before I do so and respond.

"It's, uh, it's good. Um. We're doing fifties drill. We're tapering," I explain.

"I heard—are you excited for JOs?" He crosses his arms over his chest.

"Yes," I offer. *Isn't he in college? Why is he home in February?*

"I remember JOs. Such a fun meet. But I was still competing with the girls." He doesn't skip a beat. I wonder if that's because he knows he's talking to me. *Does he talk this way to everyone, disclosing that he used to compete as a girl?*

"Do you have spring break in February?" I ask. Mom would poke me for being so straightforward, but she's not here.

"Nah, I just finished my final swim season, though, and wanted to come tell Coach Larkin about it." *Oh.* "Anyway," he continues, "this was kind of a spontaneous visit, otherwise I would have texted your mom and we could have arranged something. But you're here, so it's perfect."

"Tommy did really well on the men's team, Obie," Coach says. "He only started transitioning a few months before college—right, Tommy?"

"Yep!"

"He had a lot of catching up to do, especially in his first year, but he did pretty darn well."

"That's cool," I say, meaning it. I feel like *I* have a lot of catching up to do and I'm starting years before him.

"Listen, Obie, I said this to your mom when we chatted,

but I just want you to know I'm here for you. I know things can be confusing sometimes, and I certainly don't have all the answers. I'm still getting it all organized, too. And of course, your experience is going to be different from mine because we're doing things at different ages. But if you ever have any questions, you can always text me. If you need a friend or just a listening ear—someone who will just get it, I'm here. I don't want you to feel alone, because I know how hard that can be."

I think about that night after Coach Bolton kicked me off the team. I think about how I'd pressed my face into the pillow, wondering if I'd keep breathing. *Alone* is accurate.

"You don't have to say anything now," he continues. "I'll let you return to practice. I just wanted to give the name a face. If you need me, when you're ready, if you're ready, I'm here. If you don't, I'll still be cheering you on with my whole heart." Coach Larkin puts a hand on Tommy's shoulder and he smiles.

I don't really know what to say other than thank you. So, I do, and then I slip back into the pool behind Pooch.

"What number is this?" I ask when we're at the wall.

"That was the last one. Who was that?" Mikey asks.

"That's Tommy—" I'm interrupted by Coach.

"Okay, guys, gals, and pals, we're gonna hit some short sprints, some underwater work, and then I'll let you go for the day." She claps once. "But, before we finish up here, everyone say hello to Tommy. Some of you might already know him. He swam for Harvard, and for those of you who are sophomore or juniors, if you have questions about recruiting or college stuff, he said he'd be happy to talk to you about his experiences."

Tommy waves at everyone and then sits in the single chair that's on the pool deck. I want to ask him *What is college like? Does everyone know you're transgender like they do here?* but it's time to swim down to the deep end to practice some starts.

THINGS I MIGHT ASK TOMMY:
1. What is college like?
2. Do you tell everyone you are transgender?
3. What is dating like?

Do you like being transgender?

Chapter 29

I spot Charlie at the other end of the ticket booth and I wave. It's been almost two weeks since I went to dinner at her house. And I guess I saw her last week at Chotley's, but only for a few minutes—the shop was so busy she couldn't sit down with us. But we've been texting and Snapchatting a bunch so I've pretty much seen her face every day. She even FaceTimed me a few more times to *sing* me a few things. Apparently, that's her thing. Singing. (Melt.) And playing guitar. (Hence the finger calluses, I learned.)

"Hey!" she says.

"Long time, no see." I smile back.

"I'm sorry I'm late," she says, slipping her hand into mine. I attempt to keep my cool. *Don't start sweating, palms, don't start sweating.*

"No worries, they're not even playing the previews yet."

We settle into our seats and I hold the popcorn between us.

"I hope you like popcorn?" I should have asked before. Is popcorn a "romantic" food?

"Who doesn't like popcorn?" she exclaims.

"True. I hope you also like extra butter."

"You're in luck! I do." She smiles and stuffs a handful into her mouth. I do the same. We stare forward for a moment, suddenly awkward. Down below, by the theater's entrance, I watch a tall boy walk in, his back to us. He's alone but he seems to be looking for people.

Oh no. . . . Please don't let that be— The tall boy turns his face in our direction, scanning the seats. I freeze. I turn, following his gaze. I recognize the boys who signal to him as some of the Barracudas. I don't see Amar. I wonder if the incident with me fractured their friendship. I look down at Clyde, who has begun climbing the steps. Even though I'm sitting on a soft red cushion, I feel the cold bathroom tiles under my butt and my palms begin to sweat again.

Clyde is wearing a dark green hoodie from last year's JOs. The hood is up and his long legs take the stairs in twos. I silently curse myself for saying it was okay to sit by the aisle. I can feel my heart quicken as he gets closer. I stare straight ahead, praying he will not notice me.

"Obie? Are you okay?" Charlie leans in and whispers.

"What?" I realize I've forgotten she was there for a moment.

"You're kind of hurting my hand," she says. I realize I've been clenching my fist, with her hand in mine.

"Sorry, I'm sorry," I say, quickly releasing my grip. "I just, uh—" Clyde's more than halfway up the stairs now. I frantically look around and try not to seem so, well, frantic.

"Obie?" Charlie asks again. *Please, please, please not now,* I beg the gods.

"Oooobieeee," Clyde fake-whispers in a singsong voice that is the opposite of Halmoni's welcoming one. He bends over us from the edge of the aisle. "How's it going, buddy?" he says with one hand on my shoulder, squeezing it hard. I swallow the cry of pain.

"Hey, Clyde, hey." I try to smile. "I'm good, thanks. How are you?"

"Are you going to be so rude and not introduce me to this girl?" he hisses, and inches closer to Charlie and tries to take her hand. She snatches it away from him.

"Dude, go away," I say, giving up on civility.

"Why? What are you afraid of? Huh, Obie?"

"Nothing. I'm just here to watch a movie with my girlfriend. Leave us alone," I repeat. It's the first time I've said *girlfriend* to someone else. She's officially been my girlfriend for nearly three weeks. I forget Clyde is there for a second as I roll the word around in my mouth.

"Have you told her your dirty secret?" I am yanked viciously from my moment and almost vomit on the spot.

"Please. Go. Away," I say through gritted teeth.

"Obie, what's going on?" Charlie asks. I glance at her terrified face and stand up.

People are starting to stare at us. Although no one seems like they want to get involved—beyond loudly shushing us.

"Clyde, I'm done with your bullshit. Please leave us alone."

Clyde shoves me into my seat and leans over me again. "Sorry, you don't have your little Poochy fag boyfriend or the freakin' principal to protect you today," he says with an evil grin. My stomach turns. "I'm going to make you pay for getting me kicked out of school, faggot." *Is this a literal nightmare?* He turns to Charlie.

"So, in case he hasn't told you, he's not a real 'he' . . . ," Clyde says. Charlie looks confused. And I want to disappear. "That's right, this one's a disgusting little tranny. Guess that makes you a little lesbo," he jeers, spitting each word out. *Little. Tranny. Little. Lesbo.* My brain's repeating.

Before straightening up, he whispers in my ear, "And if there weren't all these dumb people around, I'd pummel you and your little faggot girlfriend into the ground." And then he's gone.

Little. Faggot. I hear it on a loop in my head.

I am unmoving, speechless. I want to cry but the tears don't come. I don't know what to say or do, but the lights are going from preview twilight to main movie dark and so I just sit there panicking.

What is she thinking? Is she going to leave? This is only our third official date. We've only known each other for a few months. If I were her, I'd leave. I mean, the trans thing's

*probably enough already, yeah. But then creepy jerks like
Clyde coming and threatening her? What the hell, man, what
the hell! It was one thing to mess with just me, but now also
with Charlie?*

I'm knocked from my thoughts by Charlie climbing over
me to leave. I move so she can do so more easily, unsurprised
by the turn of events. Easier this way, anyway. Then she
doesn't have to see my face when she breaks up with me. She
just gets to leave.

But then I feel a pat on my shoulder and a voice in my ear.
"Obie, let's go outside for a minute."

No, I want to say. *Let me just stay in here forever. You
know what? Don't even play the movie. Just keep the lights
off, close the doors, and leave me here.* I'm never going to
get away from guys like him. *What was I thinking*—that I
could actually compete against Clyde? But Charlie tugs on
my hand and so I get up and we hustle outside.

The lights in the hallway burn my eyes and I have to blink
several times before I can see.

"Come here," she says, slipping her hand in mine and
leading me over to one of the benches.

"I'm sorry—" I blurt. "I'm sorry I didn't tell you. I'm so
sorry he called you that. I understand if you want to leave—"

"Hey," she interrupts, and I'm surprised by her calmness.
"Hey," she repeats, my head hanging low. "Look at me."

I do. But just with my eyes.

"Listen, I don't know what just happened in there, but I

can guess that boy is a big bully. And if I'm understanding correctly, you don't have anything to apologize for." I don't move. I don't know where this is going. "I know I ask you a lot of questions, but that doesn't mean you have to tell me everything about yourself. And it doesn't mean that other people like that boy are allowed to share *your* things *for* you. Especially not the way he did."

"Clyde," I say.

"Clyde," she repeats. "Clyde!" adding an eye roll to show her disgust. The nausea in my stomach begins to subside.

"But he is right. I am—" I pause. *TRANNY FAG* burns in neon lights in my brain. I start over, breathing deeply. "I am transgender," I almost whisper. *Tall and confident,* I hear Mrs. Salmani say. "Transgender," I try again, forcing confidence.

"Okay," she says, nodding. Not like she gets it. Like she's heard me. "Listen, I'm going to admit that I've never met a transgender person before. At least not that I know of." That's fair, most people I've told haven't. "But that doesn't mean I can't learn," she continues. "I'm a fast learner. Remember? I have fourteen Rubik's Cubes. I can solve them all. Being transgender cannot be nearly as complicated as my five by five by seven Rubik's Cube." She grins.

"Yeah, probably not," I say sheepishly. Relief is pouring over me.

"Yeah! There we go," she says, and kisses my cheek. "Listen, Obie. Lots of people have lots of opinions for lots of different reasons. I really don't care deeply about them. I just like you."

"But you might get called names because some people— like Clyde—don't believe I'm a 'real' boy."

"What? Who do they think you are? Pinocchio?" She giggles. I don't. She stops and her face grows serious. "Well, then they're wrong."

"But. I mean. They'll call you names, too. Like Clyde did."

"Okay, well, neither of us can control what they say. And like I've told you, I don't really care a lot about what other people think of me."

"But I don't want my identity to hurt you."

"It's not going to hurt me. Other people might, but I'm a big girl. I can handle it."

"Are you sure?"

"Yes," she responds immediately, nodding.

I kiss her on the cheek. "I *really* like you," I say.

"I *really* like you right back." Her dimples deepen. "Should we go see if another movie is starting soon?"

My eyes widen. "You mean movie hop?"

"Yes." She eyes me mischievously. "Let's live on the edge!"

"And avoid Clyde." I nod, understanding.

"Yes, that, too."

"All righty, then! Let's go."

TODAY.

1. Clyde told Charlie I'm transgender and I thought it was all over.
2. Charlie didn't get upset. I'm really relieved about this.
3. Charlie said she wants to learn more about transness. That's nice. But I am nervous about sharing. How much should I tell her? Will she understand?
4. I like Charlie a lot. She's so nice. I like how quirky she is.
5. Mom says that everyone should be like Charlie. Mom says it shouldn't be surprising that someone was cool with me being trans. That should be an expectation. I guess that's true in theory. . . .
6. I'm sick of Clyde. I wonder if he told Coach Bolton about today.

Chapter 30

"Okay," I say to Mrs. Salmani. "I think it's done."

"Wonderful, Obadiah," she says with a glint in her eyes. "Sit tight and let me read it."

I nod and sit down at a desk. I pull out my phone.

> **ME, 3:03 P.M.:** I think I'm going to submit that essay I told you about today.

I'm not sure if Charlie will answer but I really want to tell her anyway. She's probably helping Mr. Chotley at the shop.

I'm hoping Charlie will offer again to read my essay. She'd asked before our last date because I'd mentioned I was working on it. But I'd told her I wasn't ready then. That was before Clyde outed me. I so wish I could have told her myself.

> **CHARLIE, 3:04 P.M.:** No way! That's so exciting, Obie!

ME, 3:04 P.M.: Thanks, I'm nervous about it.

I wrote about some personal stuff.

CHARLIE, 3:05 P.M.: I'm sure you did amazing.

I know you didn't want me to see it before, but if you're ready now, I'd love to read it.

ME, 3:05 P.M.: I think I want you to read it.

CHARLIE, 3:06 P.M.: Then I will!

I look up from my phone because I hear the sound of a tissue being pulled from the cardboard tissue box. Mrs. Salmani is pulling off her glasses with one hand and dabbing at her closed eyes with the other. She opens her eyes a second later and catches me watching her.

"This is perfect," she says, still teary. She puts her arm around me in a side hug. "I'm so proud of you."

I let her hug me. I know Mrs. Salmani isn't the kind of person to give empty praise.

"Thanks, Mrs. Salmani," I say into her shoulder. She might be old and fragile, but she's still tall. She's told me she used to be nearly six feet before she started getting old and shrinking.

"Let's read the end of it aloud because it's the newest part and we've given it the least attention—just to make sure you like how it sounds. And then we can submit it together."

> I am a proud transgender Korean American boy.
> I come from a German woman who survived World War II, who not only spent most of her adolescence without her parents but then moved to the United States as a teenager, alone. I come from strong Korean women who fled northern Korea on foot, carrying only the barest essentials and leaving everything else behind, who walked hundreds of miles for their freedom, who flew across the globe to find a better life for their children. I come directly from all of this womanhood—from my mother, from my grandmothers and their mothers, too. And I come from my own assigned womanhood. My expected daughterhood.
>
> And yet, here I stand today. A boy. A son. And in the future: a man.
>
> Many people use culture and difference as barriers to acceptance and love, saying that these identities cannot coexist in one person. But I am living proof that they certainly can. In all of my intersectionality, I am still here. Alive. And Korean. Alive. And white. Alive. And an athlete. Alive. And transgender. And alive.

Chapter 31

The store smells like latex and Lycra and, somehow, chlorine. Even though there's no pool here. Maybe enough swimmers come by after practice that the scent just lingers.

The guy behind the counter greets us as we walk in.

"Hey, Mikey," he says when we get closer. He's an older guy with really thick glasses and a polo shirt.

"Hey-hey, Mr. Kim," Mikey says. *Korean!*

"So JOs are coming up, right?" Mr. Kim asks Mikey. "What's it going to be this time? Speedo, Arena, Michael Phelps?"

"Speedo all the way," Pooch says. Mikey nods.

"For you, too, big man?" He pauses. "Hmm, I don't think I've ever seen you here before," Mr. Kim says to me. He's got a strong Boston accent—something I haven't heard in a while. He leaves off the r's at the end of the words. *For* becomes *foh, ever* is *evah,* and *before* is *befoh.*

"Yessir, Speedo, too, please," I say. "Gamsahabnida," I add in Korean.

"Oh." He pauses, thinking. "Cheonman-eyo?" he asks

even though it means "you're welcome." "I don't speak Korean," he admits. "I was born and raised in Southie. My parents never taught me. Sounds like your parents did. I wish mine had."

"Yeah, my halmoni lives really close to us and she makes sure we speak it even though my mom is white." I'm used to explaining myself. Most Koreans are surprised (and often delighted) when I can speak Korean because I don't look "full Korean." I've got the nose and the skin tone, but my mouth is Mom's, and my hair is light brown, almost dirty blond. And although my eyes are shaped a lot like Dad's, their color has a lot of Grandma, so I've got green flecks, too.

"Makes sense," he says.

"We got our sizes." Pooch motions to himself and Mikey, and then points to me. "But this guy needs to try on some suits. He's never worn a LZR before."

"Oh, first time!" He rubs his hands together. It's goofy. "What size is your practice suit?" he asks.

"Twenty-six," I answer.

"Okay, let's try the twenty-two and twenty-four for the fast suit, then. Usually, smaller is better." He leads me to the changing rooms, and the guys follow to make sure I know what I'm doing. Back here, the store looks almost exactly the same as the other store I used to go to with Lucy and Clyde—the one all the Barracudas go to. It's got the same wooden floors with small stalls and light spilling from behind curtains.

There's a mirror at the end of the hallway. I catch Mikey's

eye in it and he gives me two thumbs up. I try to form a smile in response. I'm a little nervous. I haven't tried on a fast suit for a while. And I've never tried on a boys' fast suit. What if it doesn't fit right in . . . that area? What if it doesn't look right?

"Here's the twenty-two and twenty-four. You should try both—but the twenty-two first. . . . Sound good?" I nod.

"Your friends will know which one's best for you," Mr. Kim adds as he returns to the cash register.

"We'll wait here, dude," Mikey says, and takes a seat next to Pooch on the bench beside the mirror.

I slip behind the nearest curtain. There's a floor-length mirror inside and a bench as well. I strip and pull the first suit from the box. Lucy always said race suits feel like "powdery sandpaper." She's right. They do. It's a very distinctive texture. I hold it up in front of myself in the mirror. It looks like there is no possible way it'll fit, but I know from having worn a girls' race suit that it likely will. It just might take some time.

"How's it going in there, Obes?" Pooch calls.

"Good, just about to squeeze myself into the first one," I answer.

I sit down and step into the legs one at a time. I shimmy it up, tugging as gently as I can at the waist. I get it above my thighs and pause to recoup before I stretch it over my butt. I'm suddenly very thankful I don't have the same parts in the front as many other boys do. How do they squeeze it all in there? As if on cue, another call comes from the other side of the curtain.

"The ass is definitely the hardest par—" But something cuts him off.

"Ow, man," he says. "What?" I strain to hear.

"No cussing," Mikey says. "Mr. Kim's not down."

"Oh, my bad."

"Careful with the badonkadonk, Obes," Pooch says instead, and they both chuckle.

"Yessir," I say.

I finally get it above my "badonkadonk" and adjust the legs, inching the material around so it's evenly stretched. Then I brave a look in the mirror.

I stare at myself. I look strong in the suit. *Tall and confident.* I push my shoulders back and stand up straighter and suddenly I can't wait for race day. *Heck. Yes.* I swell with a pride I am not familiar with. Look at that boy in the mirror. That's me. That's *me!*

I push aside the curtain. Mikey and Pooch look up from their phones.

"Daaaaang," Pooch says. "Zechariah-Obadiah, you look like a mini Nathan Adrian or something." Nathan Adrian is another swimmer who is half Asian. He's also very, very fast . . . and many consider him handsome. I don't mind being compared to him at all.

"Yeah, dude, you're going to go so fast. That suit is sick."

I grin.

"I think it fits. Only took like twenty minutes to get on—" We all laugh. Mr. Kim comes around the corner.

"Let's see," he mumbles to himself.

He tries to pinch a section of the suit—and I yelp because he pinches me, too.

"Perfect," he says, meeting my eyes for a moment. "Too tight?" he asks.

"It's tight," I reply.

"Good." He smiles. "That's exactly how you should have it. You'll go wicked fast in this one."

"Yay! Let me call my dad to see where he is." I pull out my phone and duck into the changing room. Being greeted with a message from Charlie makes me smirk-grin.

CHARLIE, 2:00 P.M.: How's the suit trying-on going, handsome?

I look at myself in the mirror again and hold my phone up. I snap the selfie and send it to Charlie along with the message, PRETTY GOOD! I THINK I'M GOING TO BUY THIS ONE. WHAT DO YOU THINK? Then I hit Dad's number and wait.

"Hey, bud, how's it going? Did you find a suit yet?"

"Yep, are you done at Target?"

"Almost. I'll be there in about ten minutes. You boys sit tight."

"Okeydoke, see you soon." I put the phone on the bench as I sit down and begin to peel the suit off.

My phone buzzes.

Outside, I tell Mikey and Pooch that Dad's on his way.

―――

After Mikey and Pooch leave, Mom tells me that Lucy came by while we were at the swim store and that I should give her a call. I tell Mom absolutely not.

"She sounded pretty upset, honey. I think she might need you," Mom pushes.

"Mom, I've needed her so many times in the past year, and where has she been?" My voice climbs to a shout.

"I know, honey, I know, but I think she knows she made some mistakes. Growing up is really hard sometimes, and I know you two are working through a lot. But I think you'll regret it if you just give up on her."

I think of the photo of me and Grandma and Lucy. I do miss her. But how come she gets to need me and I don't get to need her anymore? Why can she give up on me, but I'm not supposed to give up on her? *This is so unfair.*

"Some friendships aren't fair, Obie." Mom's doing her mind-reading thing again. "But sometimes they even out over time if you give them a chance. Go give Lucy a second chance." She hands me the phone and I dial as I walk up-stairs. I realize that Lucy's number is the only one I actually know by heart.

"Obie?" Lucy picks up after a single ring.

"Hey, Lucy," I say, unsure of how to tone my voice.

"Hi . . . ," she says. There's a silence. "I, um." She stops again. "I . . . Jenn and Chelsea are just as crappy as we knew they were." I can hear her sobbing through the receiver and even though I'm still angry with her, I feel sorry for the Lucy I remember. The one who spent every day being tormented by those girls. *She just wanted to be liked. Is that so bad?* I ask myself. *Don't I just want to be liked, too?*

"Oh, Lucy, I'm sorry," I say, meaning it. "What happened?"

"They told everyone on the team that I got with Clyde," and there my empathy goes.

"What?" I say, suddenly cold again.

"It's not true," she wails. "It's not true, I promise." *Should I believe her?*

"They're telling everyone I'm a dirty slut because after they started that rumor, Jimmy Greene started telling people I did things with him in the bathroom and Grace's mom told my mom and now I'm in big, big trouble."

"Is any of it true?" I ask, not knowing what else to say.

"Noooo," she sobs. "I told you. I had a crush on Clyde when we were kids. A big one. I never told Jenn and Chelsea because Jenn has been trying to get with him for a while. So, they got angry when Clyde asked me"—her voice trembles—"and . . ."

The fury is in my fingertips now and I'm contemplating hanging up. She's calling me because she and Clyde are *dating* and I'm supposed to be *empathetic* that people are making fun of her for that? But I decide silence is the best response, at least until she finishes.

"I did say yes at first," she admits in a tiny voice. My stomach churns and my resolve to be silent weakens. "Because I liked him for so long, Obie. I just—I don't know." She's talking fast now. "But like I said, Jenn likes him, too, and so—" But I've had enough.

"Lucy," I interrupt, trying my hardest to keep my voice level and not yell. "I am not the person to talk to about this. And I can't believe you can't see that. Clyde is the biggest bully. He's not the kid we grew up with anymore. It's like his goal is to make my life a living hell. Do you know why I pissed myself in the bathroom? Do you know?" I've failed at keeping my voice down and I'm yelling now.

"No," she cries.

"Because he beat me up. Remember how I had that bandage on my arm? Yeah. That was because he shoved me so hard into the paper towel dispenser, I needed stitches. He harasses me every chance he gets." There is silence on the other end. "He is not the friend or cute boy you thought he was when we were kids. He is a mean, vicious bully," I repeat.

"I—I—I swear, I didn't know any of that," she says almost inaudibly. "I didn't know. . . . You don't tell me anything anymore!"

"When would I have told you? When you lied so you wouldn't have to see me? When you left me on read when I called you the day it happened? When you won't make eye contact with me at school? When I see you at swim practice—oh, right. Your *boyfriend's* dad kicked me out." I spit the word *boyfriend*.

"He's not my boyfriend."

"Yeah, only because Jenn and Chelsea got in the way. I swear, you're more afraid of them than you are of losing yourself."

She doesn't say anything. I just hear her breathe. Shallow, sniffly. She inhales.

"I told Clyde yes before I even told Jenn and Chelsea that he asked me on a date," she says. Does she think she's making it better? But for some reason I let her continue. "I realized—after I said yes—that the only person I wanted to talk to about all this is you. And then I realized that I didn't actually want to go on a date with Clyde. Ten-year-old me does. Did. But thirteen-year-old me doesn't. Thirteen-year-old me just wants to feel like she fits in." *I don't want to be different anymore,* she'd said that time in the hallway. Now she sounds far away.

I don't know whether I should believe her or not. I'm silent for a while. We both are. Finally, I decide to say something Dad's said to me:

"Fitting in isn't the same as belonging."

"That's true," she agrees. "Obie, I'm so sorry I chose them over you. You're right. I don't feel like myself much anymore. I miss you. I miss us," she adds, weepy again. The anger begins to fizzle.

I've been waiting for these words for months. But finally hearing them, I have no idea what to say. I flip over the picture on my desk and stare at our three faces. I wonder what Grandma would have done. Would have told me to say. Probably that those girls are mean and not worth any more tears.

"I'm sorry those girls are so mean," I offer.

"It's all my fault. I shouldn't have even tried. I just thought . . ." She trails off. I think about how the bad guys aren't always all bad. How annoyingly complicated that makes everything.

"I get it," I say, softening more. "I do. You just wanted to be liked. Included. If Clyde offered to be my friend again, I might try, too."

But then I think about all the new people I've met who have been kind to me, who haven't cared that I am trans. Everyone on the new team. Charlie. Especially Charlie. "Listen, Lucy, we're all all kinds of messed up, you know. Chelsea and Jenn messed you up when we were kids. And you wanted to feel a part of something. I get that." I hear her sniffle.

"But you still really screwed with me. I mean, how am I supposed to feel that my"—I falter before the words *best friend,* when she hasn't been much of a friend—"that the person I thought knew me best wanted to *date* the person who put me in the hospital?!"

"But—well, I didn't know about the hospital thing." She's still crying. "I'm even sorrier now," she repeats. "Do you think you could ever forgive me? Do you think maybe we could be friends again?"

I really don't know. *I know you two are working through a lot. But I think you'll regret it if you just give up on her.* I remember Mom's words.

"Maybe," I try, hesitating. "I don't know." She stifles a sob. "It would take time. Maybe a long time. A lot has happened."

"I know. I'm really sorry I've been such a bad friend, Obie."

"Thanks, Lucy."

"I'll see you at school?"

"Yeah." And I end the call.

———

ME, 4:45 P.M.: Hey Tommy, it's Obie. I was wondering if I could ask you a question.

TOMMY, 5:00 P.M.: Hey Obie! Sure, what's up?

ME, 5:02 P.M.: Have you ever lost friends for being trans?

TOMMY, 5:10 P.M.: Unfortunately, yes. Sometimes people don't know how to step into this with me. With us. Did something happen? Do you want to talk about it?

ME, 5:11 P.M.: I'm just having trouble with a friend. I think it's getting better. I just . . . I guess I'm just worried being transgender is always going to affect my relationships.

TOMMY, 5:12 P.M.: I get that. And sometimes it will. But then those are not people you want to have around in the first place. Sometimes people need time, and I've had some folks really struggle when I first came out. But I gave them their space (and set up the right boundaries) and we've grown so much closer. Some people still haven't budged, so I've had to leave them where they were.

TOMMY, 5:14 P.M.: If anyone makes you feel like you don't belong, that is on them. It is not on you.

ME, 5:15 P.M.: Thanks, I needed to hear that.

TOMMY, 5:16 P.M.: Anytime.

ME, 5:20 P.M.: One more thing . . .

TOMMY, 5:25 P.M.: Of course

ME, 5:26 P.M.: What about dating?

TOMMY, 5:27 P.M.: Gosh. Dating is so tough. For everyone. Don't let anyone trick you into believing dating is easy or something for cis folks. Most of my friends are cis and let me tell you, they've got issues, too.

ME, 5:30 P.M.: Haha that makes sense.

TOMMY, 5:31 P.M.: But in all seriousness. You should decide when and how and where you tell someone. You never owe anyone an explanation. You are not lying if you do not tell someone.

ME, 5:32 P.M.: So I'm dating this girl. I hadn't told her. And this bully from my old team ran into us at the movies and he literally told her. At the movie theater.

TOMMY, 5:35 P.M.: Omg I'm so sorry, Obie. That's so unfair and mean . . .

TOMMY, 5:35 P.M.: How did she respond?

ME, 5:38 P.M.: She actually was good about it, I think? She just said she still likes me and wants to learn.

TOMMY, 5:39 P.M.: Well that's good! I'm really happy to hear that.

ME, 5:41 P.M.: Yeah. I just . . . I don't know how to help her learn?

TOMMY, 5:42 P.M.: Oh, that makes a lot of sense! I would just recommend being honest and open about your experience. If you can. And you can start small. You can say no if she pushes. You can say no whenever. The same idea applies from what I said earlier: you don't owe her anything. Not even an explanation. So take your time. Ask for her patience. Be patient with her. Be compassionate with yourself. If you have any specifics you want to chat about, I'm happy to help you work through those, too 😊

It's almost dinner by the time we stop texting. I hadn't expected myself to be as open with Tommy as I was. Maybe it's because I know he gets it. I grumble to myself. I guess Mom was right. Ugh. It *is* nice to talk to someone who has gone through the same things as me.

I even ask him the last question I wasn't sure I'd ask.

ME, 6:12 P.M.: Do you like being transgender?

TOMMY, 6:15 P.M.: Yes. I'm not going to lie and say it's easy. Of course it's not and I know you know that. But it's also beautiful. Being transgender is one of my favorite things about myself. Sometimes I think it's my superpower.

ME, 6:16 P.M.: Really? Why?

TOMMY, 6:17 P.M.: Really.

TOMMY, 6:17 P.M.: Not many people know what it's like to walk the world being perceived as different genders. That brings so much amazing perspective. And not many people have to fight for their gender and their truth the way we do. In order to be ourselves, we have to learn about ourselves in ways most people never do. That's a gift. So yeah. Being trans is hard but life is hard. And I love being trans, Obie. I hope you do, too.

My superpower, I repeat to myself.

Chapter 32

"Jason, thank you, yes," Mrs. Salmani is saying. For once, I'm not paying close attention to what's going on. I'm not sure what Jason said or what question he was answering. I'm thinking about JOs. That's a lie. I'm thinking about seeing Clyde and Coach Bolton *at JOs*.

He had a huge crush on you, I hear Lucy say. I try to imagine how I'd feel if Charlie told me that she was transgender. If she wanted to transition. I mean, the name would be perfect. But I think that yes, maybe Charlie being trans would change us—because I don't think I like boys. But I don't think it would make me act like Clyde, either.

Charlie says she thinks part of how he acts is because he's so insecure. I agreed. I told her about how Clyde's mom died when he was born and how not having her around must have been super hard on Clyde, obviously, but also his dad. I couldn't imagine living without Mom. Charlie had gotten all quiet then. Afraid I'd said something wrong, I asked if she was okay.

"Remember how when you came over for dinner there was that weird moment about my dad? And how I never talk about him?"

"Uh-huh." I had thought about asking a few days ago, but I decided I should let her get to it on her own time.

"He died. When I was three. I barely remember him. But sometimes it still hurts. I used to get really sad and angry all the time. But Mom and I talk a lot about how we feel. Which helps." She had paused. "But if I didn't have her, I think I would still be angry or sad all the time. I hope I wouldn't be like Clyde, but I guess what I'm saying is that it's hard. I got lucky because my mom is awesome. And we get to see my Cuban family in Miami during the holidays like I told you about. So I feel like I stay connected to my dad. But from what you've said, Clyde's dad and family are pretty awful. Maybe Clyde's stuck, too."

I had stayed quiet. I didn't know what to say. A part of me was furious because it felt like she was taking his side. After a few moments, she had kissed my cheek and continued.

"Either way, no one should treat you like he does. He really has some issues. . . ."

I'd looked away. *I don't want to care about his issues,* I'd thought. But maybe she's right. This is about Clyde's pain, not me. I lift my palms from where they've been resting on my notebook. The paper is wrinkled around my handprints like after Dad accidentally leaves a ring of coffee. My sweaty palms. Oh, joy.

"Goodbye, Mrs. Salmani," I say as I pass her desk. She catches my forearm, her eyes wide. "Is everything okay?" I ask, immediately nervous.

"Yes!" she exclaims. "Everything is marvelous. Obie-jaan, you made it to the next round."

"What?" I say, staring at her. "I—"

"You're one of the finalists! That means you wrote one of the top ten essays."

"I—I did?!" I seriously cannot believe this. I had all but forgotten about my submission.

"Yes, you did." She grins at me. I set my backpack down. *I made it?* This means that a bunch of judges read an essay about me—so they know that I am transgender. And they think it's one of the top ten?

"How many people submitted essays?" I ask. I mean, it's probably like forty. Maybe it's just twenty, I laugh to myself.

"I think the website said they got a record number of submissions this year. Two thousand-something?" *Holy cow. That is not twenty.*

"You wrote a really terrific essay, Obie. And the revision about your halmoni"—she pronounces *halmoni* impressively well—"was really the cherry on top."

"So, what do I do now? What's next?" Will I have to write more essays? (Would that be bad? Do I want to?) I can imagine Jae-sung's reaction: You *won* something and the *prize* is *more* work?

"In a month or so, the organization will release a secondary prompt to which the top ten essayists must write a response. Then a committee will judge those to determine the winner."

"Okay."

"You don't have to think about it now. Or ever, really," she continues. "If you decide you don't want to write the final response, that's totally fine." Like Halmoni, Mrs. Salmani is one of those old people who mean *fine* when they say *fine*. "I promise, I don't mean any pressure. I'm so proud of you already, and I hope you are, too, Obadiah. You claimed your story with such courage and eloquence."

"Thanks, Mrs. Salmani."

"Tell your parents about it, though, okay?"

"I will." I nod. "I think they'll be proud. My halmoni, especially." I beam. Halmoni will be so proud.

"Wonderful," Mrs. Salmani says, putting a hand on my shoulder.

———

The rest of the day goes by in a distracted blur. I'm not really sure what's up with me today. Maybe I'm starting to feel the nerves of JOs.

I take a bathroom break during the last period of the day, wandering the long way through the school to find the boys' bathroom near all the lockers by the entrance. Luckily, the bathroom visit itself is uneventful, but when I exit and walk down the hallway, I spot Jenn and Chelsea. They're crouched in front of a locker, taping a piece of paper over it. It could look like they were decorating the locker for someone's birthday, but something doesn't feel right. The paper is too plain, not like birthday or holiday wrapping paper. And Chelsea and Jenn are whispering to each other. I take a few quiet steps backward, retreating into a nearby doorway that's hidden by a pillar. I pray they cannot see me.

I watch as Chelsea takes an enormous red marker and begins to write on the blank page. My stomach drops.

Chelsea writes, **LUCY WEAVER IS A DIRTY SLUT.**

Jenn giggles, covering her mouth. Chelsea is whispering and I strain to listen.

"That'll teach her—" I catch. My phone buzzes in my pocket. Thank goodness I put it on silent. I read the notification.

CHARLIE, SNAPCHAT.

Good call, Charlie. I open the phone's camera and check to make sure the sound is off. Jenn and Chelsea haven't stopped whispering. I lean past the pillar to see that they are still crouched in front of Lucy's locker. Jenn says something I can't make out and Chelsea smirks, nodding.

"Do it," Chelsea commands, not bothering to be quiet.

Jenn turns to the paper-covered locker. She draws a caret beneath the space between **DIRTY** and **SLUT**. Then she writes in even bigger, block letters: *FAT*. As she does this,

I hit the shutter button on my phone's camera. About ten times. *Got 'em.*

I Snapchat Charlie a picture, too. I write: WENT TO THE BATHROOM AND FOUND THESE GIRLS DOING THIS TO LUCY'S LOCKER. Charlie doesn't know a lot about Lucy. But Lucy's name has come up a few times and I've told Charlie Lucy was a childhood best friend but that she's gotten mixed up with the wrong people.

I flip the camera around to send Charlie another snap. I make a confused/scared expression and caption it, WHAT SHOULD I DO??

As I wait, I weigh the pros and cons.

One. Do nothing. Pros: I don't have to do anything. Cons: Lucy gets hurt and even though Lucy has been pretty crappy to me, I wouldn't enjoy being crappy to her.

Two. Wait until the girls leave and then take it down and pretend like it didn't happen. Pros: Lucy will never see the signage. Cons: The girls might do it again another time. Scratch that. They *will* do it another time. I mean, they have been like this since we were in kindergarten. Cons: The girls will not get in trouble for what they did.

Three. Go confront the girls now. Pros: Nope. Bad idea.

Four. Go get a teacher now. *But who? Mrs. Salmani?* I feel like the principal might not believe me. *But that's why you took the pictures,* I remind myself. *Yes, I sound like a crazy person having a conversation with myself.* Anyway. Get a teacher, tell them, show them the pictures. Let them deal with it. Pros: I don't mess with the evidence or engage with the perpetrators. *Hehe, I feel like an investigator.* Hopefully, Jenn and Chelsea will be held responsible for their actions. Cons: Lucy might see the sign. I might be considered a tattletale.

My phone buzzes three times in rapid succession. I unlock it.

CHARLIE, 2:35 P.M.: That's horrible. Who does that??

CHARLIE, 2:35 P.M.: You need to tell a teacher now

CHARLIE, 2:35 P.M.: Show them the picture you sent me.

I'm about to reply but I hear footsteps approaching. I hold my breath. The high heels are distinctive. *Who even wears high heels in middle school?* I want to ask. Instead, I pray they don't spot me as they walk past. I pull my headphones from my pocket, desperately untangling them as I do so. I shove the buds into my ears in case they do look. Maybe they'll think I was just listening to music, skipping class. *Yeah, right. Definitely not the skipping class, but whatever.*

Just as the steps sound like they're right on me, the bell rings and I'm knocked aside as the door I've been standing against opens and kids pour out. Through the masses I see Jenn and Chelsea and I push myself through the people toward Mrs. Salmani's room.

I bump into more people than I think I've ever bumped into before. I almost fall as I break out of the main crowd and run down the familiar linoleum tiles into Mrs. Salmani's classroom. *Please be there. Please be there. Please be there,* I pray under my breath.

I fling open the door so loudly that it slams against the wall and Mrs. Salmani, who is sitting at her desk drinking a Martinelli's apple juice, jumps, spilling a bit of the juice on herself.

"I'm sorry, Mrs. Salmani, but you *have* to come *right now.* Jenn and Chelsea put up a horrible sign on Lucy's locker and I don't know what to do but she's going to see it if we don't do something and it will crush her"— speaking at new levels of fast. I'm panting. Whether Mrs. Salmani has clearly understood or not, she stands immediately.

"Okay, show me." We can't run—Mrs. Salmani is too old. But she's keeping up. Most of the students have cleared the hallways already.

We round the corner, but Lucy's already there. *Dammit,* I want to scream as I see her, crumpled on the floor.

She's sobbing loudly. Two girls I've seen hanging out with Jenn and Chelsea are taking pictures from about ten yards away but she doesn't even notice. As I kneel down next to Lucy, Mrs. Salmani's on the girls.

"Are you two trying to get suspended?" Mrs. Salmani yells. "Just who do you think you are, taking pictures of a girl crying like this?" She starts toward them. They put their phones away and back up, afraid. I've never heard Mrs. Salmani like this before. "Don't you dare put those away. Show me that you've deleted those pictures. Right now," she commands. Both girls remove their phones from their pockets and silently do as they're told.

I've got Lucy wrapped in a hug as she continues to sob into my shoulder. I want to punch something or someone. And some of me wants to scream at Lucy, too. *How could you let them do this to you? AGAIN?* But now I know nothing's that simple. I remember after the bathroom incident, I didn't want anyone trying to explain to me why it had happened. Or what I could have done differently. So I just keep holding her.

"I should have—" she chokes. "I should have listened, you were right, I'll never be—"

"You're never going to be one of them because you're not a bad person, Lucy," I say quietly.

"I was terrible to you," she sobs. I consider this.

"I'm not sure bad people feel bad when they do bad," I

say. "Mom always says that there's a difference between being bad and doing something bad. You *did* some bad things to me. But *you* are not bad." I think about our last conversation on the phone. "I think I can forgive you," I realize aloud. She pulls away from our hug and looks at me, just on the verge of full-on ugly-crying.

"Really?" she asks, her voice breaking.

"I think so," and I mean it. "Also," I begin. "I don't think I've been the best friend to you, either . . . ," I admit, looking down.

"Obie, no," Lucy says, reaching for my arm.

"No, I mean it. You were right, I didn't tell you anything about what was going on. I tried, but I could have tried harder. When Bolton kicked me off that team, all I could think about was myself."

"But that makes sense. What's happened to you is horrible, and I wasn't there for you. I'm so sorry. . . . I just want my best friend again."

"Me too," I say, hugging her again.

"Ms. Weaver, we need to report this to the principal," Mrs. Salmani says gently. "Whoever did this must be held accountable." Lucy's eyes widen.

"That'll just make everything worse," she wails.

"I felt like that, too, Lucy," I say, "when Clyde beat me up. But after I went to the doctor and Principal Franklin expelled Clyde, I did actually feel a little better. Like I wasn't all alone. Like the adults really stuck up for me." She looks at me, still sniffling. "It's not like telling the principal and getting them in trouble is going to stop them completely. It probably won't. Clyde is still an asshole to me. But it made me feel just a little more powered."

"Empowered," Mrs. Salmani corrects me gently.

"Empowered," I repeat, nodding.

"I took a picture, too," I tell her. "Of them writing it. That's why I brought Mrs. Salmani here. I saw them doing it. I didn't know what to do—I—" I falter.

"Obie-jaan, you did the right thing." Mrs. Salmani smiles and I feel myself relax slightly.

———

ME, 6:45 P.M.: Sorry I took forever to reply. Just got home. I told Mrs. Salmani and we went and told the principal together.

CHARLIE, 6:59 P.M.: No worries, I figured. I'm glad you told someone. Proud of you, handsome ☺

ME, 7:03 P.M.: Thanks, Charlie ☺ it was hard to see Lucy so upset.

CHARLIE, 7:04 P.M.: That makes sense. What's going to happen?

ME, 7:04 P.M.: Idk

ME, 7:05 P.M.: I think they're going to get suspended. I forwarded the principal the photos and everything.

CHARLIE, 7:07 P.M.: That's good. They should be. Mean girls that they are. I wonder if they wear pink on Wednesdays.

ME, 7:09 P.M.: What?

CHARLIE, 7:10 P.M.: 😔 You really don't watch movies do you???

ME, 7:11 P.M.: Sorry 😬

CHARLIE, 7:12 P.M.: It's from Mean Girls. It's a movie. And I think those girls belong in it.

ME, 7:12 P.M.: Haha okay we can watch it sometime

CHARLIE, 7:16 P.M.: We have to start with the basics first tho. Disney classics first. Like Atlantis the Lost Empire.

The conversation shifts into lighter banter and I Snapchat her a little, too. Gosh, she's pretty. I tell her so, lying faceup in bed.

"Whatcha doing?" Jae-sung pops into my room and I drop my phone on my face.

"Ouch!"

"Haha, loser," Jae-sung snickers. He jumps on my bed and keeps jumping so that the entire thing shakes.

"Dude, I think we're getting too heavy for you to do that. My bed sounds like it's going to crack in a second."

"Nahhhhh, you're still too tiny." His voice climbs high as he says *tiny,* but then it cracks and I crack up.

"TiNy," I say, mimicking him.

"Aw, shut up," he says, but he's smiling.

"So. What's got you all grinny, huh?" he asks again.

"Just talking to Charlie," I say.

"Rule Number Seven. Take good selfies," he declares, nodding theatrically. Maybe he should be an actor.

"What counts as a 'good' selfie?"

"Hmmm. There's not really a universal code for that. Gotta feeeeeel the moment, brooo." He leans into the words *feel* and *bro*.

"And. Rule Number Eight. Take bad selfies after you get past the First-Date Feeling."

"What's the First-Date Feeling?" I ask, confused. We've been on plenty more than one date. Does that mean the First-Date Feeling is gone?

"It's when you feel comfortable. You know. When you go on a first date, you've got a First-Date Feeling. You want her to think you're perfect and amazing and you maybe don't show all of your, um, not-perfects. You get me?"

I nod. This makes sense. I didn't share everything about myself on the first date and I definitely felt like showing her only my best.

"Also, just to be clear. We're not talking about being trans here. Some of the things you decide not to show aren't not-perfect. They might just be things you're not ready to share yet."

"Okay," I say, not sure I completely understand.

"So when you feel like you can share more, like—when you can tell her more about having a bad day. Or when you can tell her about what makes you sad. OR"—he jiggles his eyebrows up and down and looks at me sideways—"or, when you can fart in front of her." I roll my eyes, but he keeps going. "That's when the First-Date Feeling is gone. Or maybe it's just smaller. Anyhoo. When it's gone. Then you take bad selfies. Because then you're being more real. Trust me, this is a good thing."

I'm not sure his logic makes complete sense but I nod anyway. Close enough.

———

Before I start my homework, I send one last text.

> **ME, 7:45 P.M.:** Hey. I'm really sorry about what happened today at school. I know how it feels. It doesn't matter what you did. It's not your fault. Those girls are so mean. If you want to talk about it, I'm here.

My phone lights up almost immediately with a call, and I quickly hit the green ACCEPT button.

Chapter 33

I t's still dark outside when Dad comes to wake me up. I'm awake before he's even opened the door, of course.

"It's time," he says softly.

Like usual, I don't reply with my voice. Instead, I'm already rolling out of bed. I slip into my Speedo and wander, lights still off, into the bathroom to brush my teeth. I stare into the mirror, late moonlight illuminating my body. My reflection is crowded by sticky notes. I read over some favorites:

SO MANY PEOPLE LOVE YOU, DON'T FOCUS ON THE ONES WHO DON'T. Mom left that one after I'd come out at school.

ONE MORE STROKE. A reminder from earlier in the season, before making JOs.

DON'T LET THEIR WORDS GET TO YOU. BEAT THEM, INSTEAD. Pooch's text after Clyde bullied us at Invitational.

I'M PROUD OF YOU. A line from a letter Charlie wrote me after the Clyde disaster at the movies.

MANIFEST YOURSELF. Mikey from the Bowdoin meet.

Jae-sung had insisted on coming to the meet, even the morning sessions. I'm not sure if he's coming to get out of school or to support me, but either way, he's here. Somehow, he manages to fall sleep again on the way to the pool. I am far too nervous to even think about closing my eyes. *It's JOs!*

I think about Coach Bolton's face the last time I saw him. Or rather, the last time he yelled at me to stay away from Lucy and his team. I still miss his practices and excellent stroke advice. I used to say I missed swimming with my best friends, too, but now I'm not really sure if that's true. Lucy and I only just started really talking again, and I never want to interact with Clyde again. So that doesn't leave many friends on the Barracudas. And here on the Rays, I've got Mikey and Pooch. Maybe I don't miss the 'Cudas so much anymore. . . .

"You're going to do great," Dad announces. Sometimes parents really can read your mind. "Don't worry about those other guys. Their insults, those are about who *they* are, not who *you* are. You just get out there and show them what you can do."

I try to smile but instead feel tears stinging. Dad looks at the road and then at me. I wonder what he's thinking. He squeezes my shoulder and I hear Mom in my head saying, *Hands on the wheel!*

"I'm really proud of you," he says, "no matter what place you get." I want to believe him. I think I believe that he believes that. But I'm still stuck. If I don't win, Coach Bolton and Clyde will never see me the right way. Coach Bolton was so explicit. If I can't beat his guys, I'll never be man enough. Dad doesn't offer more thoughts. I watch as the sun begins to rise and I imagine that all the other swimmers are watching the sunrise, too.

———

At the pool, I jump out of the car, swim bag slung over my shoulder. It's as big as I am—filled with two towels, my brand-new race suit, my goggles and cap, and the enormous bag of snacks Mom packed for me last night. She's not with us for morning prelims because she had some important meeting, but she'll meet us for finals this afternoon. I don't mind at all—the amazingly organized food bag is how she shows her love.

"Obie," someone's voice calls. I turn around to see Lucy rushing over. I steel myself. Even though we're talking more, things are still awkward. Mom says it's a slow process. I'm trying to trust her on that one. "Obie! Are you swimming two hundred fly today?"

"No way! Are you?" I answer as we head toward the building's entrance together.

"Ugh, yes. Coach Bolton hates me." I feel something shift in my chest and I blink to push away the discomfort.

"Oh, sorry. I didn't mean, I mean . . ." Lucy trails off.

"I know what you mean," I say, forcing a smile.

"Well, good luck," Lucy says nervously. "I'll cheer for you. I don't care what Bolton says."

Really? I want to ask. But I don't.

"Thanks," I say instead. "See ya later," I add as we veer toward our separate locker rooms.

———

To my surprise, I feel fantastic in warm-up. The water is so wonderfully cool against my skin and my arms glide easily through the blue, almost as if they are cutting a path for the rest of me. I feel light and grounded all at the same time— the way the water always holds me. With each push off the wall, I feel my strength growing, my confidence and excitement building. *Maybe I really* can *beat them,* I think. *Maybe today is the day.*

Coach Larkin calls everyone to the end of the lane to do pace. Everyone must do two 25s or two 50s at race pace to prepare. She says we'll take turns to make sure everyone gets clear water and an accurate time.

Mikey goes before me. He hits a solid 32.0 on both his 50s. Spot on. Coach gives him a high five and he offers me a fist bump as he goes to warm down.

I ask to do the same two 50s as Mikey to prep for 200 IM, one 50 fly-back and one 50 back-breast. Practice transitions. Coach nods.

"Ready, go." And I push off the wall.

"Thirty-one point six, nice job, boss." Right on pace. And a little faster than Mikey.

"Thirty point nine, whoa," Coach calls. I grin even wider this time. *Faster* than pace! If I keep that up, I could definitely win.

"Slow down there, Obie," Coach says with a smile. "Don't get too excited just yet. It's just prelims." I nod. She's right. All I have to do this morning is make it back top eight for tonight.

"Warm down a bit and then go change into your race suit."

"Yes, ma'am."

I excitedly hop out of the pool and find Pooch on the bench.

"Wanna go change now?" he asks.

"Yeah, dude, let's go. This suit is going to take me a year to get on."

"Me too. I think I grew since we bought it."

"You probably did," I say, looking at him. "You a beast."

"I know." He puffs out his chest and we laugh.

———

In the locker room, we find a relatively quiet corner. I strip off my Speedo and pat myself dry. It's so much harder to work these suits on when your skin is wet.

"Yo, I'm going to go pee before I squeeze into this mess," Pooch says, but I'm too focused on my suit to reply.

I've almost gotten the suit above my butt—my badonkadonk—when I see someone set his stuff down a few lockers away. Reflexively, I turn away as I finish pulling the suit all the way up. Then I sit down. The guy a few lockers from me looks up and I straighten immediately.

"Hey there, Obadiah." Clyde uses my correct name but spits each syllable like he's tasting something he hates.

"Uhh, hey, Clyde," I say nervously.

"Ready to get creamed today?" he says, his voice low and somehow more threatening than when it's loud.

"No," I answer.

"Didn't think—"

But I cut him off, continuing, "Because I don't plan on getting creamed."

"Oh, but you will," he says, standing up. He towers over me. Suddenly the race suit doesn't feel as cool or strong as it did in the store dressing room. Suddenly it's way too tight and I'm all out of air. I take a deep breath. I know I am shaking.

"Clyde, if you bully me again on the pool deck today, I will get you suspended. I've already talked to an official."

"What?" he snarls. "I thought you'd be smarter than that." *Where is Pooch? Why is he taking so long to pee?*

"I'm sick of you taunting me. If you want to beat me, beat me in the pool. Stop making yourself feel bigger by trying to make me feel small."

"HA!" He laughs but it seems forced and he looks confused. I finally see Pooch approaching us out of the corner of my eye as I lean down to get my stuff.

"Seriously, Clyde, you need to grow up." Pooch grabs his towel and looks at me. He cocks his head as if to say *you okay?* I nod. He checks something on his phone as we walk away.

"I'm older and taller than you, I'm way more grown—" comes Clyde's pathetic response.

"Then act like it," I say.

"And remember what I said," Pooch says loudly, his back to Clyde. "You say anything to my friend Obie here and you'll get disqualified real fast."

"Screw you, guys, you're both f—"

"Ah-ah-ah! What did I tell you about that word, my friend?" Pooch says loudly, lighting up his phone to show Clyde. The screen clearly shows the voice-recording app— and it's already recording. He must have been recording the whole time. . . . *Smart guy.*

"You say it, I report you. It's that simple." We walk away, leaving Clyde in angry silence.

Chapter 34

I touch the wall, gliding in. I pop my head up to see Pooch leaning down over me. Just like at practice.

"Easssyyyy," he says, dragging the word out, "money." He gives me a high five. I slap it.

I look over at the board and feel my chest swell. 1:57.90. The fastest I've ever gone.

I'm suddenly a little less tired.

I also won my heat—and by a good margin, so that bodes well for finals.

"There's only one more heat left, Obes." Pooch nudges, grinning. "You're gonna make A final!"

"Shh, don't jinx it! Who knows, they could all beat me."

"Aw, c'mon, it was circle-seeded," he whispers knowingly. He's right. This means that the fastest people are distributed across the last three heats, down the center lanes.

I stay with Pooch to watch the next heat because Mikey's in it. Pooch and I shriek over Mikey's lane at every turn, but it's not a particularly close race. This is the final heat and

Clyde is already pulling away from the others, up first per usual. He's always had the most beautiful underwaters. It's like he's an enormous torpedo. Fly is his best stroke, unlike me. He gains himself a pretty hefty lead, and no one runs him down.

Clyde cheers for himself when he finishes. As Mikey comes in third—with a great time for a morning swim—Clyde pumps his fist in the air and looks over at Coach Bolton for approval. I follow his gaze and see Coach Bolton give a slight nod. Clyde slams his fist into the water, making a huge splash. He doesn't wait for the rest of the swimmers to finish. He just climbs out of the pool and sits on the edge.

"Well. There's the jackass," Pooch says beside me. Swimmers are supposed to wait in the pool until the last person finishes and then exit together. They even announce it over the PA. I'm surprised Clyde doesn't get scolded by the officials.

"Yeah."

"And you get to race him tonight," Pooch says, bumping me in the shoulder.

"Yeah. . . ." My stomach hurts and I can't tell if it's because I haven't warmed down yet or I'm nervous. Probably both.

We wander to the warm-down pool, meeting Mikey there. He leans over, his hands on his knees. He's very out of breath.

"Oooof," he says. But he doesn't look upset.

"Nice job, dude!" I clap him on the back.

"Thanks, man," he wheezes. "It's going to be a helluva race tonight." He smiles at me. "You ready? I think we'll be right next to each other—third and fifth seed."

"Yeah, let's do it." The thought of racing next to Mikey makes me feel better—it'll be just like practice. I can do that. I do it every day.

———

All four of us pile into the car for finals. I curl into my seat, my enormous swim bag between me and Mom. Jae-sung demanded the front seat because he's fifteen now, which supposedly makes you old enough. His big body fits better up there anyway.

I rub my eyes. I'm still pretty groggy from my between-session nap. I've finally gotten myself to take those. I used to have way too much trouble falling asleep, which just got me even more anxious. But Coach Larkin says taking a nap after prelims will help you swim fast in finals. Like I mentioned, she's all about incorporating good rest.

My phone buzzes.

> **TOMMY, 3:45 P.M.:** Hey Obie, it's Tommy. Just wanted to wish you good luck tonight. I know you're gonna crush it. Go show em!

I smile and slip the phone into my pocket. I'll reply later.

We pull up to the pool and I hop out of the car, bag slung over one shoulder.

Jae-sung calls out, "Wait." I turn around. "Come back, I have to tell you a secret."

I walk over to the passenger-side window.

"Come closer."

"Why?" I ask, but I oblige, leaning down so my face is almost in the window. He cups his hand around my ear.

"You're going to crush it," he whispers. I stand back up, smiling.

"You're a weirdo," I reply.

Then he shouts for everyone else to hear, "MY LITTLE BRO IS GONNA CRUSH IT TONIGHT. MY LITTLE BRO IS GONNA CRUSH IT TONIGHT!" I roll my eyes as I head for the doors, but I'm grinning like crazy.

"Thanks, Jae-sung," I say softly to myself.

———

I try not to stress about the fact that my muscles are sore during warm-up. I feel heavy on the walls. It's been a long meet. I chat with Coach Larkin before I walk over to the ready room.

"Focus on your turns. Your underwaters are probably the strongest in this heat. Hit those hard. Don't go out too fast. Let them play. Rail on that breaststroke." I nod, my throat feeling tight and my fingers tingling.

"Stand up tall, Obie. You've got this," Coach says, her hand on my head. *Tall and confident,* I think. I glance up into the stands and find Mom and Dad. Charlie's standing next to them, holding a big sign that says OBIE WON A KENOBI. I giggle. Jae-sung jumps up and down, waving at me. An older woman next to him is waving, too. I turn around, looking for who she is waving at. No one is behind me. I look up at her again and squint. *Mrs. Salmani?* I wave back, my smile bigger and my nerves calming. "Hi, Mrs. Salmani," but my shout is swallowed by the pool.

———

Behind the blocks, I stare at my toes on the small clay tiles. They're like mini-linoleum tiles. I look at the water. The consolation final—the people who placed ninth through sixteenth this morning—is finishing into the wall and I'm not sure my heart has ever beat this fast. My tight silicone cap creates an echo chamber, the material stretched over my ears like little drumheads. My hands and feet are suddenly freezing, so I tuck my hands into my pockets, wrapping myself in my long swim parka.

I notice someone moving kind of funny at the end of my lane and I squint to see who it is. It's Lucy. Her hands in the air. Doing our stupid dance. *Should I do it?*

She pauses for a moment, looking at me, her arms still raised above her head. *Screw it,* I think, and I dance along with her, grinning as we end with the point.

"Swimmers, please exit the water," the official says over the microphone. As they climb out, I hear their labored breathing and suddenly I'm terrified of how much this race is going to hurt. I can feel my stomach in my throat. *Can I choke on my own stomach?*

"Announcing your championship finalists. In lane one—" I stop listening as I adjust my cap. The silicone squeaks against my goggles and I adjust those, too, spitting into the lenses to clear any fogginess. I jump up and down three times, just like I do before every race. I take off my parka and lay it carefully folded on the chair behind the block. I feel the blood draining from my feet and hands again and realize my breathing is far too shallow. I pause, staring at the blue water, and force several deep breaths. They are loud and they bounce around in my echo chamber cap. I try to focus on this sound. In, out. In, out—

"And in lane two, from the Manta Rays, Miguel Garcia!" Our team roars from the edge of the pool and somehow I hear Pooch's yell. *"GO, MIKEYYYYYY!"* I grin, a small break from my nerves. Mikey jumps up and down and does his Michael Phelps pre-race imitation. He gives me two thumbs up as the announcer moves to me.

"And in lane three, Obie Chang!" The announcer emphasizes my name like they do for stars on TV: *Ohhh-beeeeeee Chaaaaaang!* Pooch screams, "That's my boy!" and Lucy is cheering at the end of my lane. My chest is bursting with nervous excitement as I hop up and down three final times. *This is it.*

"In lane four, your top seed for the night, Clyde Bolton!" I wonder if the cheering for Clyde is louder than it was for me. *Pretend every cheer you hear during announcements is for you. Because it is. Even people cheering against you—that's for you. It's motivation. Take it and run with it. Or rather, swim with it.* Dad's words play in my brain. *Okay,* I think. *More cheering for me.*

I stop listening as the announcer finishes the last four swimmers. The eight of us stand behind our respective blocks, each with one foot on the step, poised and waiting. The whistle blows three short bursts. The signal to step onto the blocks. I feel the rough sandpaper beneath my bare feet. I tuck my big and second toes of my right foot over the edge of the block and position my other foot a step behind. Ready. The official blows one more long, rolling whistle, ending with a sharp and quick *weee-eet!*

"Swimmers, take your mark—" And the buzzer goes off.

It's like I leave my body for a moment. I watch myself dive in, toes pointed, arms in streamline. I see the water crashing over all of us, our bodies leaving white water tunnels just beneath the surface. I see Clyde stretching ahead with those perfect underwaters. And that's when I snap into it.

KICK, I yell at myself, *KICK!* And I do. I break through half a stroke behind him. I can see the tips of his arms with each stroke. I press into my second turn and we're on our backs. My weakest stroke.

Keep your kicks up. Use those legs. Spin those arms. What if I use Coach Bolton's technique tips to beat his kid? How fantastic would that be?

Focus, Obie.

Just make it to breaststroke.

We flip at the far wall and I'm facing Mikey's feet as we kick underwater. He's almost a full body length ahead. *Shit.*

I break out and feel the fatigue beginning to build in my legs.

Just make it to breaststroke.

I turn, this time right alongside Clyde. We turn at exactly the same time. Hell, yeah. Let's go.

Don't get too excited. Focus. Catch, pull, drive. Catch, pull, DRIVE.

I'm closing the gap between me and Mikey with each stroke, leaving Clyde behind. I know if I can make a big enough gap here, Clyde won't be able to catch me in freestyle. *C'mon.*

We turn into the last leg. Mikey, Clyde, and I push off the wall together. The crowd is roaring. I wonder if we tied that split. I'll have to ask Pooch. I'm pretty sure that was him screaming into my face as I turned into the last 50.

Clyde pushes ahead with his underwaters and I scream at my muscles. *Go, go, go—*

But there isn't anything left. I kick as hard as I can and break out a stroke behind him. Mikey is between us, a little ahead of me but still behind Clyde.

Head down, why are you swimming like Tarzan, Sarah— I hear Bolton using my old name in my head. I put my head down and scream at him like I should have last year: "My name is Obie!"

But I can't catch them. I touch the wall half a second after they do and stare at the time board.

I failed. I can't believe it. I lost. The "4" next to my name seems brighter than everything else. *Fourth?* Who got third?

I feel the anger welling up inside, mostly at myself. I pull off my cap and am about to furiously throw it across the pool deck when I catch Pooch's eye. He's grinning and holding two thumbs up. I can feel his excitement from across the pool. He must have run around from the other side to cheer our last lap. I have to smile.

"Great job!" he mouths. Tears sting my eyes. I should have kept my goggles on.

"Swimmers, please exit the pool," comes the garbled instruction from the official. I pull myself from the pool, exhausted. It's like I can feel every single muscle in my body. Some I didn't even know I had.

I go to walk back and feel someone give me an enormous hug from behind.

"DUDE!" Mikey screams in my ear. "Dude, we totally crushed it, that was the shit!" He's out of breath.

"DUDE," I exclaim. "You're the man, I can't believe you beat"—I nod behind us—"Clyde. I mean, that's insane." He grins.

"Thanks, man, I'm pumped for both of us. I mean, you didn't even think you were going to make JOs. And you just got fourth. At JOs. Imagine what you'll do next year."

"But—" I falter.

"No buts or badonkadonks, dude. We both crushed it."

Coach Larkin is waiting for us by the team area as I trudge back, still feeling defeated. Everyone gives Mikey and me high fives and I look across the pool deck to see Clyde sitting on the bench, head low. Coach Bolton is clearly yelling at him. I remember that yelling. Watching it now, maybe I don't miss it so much anymore.

The tightness in my chest subsides slightly.

"Look at me," Coach Larkin says sternly but gently. My eyes flit up and then down to my feet. "Look. At. Me," she repeats, and tips my chin upward. I feel like a small child, but I don't really care.

"I know what you're thinking. But you did not fail. I don't care what Bolton told you. He is wrong. You only started competing against the boys one year ago and now you are the fourth fastest thirteen-to-fourteen-year-old in this entire area." I open my mouth to argue, but she cuts me off. "So, no, you did not get first. No one can argue with that. But that does not make you a loser. There are more things than winning a race that constitute glory, Obadiah." She lets go of my chin, but I stay looking at her.

"Being yourself here today, *that* is real glory. Fourth place? That's only the cherry on top."

I stare at her, wondering what it would be like if everyone thought like her. *What if everyone didn't care that I was supposed to be a girl first before I realized I'm really a boy? What if no one cared what parts I have in my pants?*

"Go warm down. And come see me when you're done and we'll talk about your race."

Still feeling a little heavyhearted, I wander over to the warm-down pool. I meet up with Mikey on the way and I smile for real this time. I give him a big high five.

"Proud of you, man," I tell him.

"Showed that punk what's *up*," he says, bouncing up and down.

"Boy, am I happy you beat him," I say, nodding. "Might be the best part of the whole day."

We stand at the edge, watching the water—which is choppy with so many awkward fourteen-and-under bodies. Mikey slides in and waits at the wall for a few moments and then pushes off.

I wait for a break between the circling swimmers. I let myself fall in, the water enveloping me as it crashes over the top of my head. I breathe out, blowing bubbles and a small sob along with it.

It's okay to cry, I hear my dad say. *Don't let anyone tell you boys don't cry. Boys do cry.*

I sob as I swim, letting my goggles fill with tears. *What could I have done better?* I think to myself. *I nailed every turn and I swam as hard as I could. Maybe my best just isn't good enough. Maybe they are right. Maybe trans boys can't* really *beat cis guys.* But then I hear Coach Larkin's voice. *Fourth place? That's only the cherry on top.* And I wonder if maybe this really was a victory.

When my sobs have quieted, I stop at the far wall for a moment to empty the tears from my goggles. I stand in the corner of the lane, the crashing of other swimmers' flip turns dousing me every few seconds. I'm at the Junior Olympics. I think about the last time I was here. I was wearing a one-piece suit. I was swimming against the girls. I had actually won or made the podium—the top three—in all of my events. Coach Bolton had been gunning for me to make my Nationals cut, which I'd been so close to.

And I was miserable.

It didn't matter how many events I'd won. Or how many personal best times I'd swum. After every session, I'd sit in the bathroom—the girls' locker room—and cry in a stall, silently. It didn't matter how much I tried to be okay with it—competing as a girl felt like I was betraying myself. I felt like a shell of a person.

I push off the wall again, and I feel the water rush past my bare chest. I do a few dolphin kicks before breaking the surface. *Look at me, wearing a boys' suit. Swimming against the boys.* Beating *the boys. A hundred and fourteen boys swam this event, and I got fourth.* I feel a proud anger rising in my chest. This is not something I've felt before. Instead of having an elephant crushing my lungs, I feel like the elephant is inside, demanding freedom. Or maybe I am the elephant, standing tall and proud and grounded—and the slightest bit angry, too.

Coach Bolton never believed in me. He only ever cared that I won. That I made him look good. So, yeah, maybe he'd care about me now if I won the boys' races, too. But so what. I got fourth. That means I beat 110 other boys.

I'm excited by this new feeling. And scared, too, if I'm honest. *Does this make me arrogant?*

I flip at the wall and push off. I'm no longer at a smooth, easy, warm-down pace. I'm swiftly increasing to strong, confident strokes. Usually warm-down is a 300, maybe a 500, but I feel so good I flip again, heading into 625 yards. I think about Lucy at the end of my lane, her two thumbs up. I wonder if this means we can be real friends again. I think about Dad's words from the car. *Their insults, those are about who they are, not who you are.* And then something Mrs. Salmani had written on my first draft: *Just because they are mean to you doesn't make it okay for you to be mean to you, too.* I should probably make that a sticky note.

Screw you, Coach Bolton. I know who I am. Maybe you're having trouble with who you *are.* In all this time of repeating Bolton's words in my head, I realize that I have never once asked what being "man enough" even means. If someone is a man, aren't they just that—a man? And then it hits me: *There is no man* enough. *There is just being a man. And winning has nothing to do with my manhood.*

As I flip, completing 700 yards, I feel a kickboard on my feet. I stop and look up. I am so startled by the face staring down at me that I almost fall right back underwater.

"Get out. I want to talk to you," Coach Bolton says in his usual gruff voice. I look around for Coach Larkin or Pooch or any reinforcements. The proud anger I'd been feeling has pretty much evaporated and I feel like a tiny ant. I want to scream *HELP!* But that probably wouldn't be the best plan. Coach Bolton must notice my nervousness and says, "Don't. It's fine. I just want to talk." He's got a weird look on his face. Not one I've ever seen before.

"Come," Bolton says, and motions for me to follow him. We walk over to an empty bleacher near the locker rooms and Bolton sits down. I don't.

"L-li-listen, I, uh, I wanted to tell you," he stutters.

I can't place his expression. Sadness? Fright? Nervousness? *Is Coach Bolton afraid of talking to me? Shouldn't I be the one to be scared?* I say nothing. I just wait, staring at the tile beneath my feet. I should be wearing my flip-flops. Mom always tells me I'll get athlete's foot if I don't. Well, add that to the list of things. Death by Bolton. Athlete's foot.

"I, uh, I . . . Well. That was, uh." He takes a deep breath.

Bolton has never been a man of many words, but him having this amount of difficulty speaking is so strange. Is he okay?

"That was a good race," Bolton mumbles.

What? I look up to see that he is now staring at the tiles on the floor, too. His eyes meet my incredulous gaze for half a second, and then return to the floor.

"That was a good race," he says again. "And, I, well. I— I'm proud of you." Coach looks up as he says *proud* and I feel confused. I have been waiting for years for this moment. To hear him say he's proud of me. I freeze. *Is this a joke? Is he going to make fun of me next?* As if anticipating my disbelief, Bolton continues.

"I mean it. And, I, uh, I wanted to apologize. I still don't understand. I really don't. But if you're going to go through all this trouble to be here, to compete with the boys . . . you must really mean what you say. You must really feel it." Bolton takes another deep breath and I continue to stare. "You did good today," he says.

I feel a small, tentative smile on my face that is suddenly overcome by anger. I want to shout, *WHERE WAS YOUR PRIDE WHEN I WAS STRUGGLING? WHERE WAS YOUR SUPPORT WHEN I CRIED EVERY DAY*

AFTER PRACTICE BECAUSE YOU SAID I'D NEVER BE ENOUGH? WHERE WAS ANY OF THIS WHEN I NEEDED IT?

And then with a sudden rush of pride: *I DON'T NEED IT NOW.*

Bolton must notice the shift in my expression because he repeats himself: "You did good today, Obie." He uses the correct name for the first time. I swallow and straighten.

Tall and confident, Obadiah.

"I did," I say, nodding. And before he has a chance to reply, I turn and walk over to my team. I don't look back.

After

I flip to the end of my journal. To the list I started almost a year ago.

I read the names aloud, one at a time, almost like a prayer.

PEOPLE WHO BELIEVE I'M MAN ENOUGH:
1. Mom and Dad
2. Jae-sung
3. Mrs. Salmani
4. Grandma
5. Halmoni and Harabuhji
6. Coach Larkin
7. Pooch and Mikey
8. Charlie

I sit in the silence for a few moments. Then I dig around for the extra thick black Sharpie I used to decorate posters last year. I add in big block letters—

9. ME

Living Proof by Obie Chang

Write about how your identity does or does not conflict with your ancestry and culture. How does your identity connect you to or disconnect you from your ancestry and your history?

As a Korean American transgender boy who is an athlete and student, I have spent my life feeling stuck in between. Perhaps the first and most obvious in-between I experienced is my half Asian identity. I am never Korean enough to be considered truly Korean, and I'm always the Asian kid in a room filled with white people.

My father is Korean American. He moved to the States with his family before he can remember. In Korean, the word for *transgender* is "transgender," just said in a Korean accent: "teu-laen-seu-jen-deo." I am "teu-laen-seu-jen-deo."

When I figured this out three years ago, I had no idea how to tell my Korean family. I worried because I wasn't sure how to translate this. But what made me actually afraid was that my Korean family are immigrants from a country where there was and still is little to no exposure to or visibility of LGBTQ+ people. And they're also devout Catholics. I was terrified being a transgender boy would disconnect me from my Korean family.

My mother is a white woman born to a German immigrant and a Midwestern farmer. When I was first learning about transgender people, my mother confiscated my computer because when I entered "transgender is" followed by a space, Google suggested the following searches: "Transgender is unnatural," "Transgender is a sin," and "Transgender is an abomination." That is, even though *transgender* exists in the English language, people still don't truly understand what it means.

And to be honest, neither did I at the beginning. I used to think that transgender people were people who randomly elected to get sex changes for no reason. I didn't realize that being transgender is not an action. It is an identity. It is who I am. It took me a long time to find the words to describe myself and when I finally did, I still stumbled speaking them.

When I came out to my Korean grandmother, my halmoni, I read her a letter. Because I could not translate the word *transgender*, I attempted to explain what it meant in detail. I closed the letter by saying, "I love you, always." My halmoni told me that she already knew. As my dad teared up, Halmoni continued: "You can be a boy, a brother, a husband," she'd said. *Whoa, Halmoni, slow down—husband?!* I'd thought to myself. "You can be a man." She paused. "But, in Korean culture, it is the *daughter's* responsibility to take care of the parents. Your mom and dad have no more daughters now. It is still your responsibility, Obie, to take care of your parents." I had just nodded, relieved. *Of course, Halmoni.*

I am a proud transgender Korean American boy. I come from a German woman who survived World War II, who not only spent most of her adolescence without her parents but then moved to the United States as a teenager, alone. I come from strong Korean women who fled northern Korea on foot, carrying only the barest essentials and leaving everything else behind, who walked hundreds of miles for their freedom, who flew across the globe to find a better life for their children. I come directly from all of this womanhood—from my mother, from my grandmothers and their mothers, too. And I come from my own assigned womanhood. My expected daughterhood.

And yet, here I stand today. A boy. A son. And in the future: a man.

Many people use culture and difference as barriers to acceptance and love, saying that these identities cannot coexist in one person. But I am living proof that they certainly can. In all of my intersectionality, I am still here. Alive. And Korean. Alive. And white. Alive. And an athlete. Alive. And transgender. And alive.

ACKNOWLEDGMENTS

The summer of 2017, I walked into the massive New Orleans Convention Center alongside Sara Farizan and Ellen Oh. *Fresh Ink,* which included a short story I'd written, had just been published and we were there to speak about it at the American Library Association's Annual Conference. This was my first publication.

"Authors, come over here," one of the conference staff called to us. The word *IMPOSTER* shone in my brain. I trailed behind. Sara fell into step with me.

"I'm not a *real* author," I whispered to her. "I don't feel like I can claim that."

"Yes, you are," she said, smiling but firm. "You are absolutely an author. You wrote something. So you are an author. Don't let anyone tell you otherwise."

Though I still had trouble believing her—and in myself—I have held tightly to her words ever since.

This is to say that in the end, this book is not here

because *I* wrote a story. *We* are not here because I wrote a story. We are here because of a village of people's help. We are here because of Sara's crucial encouragement. Because of the educational resources I had access to and the teachers who taught me to read and write. Because of the supportive actions of my loved ones. Because I had access to gender-affirming health care that saved my life, thus allowing me to write at all.

A myriad of privilege and support and love went into this book. I and this book are here because of everyone who ever told me—explicitly and through their actions—they love me. So here is a non-comprehensive list of people who helped write this book:

My team at Crown—Elizabeth, Kris, Laura, Melinda, Bob, Dion, and of course, Phoebe Yeh, my editor. Phoebe was the first to insist I write a book; without her persistence, these words might never have made it into a document, much less a published book.

Marietta, my agent, who will fight with fire and love for my work and my humanity, who has showed me what true allyship in a professional space can look like.

Ellen Oh, my mentor and late-night texter, whose expert advice made this process all the smoother.

McKenna and our early-morning work sessions during which I wrote this manuscript.

Kevin, my best friend, who brought a safety and kinship to our friendship that I had never before experienced.

Daniel, whose joy and thirst for life are intoxicating.

My friends, who were the first to welcome and affirm my transness, creating a safe bubble that was critical in the beginning months of my transition. My friends, who provide meaningful company that reminds me I am more than just transgender.

Janet, who was the first person to welcome me on my new high school team and has always been a beacon of balance and grounding.

Every teammate I've ever had.

Ron, my favorite coach, who sparked in me and nourished my love of competition.

My college coaches, Stephanie and Kevin, who prioritized my happiness and humanity by offering me a spot on the men's team at Harvard and made my journey possible.

Josephine, who first taught me to see myself and in doing so, not only saved but helped me rekindle my own joy for my own life.

Deb, who has been one of the most important safe places in my adult life.

Lida, who, amidst the social disaster that was middle school, was a safe place for me and able to truly nurture my love of learning.

Clay, my eighth-grade English teacher, who gave me my first C grade and whose class was simultaneously the birthplace of my love of writing.

Desireé, who, through her raw poetry, writing, and the

Heart of It retreat, reminds me that writing the truth however we can is the only thing that matters.

Every trans sibling who showed me that my life was
possible. Because of Sam, Elijah, Dominic, Saren, Kase, Jah,
Taylor, Caden, Chase, Skylar, Asher, Levi, Emmitt, Michael,
Dana, Max, Santiago, and so many more.

Each Instagram follower and supporter—and Instagram
itself, the first place I ever asked for my proper pronouns,
the first place I ever said, "I am transgender."

My brother, who always pushes me to think beyond myself and my own echo chamber.

My father's parents, who will never read this but would
not need to do so to support me.

Dearest Halmoni, Kumja, and Harabuhji, my immigrant
Catholic grandparents, who could have used every excuse
to reject me but chose instead to lead with love, who are
examples that all of us can and should follow.

My partner, who is one of the few (if not only) people
who will examine my work more carefully than I do, who
will always fight for me, whose soft love and home together
I have spent a lifetime craving, and whose patience I do not
always deserve but for which I am endlessly grateful.

And, of course, my parents. My parents, who never doubt
me. My parents, who believe in me more than I do myself.
My fiercest cheerleaders and loudest supporters. My father,
who is the most resourceful and curious person I know, who
I hope I've taken after, if only a fraction of the degree. And

my mother, who edits everything I write (including my Instagram captions), who has given me all I need to be an author, who is the reason I write in the first place.

Finally, I am here because of you, treasured reader. You chose to pick up this book and support my work and trans kids. Thank you.

AUTHOR'S NOTE

For my cisgender (not transgender) readers—

I'm so glad you made it here. Thank you for reading and for spending time with Obie in his world. I wrote this book in hopes of sharing a piece of our humanity as trans people with you. Trans folks are often reduced to our transness, but that is not all we are. Obie is Korean American. Obie is kind and silly and nerdy. Obie is a teacher's pet. Obie struggles with friendships. Obie loves pickles. Obie is a swimmer. Obie likes sandwiches and English class. And Obie is transgender.

But while Obie is transgender, he also cannot possibly represent all transgender children or people. Obie is just *one* trans kid. And despite Coach and Clyde Bolton, Obie is one trans kid with a lot of support and resources. So many trans kids do not have what Obie has. So many parents are not as supportive, loving, and affirming, so many parents do not allow or have access to gender-affirming doctors, so many coaches are not supportive like Coach Larkin, and so on. I wrote this support and kindness for Obie because I wanted no barriers for you to understand Obie—and I wanted to prove the possibility and provide examples of this kind of love and acceptance. Because this kind of love and acceptance is absolutely possible. Unfortunately, this does not mean it is common. But it absolutely should be and I am advocating and fighting for the day it will be.

Obie also fits many traditional "boy" roles—he dates a girl, he is an athlete, he wears the same kinds of clothes as his brother and male teammates. I wrote Obie this way so there would be no barriers for you to understand him. But Obie would be no less valid if he were gay, no less valid if he were nonbinary or presented in an ambiguous way. Obie would be no less of a boy if he didn't wear traditional "boys' " clothes or wasn't an athlete. Obie would be no less trans or a boy if he didn't want to take testosterone or couldn't.

Your acceptance and love toward trans people should never depend on how we look or what pronouns we use. Trans people are valid however they identify and however they present themselves.

For my transgender readers—

It is okay if you are not like Obie. There is *no one way* to be transgender. There are as many ways of being transgender as there are trans people. So don't let anyone else tell you who *you* are. You know yourself best. Trust that.

Please also remember that if the people around you do not accept you as Obie's loved ones do, that is *not your fault*. It is *not* a reflection of who you are or your character; it is a reflection of theirs. Their attempt to invalidate who you are does not mean *you* are invalid. It means a whole lot about that person, their character, their insecurities and fears, their views of the world. . . . This does not mean you can't feel upset about it. Of course, it hurts—and I encourage you to validate this anger and pain. Tend to those wounds, but do not pick up their words and use them as weapons against yourself.

If you are struggling, know that you are not alone. I know that feeling. I know the pain of wondering if you have a place in this world, and I'm here to tell you that you absolutely do. And you might find that in the same home you're in now, but you might also find it elsewhere. If you feel stuck, know that you will not always be stuck where you are. I know you are resilient because you've made it here. You are reading this book. You are looking for ways to find yourself and you are succeeding. Even just by reading. Keep going. You belong here. We need you.

RESOURCES

MENTAL HEALTH

For LGBTQ+ folks struggling or contemplating suicide, please reach out to the Trevor Project at +1 (866) 488-7386. The Trevor Project is available 24/7 specifically for LGBTQ+ folks. They provide services over text and chat in case you aren't in a safe place to talk aloud over the phone. Find those resources at TheTrevorProject.org/get-help-now.

For trans folks struggling or contemplating suicide, please reach out to Trans Lifeline at +1 (877) 565-8860 in the USA and +1 (877) 330-6366 in Canada. Trans Lifeline is staffed by trans folks and provides peer support for trans folks in need. Visit their website at TransLifeline.org.

For parents of trans folks who want to learn more about how best to support your trans children, please visit pinkmantaray.com/parents.

For allies—that is, folks who are not transgender but want to support those who are—who are curious to learn more about how to be the best ally they can be, please visit my website at pinkmantaray.com/obie.

GLOSSARY

Language is incredibly important, especially when talking about marginalized folks and our experiences. Of course, language evolves rapidly, as communities do, so it can be difficult to keep up. Remember that while it's okay to make mistakes, it's not okay to use habit or ignorance as an excuse. If you mess up, apologize and make concerted efforts to learn and use the most respectful terminology going forward.

Transgender: an adjective used to describe someone who does not identify as the gender they were assigned at birth. Do NOT use: "transgendered," "a transgender," or "the transgenders."

Trans man: a man who was assigned female at birth. Do NOT use: "transman," "fake man," "woman who turned into/wants to be a man."

Trans woman: a woman who was assigned male at birth. Do NOT use: "transwoman," "fake woman," or "man who turned into/wants to be a woman."

Trans masculine: an adjective used to describe a transgender person who was assigned female at birth but who does not identify as female. This is an umbrella term.

Trans feminine: an adjective used to describe a transgender person who was assigned male at birth but who does not identify as male. This is an umbrella term.

Cisgender: an adjective used to describe someone who does identify as the gender they were assigned at birth. Do NOT use: "normal person."

Cis man: a man assigned male at birth. Do NOT use: "biological man," "real man," or "normal man."

Cis woman: a woman assigned female at birth. Do NOT use: "biological woman," "real woman," or "normal woman."

Nonbinary: describes someone who does not identify within the gender binary. For some folks, this means identifying somewhere between the binary ends of the spectrum (male and female), for some it means identifying with a combination of genders, and for others it means feeling a complete lack of a gender. For many folks, being nonbinary entails liberation from the stereotypes and gender roles attached to the gender they were assigned at birth. Some nonbinary folks consider themselves transgender, some nonbinary folks do not.

Note: Many folks use the term "enby" as a short term for nonbinary. This is the spelling of the abbreviation "NB," but folks have strayed away from using "NB" to refer to non-binary folks because "NB" is used more widely as an abbreviation for non-Black folks.

Genderfluid: describes a person who does not identify themselves as having a fixed gender.

Gender identity: the internal sense of one's gender; does not have to match assigned gender at birth.

Sex: usually refers to one's anatomy. I encourage folks to use the term "gender assigned at birth" instead of "biological sex," because, in reality, there is no one way to define biological sex. There are five major components of biological sex: chromosomes, hormones, expression of hormones, internal genitalia, and external genitalia. Visit pinkmantaray.com/sex.

AFAB/AMAB: "assigned female at birth" and "assigned male at birth." These are respectful and accurate ways to describe what gender someone was assigned at birth, instead of saying "what someone was born as."

Gender expression: how we communicate our gender to others. These are things like the clothing we wear, the ways we look, how we act, mannerisms we use, and more. This is best defined as a social construct influenced by culture, epoch, and systems of power such as white supremacy and patriarchy.

Gender-affirming: the acceptance (through explicit language or practices) of someone's true gender and treating them in ways that actively affirm them living authentically in that gender. E.g., gender-affirming health care, gender-affirming language, gender-affirming policy.

Gender dysphoria: the discomfort or distress that arises from the incongruence of gender identity and gender assigned at birth.

HRT/GAHT: hormone replacement therapy or gender-affirming hormone therapy. Hormones (usually testosterone, or "T," for trans masculine folks and a form of estrogen, or "E," for trans feminine folks) taken for gender-affirmation.

Sexuality/orientation: the classification of one's enduring romantic and/or sexual attraction toward others, usually based upon which gender or genders a person is oriented to.

Transition: any step(s) a person takes to affirm their gender identity. This might include surgery, hormones, pronoun changes, wardrobe changes, haircuts, and more, but it can also exclude any or all of these things. There is no one way to transition.

Misgender: the act of referring to someone in a way that does not reflect that person's gender identity. For example, using incorrect pronouns, calling someone by an old name (a deadname), or using an incorrect prefix (e.g., Mr. or Ms.). Misgendering can be especially painful for trans individuals because it calls forth a history of not being seen as who we truly are.

Deadname: refers to the name someone was given or used before they transitioned and/or discovered their true gender identity. This term is an adjustment to the term "birth name" for a few reasons, namely that these names are dead. Some people also feel that when deadnamed, a small part of them dies. Like misgendering, deadnames often drag forth a great deal of pain and trauma for trans folks, for having to live as someone they are not. Some folks also refer to deadnames as "old names," as Obie does in this book.

FURTHER READING

All the following links are amassed at pinkmantaray.com/obie.

How to Be an Ally:
pinkmantaray.com/allyship

Things NOT to Say to Queer People:
pinkmantaray.com/bullying

Things NOT to Say to Trans People:
pinkmantaray.com/dontsay

A Sex-Ed Lesson: What is "biological sex"?:
pinkmantaray.com/sex

Pronouns:
pinkmantaray.com/pronouns

Resources for Parents of Trans Kids:
pinkmantaray.com/parents

Coming Out Advice:
pinkmantaray.com/coming-out

Swimming & Being Transgender:
pinkmantaray.com/swimming

Transition Information:
pinkmantaray.com/transition

ABOUT THE AUTHOR

Schuyler Bailar (he/him) is an internationally renowned inspirational speaker, inclusion advocate, and diversity advisor. A graduate of Harvard University, Schuyler was also the first transgender athlete to compete in any sport on an NCAA Division I men's team. Growing up, Schuyler never saw anyone else like him—not in media, not in sports, and certainly not in books. He wrote *Obie Is Man Enough* for all the kids who don't know where or how to find themselves, either, trans or not. Because the journey is never linear or simple, but we dive in anyway.

As a top-ranked athlete, Schuyler's difficult choice—to transition while potentially giving up the prospect of being a champion swimmer competing as female—was historic and timely. His story appeared everywhere from *60 Minutes* to the Olympic Channel. Schuyler continues his advocacy work through social media, speaking engagements, life coaching, and consulting. He is a contributor to the YA anthology *Fresh Ink,* holds ongoing advisory roles with leading eating disorder treatment organization Monte Nido & Affiliates and trans health-care company Plume, and is a research assistant at Harvard University.

pinkmantaray.com
@pinkmantaray 📷
@sb_pinkmantaray 🐦